THE

SWEET RELIEF

OF MISSING

CHILDREN

THE
SWEET RELIEF
OF MISSING
CHILDREN

Sarah Braunstein

W. W. Norton & Company

New York · London

For information about permission to reproduce selections from this
book, write to Permissions, W. W. Norton & Company, Inc.,
500 Fifth Avenue, New York, NY 10110

For information about special discounts for bulk purchases, please contact
W. W. Norton Special Sales at specialsales@wwnorton.com or 800-233-4830

Manufacturing by Courier Westford
Book design by Chris Welch
Production manager: Anna Oler

Library of Congress Cataloging-in-Publication Data

Braunstein, Sarah, 1976–
The sweet relief of missing children / Sarah Braunstein. — 1st ed.
    p. cm.
ISBN 978-0-393-07659-2 (hardcover)
1. Missing children—Fiction. 2. Runaways—Fiction.
3. New York (N.Y.)—Fiction. 4. Psychological fiction. I. Title.
PS3602.R3895S94 2011
813'.6—dc22

                              2010037720

W. W. Norton & Company, Inc.
500 Fifth Avenue, New York, N.Y. 10110
www.wwnorton.com

W. W. Norton & Company Ltd.
Castle House, 75/76 Wells Street, London W1T 3QT

1 2 3 4 5 6 7 8 9 0

For Anna Braunstein
and Norma Garson

This girl I know, she's a Cadillac stunner

This girl I know, she's a nuclear reactor

I tell you she's supersonic, quadraphonic

This girl I know, she's here and there

This girl I know, she's split

She's gone to pieces

She's everywhere

—"Pipe Dream," Roger Ranger

PART 1

LEONORA

The girl had received all her immunizations. She had been inoculated. She had been warned in school assemblies and by her mother and father and several aunts. One of these aunts had a serious-looking mole on her cheek, a sharp chin, a stern, pale mouth, and she wore no jewelry except for a black-stoned ring on her middle finger, all of which gave her the appearance of a witch or intractable schoolmarm. The girl took these warnings seriously—the aunt's most of all. She knew to watch her back. She knew to avoid slow cars driven by men in sunglasses. She knew, at home alone, to say to the stranger on the phone, "My mother's in the shower now. Shall I have her call you back?"

She would never say she was home alone, nor take the short-cut through the alley. All these warnings, all this advice, the real message was: You are precious. You are precious but you are not free. You can't be both.

Did anyone get to be both things at once? It was unlikely.

The girl knew her family's code word. If someone unfamiliar tried to pick her up from school, he had to know the code word. He had to say it aloud. If he didn't? She was to go to the principal's office. She would have. She was staunch, confident.

She bore an obligation to the future to remain safe. The future was the tiny spray you feel on your face when you peel an orange, a simple promise.

The code word was—

It was not something she told anyone.

As a baby, she had been fed iron-fortified rice cereal and homemade purees; she had worn a pink satin headband. The headband, the booties, the yellow-haired doll propped in the corner of her crib, the expression of awed, nervous delight on her mother's face, all this said: *A girl! A girl!* Later, vast quantities of vegetables: peas, succotash, lima bean soup. Her parents rarely served dessert. Occasionally a graham cracker, maybe a small bowl of vanilla ice cream. No sugar cereal, no candy bars. When she had a cough, her mother squeezed lemon and honey into a mug of hot water. The girl ate and drank whatever was put before her. She dried the dishes with a gingham cloth. She obeyed.

Early on her mother taught her about the wage gap, the suffrage movement, the sheer poverty of certain minds, some of which—but not all—were male. It was never too early to illuminate the harsh truth of the matter for a girl. Boys could play, could treat the world like a junkyard to be rummaged through, but girls needed a different set of eyes. Girls needed to be wary and strong and curious but not too curious. "Say 'feminist,'" the mother coached, and the girl, as a toddler, said it. Still, she was given the traditional things, babydolls and pink. Her hands mastered the rhythms of needlepoint. Her mother knew how to accept a paradox: a girl could be anything, could shatter the glass ceiling, but she was still a girl. Girls liked lace; they loved bows. Give a girl a pink something, give her a doll that tinkled in its pants, she'd be happy.

She was happy, this girl.

Even when the sadness of life pressed up against her, even when she learned about the wage gap, corporate greed, the fact of death. This last truth, death, came one afternoon in the back of a taxicab. The girl, her mother, and her aunt were going to a museum. The mother said, "Hildegard passed away last week. From Meals-on-Wheels. The German? Her daughter's coming from Florida to collect her things."

"Godspeed," the aunt said.

"She was ready, I suppose."

"Passed away?" The girl was maybe four.

"Died," her mother said.

A silence.

"Death," her aunt said forcefully, and patted her lap like she was beckoning a puppy.

"Oh," said the girl, but she wasn't sure exactly what it meant.

The aunt raised a dark brow. "Like the end of days. On a personal level. Like, you know—" But she just snapped her finger.

"It means the body goes to sleep," her mother said gently.

"Not sleep," the aunt chastised.

"No, that's right. Not sleep. Not exactly."

"The body stops working," said the aunt. "Lights out."

"It rests," her mother added.

"Rests?" The aunt scowled. "Not really."

"Rests, sure."

"That gives her the wrong idea."

Her mother said, "Who *doesn't* have the wrong idea?"

"It goes to the cemetery. It's buried," the aunt said.

The girl pictured a hole in the earth. In the hole was a white bistro table with two chairs and, above it, to block the sun, an umbrella with crisp stripes of red and white.

"Everyone dies," the aunt said.

"Someday, yes," the mother agreed in a softer voice than usual. "Hildegard was very old."

The girl pictured rheumy Hildegard in her flannel housecoat on a bistro chair. Sometimes she'd accompanied her mother to deliver the woman's meals.

"We *hope* it happens when we're old," her aunt added, "but there's no saying."

"Everybody?" the girl asked. Nothing was true for everybody: her mother had said so.

"I'm afraid so," said her mother.

The cab jerked to a stop. The girl felt cold. She had not known it would end. She knew she would grow up, yes, but hadn't realized there would be a time when her body would stop. Her mind placed another person at that underground table, across from Hildegard, strange Hildegard who kept a dozen spare flashlights in her apartment, a flashlight on nearly every surface. The other person at the table was the girl. Her! She was wearing her favorite pink nightgown.

They got out of the cab. Briefly she was frightened, wished she hadn't asked. Isn't it better to be confused than to know? Her mother and aunt had changed the subject; now they were talking about a woman so desperate to have a baby that she advertised in the newspaper. The girl was frightened but not for long, because soon they were in the museum, standing before a painting of a fat gentleman in a festive tricornered hat. He was holding a bottle of beer. The hat, the beer, the expression of wicked, heaving delight on the man's face—

"Is he dead?" she asked her mother.

Her mother read the placard on the wall. "He lived two hundred years ago," she said. "He's certainly passed on."

His face was red and happy. He was making the most of it. He made the girl feel better, and her sense of permanence returned. Later they bought postcards of paintings from the gift shop. The girl spun the rack, looking for that man with the beer, but couldn't find him, and she was too shy to ask.

So she learned about failed fallopian tubes, about Cambodia and Medea and illiteracy and toxic shock and still she was happy, still she dried the dishes obediently with a gingham cloth. "What a happy girl!" people said, and she was proud to hear it. It was her duty to be happy. It was her duty to be curious but not too curious, to be pretty. She understood that you could be too curious but you couldn't be too pretty.

Was she pretty? You wonder, even if you don't ask. Either she was or she wasn't. It's a detail, one of many, but it's everything. Three stitches to repair a cut on her chin. These were sewn by a genius—a plastic surgeon, highly regarded, whose face conveyed the taut smoothness of plastic—to ensure there would be no scar, or just the slightest scar, a tiny pale c like a baby's fingernail clipping, noticeable only in a particular light if, say, you tilted her head back, tilted it as a lover might with his thumb when he meant to kiss her. But she was just a girl. No lovers tipped her head. Her parents paid the plastic surgeon because, yes, she was beautiful, and beauty has no price.

Soon a brother was born. He was cute for a while, around his second year, with that pudgy, incurious, pink face. Later he was just a boy, not handsome, not ugly, the poor kid. How could he compete? The girl possessed calm confidence, concern for the lower classes, a dimple in her right cheek. The girl had an innate, stately grace. Sometimes she peed her pants when she laughed, sometimes she tripped, and isn't this the finishing excellence in a perfect girl? A touch of clumsiness. It reassures.

The girl knew her family's code word, the word a stranger would have to know for her to trust him. She practiced what to say when a man failed to speak the code word, practiced the purposeful stride back to the school—she would not run, would not show fear, would simply stride into the principal's office, would say to Mrs. Levenson, "Excuse me, but I believe there is a man who means me harm." Her voice would be stern and calm. She liked that phrase: he means me harm. It belonged to another time.

The brother forgot the code word. He knew he was safe. He could take a stick and drum the tops of strangers' garbage cans all the way to school, and if someone stuck a head out the window? He'd run. If some creep tried to abduct him? Screw the code word. He'd knee the dude in the balls.

But she was a pretty girl, raised in a religion of immaculate self-protection. She rubbed lotion on her elbows and heels. She practiced walking with a book on her head. She loved rags-to-riches stories, loved that show *Lauren Rules the West,* about a clever orphan girl who becomes mayor of a small town. She loved hopscotch on the sidewalk in front of her building, loved her brother, loved celery with peanut butter. She felt sure that the world was vast and exotic, full of light and darkness both, and maybe one day she'd go to India? Maybe one day to the Wailing Wall? The Grand Canyon? She wanted to see great places. She wanted that feeling she got when she climbed the stairs inside the Statue of Liberty, that rising heat in her chest that meant: *We are littler than we imagine, but together we make something bigger than we believe possible.* Light and darkness. She was a Libra—she felt the presence of two scales inside her. As she saw it, it was her duty to forget about death with one part of her mind while thinking about nothing but death with another. How did you do this? She wasn't sure. She was working on it. In the meantime she wanted to fix things, to be a social worker, a nurse, someone who tends to those who are not pretty or raised in brownstones, those who do not sleep beneath a shelf of good-luck charms—polished stones, onyx, jasper—who do not read books about gifted animals or have mothers singing "Take Me Out to the Ballgame" as they tuck their children into bed. No one got to be precious and free. Everyone died. It was her duty to remember this, to remember and forget at the same time, to teach other people how to do the same.

She loved Crackerjack. She loved the home team with all her heart.

She was twelve; her name was Leonora; she would disappear.

1

The boy wanted a new name. He'd read about boys in Africa who at a certain point in time officially became men, and to celebrate they're given special spears, tiny as toothpicks, which someone else inserts into their penis, and also they get a bride and a mask. There was a ceremony full of bloody cattle and drums where something that represented your old name, a symbol, got thrown right into the fire. It crackled and was dead. He could go without the penis spear, the bride, but loved the idea of a new name, of igniting the old one which was incidental, a *word*, his own word so plain and flat it made him feel middle-aged. What was the special age for those kids in Africa? When were they allowed to shed themselves? Probably not ten, he reasoned.

Tonight was his birthday. He was ten. It was a Saturday evening early in the spring of 1980. The Miracle on Ice had happened, and it felt to him like that was it, that was the miracle for his era, and he was sad. Once upon a time miracles were bigger, Jesus or Joan of Arc for instance. It was a quiet disappointment, to live in an age where miracles were relegated to sports. He didn't have anything against sports—if he became a professional athlete he had a name chosen: Felix Castoff. (If he became an actor: Gregory Dubuque.) Sure, he was proud of that hockey team. He loved America, loved the underdog, loved the myth that Americans had underdog souls, but the word *miracle* made him feel somehow gypped.

Most of the time he felt trapped by his childhood. It was like watching TV, a decent show, and then a commercial comes on and lasts too long, an advertisement for oldies but goodies, song titles scrolling endlessly across the screen, when all he wanted was to discover the fate of the bank robber or the bound-and-gagged girl. He hated commercials but loved television. The girl always got untied, she was always okay, and if she wasn't it was because she was the wrong kind of girl to begin with.

His mother went by "Goldie." Her real name was something she never spoke aloud. He assumed it must be hideous, for her eyes narrowed and mouth puckered whenever he asked about it. At some point he'd stopped asking. But then, one day, poking around in her drawers, he came upon an official document and saw her real name, there in clear type: Maureen Lynn. Maureen Lynn? What was so shameful about Maureen Lynn? He couldn't ask her.

He called her "Ma." She called him by his name, or sometimes "Sugarlump."

Maybe in some part of the world turning ten meant freedom, meant you were given a bow and arrow or a bazooka and told to go off and forge your path, but not here. They sat across from each other at a card table. A vase of white carnations between them, a birthday cake, a white balloon tied to the back of his chair. His name was Paul, but it didn't have to be forever.

"You're a big boy now," Goldie was saying. "It's time you get the straight story. You want the straight story?"

He said he wanted to eat cake.

Goldie didn't seem to hear him. She said, "Let me tell you loud and clear: the truth has not vanished from the earth. Don't believe the hype."

"The hype?"

"People are still capable of honesty. Not just Christians. Regular folks. You and me."

It pleased him, he couldn't help it, that she called them "regular." Was it true?

On the table the cake beckoned sadistically. It wasn't fair, making him look for so long. A matchbox car sat buried to its axles in frosting. No one made a cake like Goldie. Her cakes were gritty, riotously sweet, pleasantly chalky.

"I'll give you as much truth as you can take. When you don't want any more, you say so. Say the word and I'll stop."

He agreed to this plan.

"Truth number one: Your father was a fraud and a dud. You know what a dud is?"

He didn't.

"A dud is can't get it up for more than thirty seconds." She cocked her head, paused. "You know what I mean by 'it'?"

She poured herself more gin.

"His weenie," she said. She laughed.

"Yes," he said.

The matchbox car was red with a blue stripe across its top. He wanted to lick its undercarriage. His hunger distressed him, by and large. He had a memory of a man—his father?—it wasn't clear, the memory was dim, there had been many men. This one was sitting on the floor of the kitchen eating marshmallow Fluff, scooping it from the jar with his fingers, no spoon, wide-eyed, desperate, in the manner of a bloated raccoon. He said, "Why is he a fraud?"

His mother took another swallow, set her tumbler on the tabletop. "He's a fraud because he told me he'd put me through college, and told me he'd never met someone so pretty, and that he never wanted to touch another lady on this good green earth and that he'd be honored to have me as his last."

He asked what was the difference between a fraud and a liar.

She thought about it. "A fraud is someone whose whole being, body and soul, is full of lies, all the organs, the skin, not a pore free of them. A liar is a person who tells stories now and then. You and me, we're just liars."

He wanted to lick the wheels of the car, but his mother held him at bay. She was the guard of cake, guard of everything.

"Your father once carved an animal out of my complexion soap. Then he yelled at me when I used it to wash my face. That soap was not cheap."

"What kind of animal?"

"How should I remember?"

She wore a red dress with a draping cowl-neck, a red-beaded necklace, and cork-heeled sandals. Her perfume evoked baby powder. The heavily plucked brows, teal liner, gave her eyes a slight bulge. She'd been drinking steadily for nearly an hour, growing impulsive, spiteful, knowing.

"Truth number two—I need a cigarette. That's not the truth. Well, it's *true*, but it's not the one I was getting at. Go in Mama's purse and grab a fiddlestick, Paul."

He obliged. It helped to have tasks. It helped when he had a mother whose demands could be met. A friend at school had a chore chart affixed to his refrigerator; Paul longed for such a thing.

He lit the cigarette for her. She took a drag, closed her eyes. "He'll be here soon," she said, exhaling, and he heard a flicker of apprehension in her voice. "Mister Clover."

He returned to his seat across from her.

He wished Mister Clover would ditch them, and he said so. He knew he wasn't supposed to say it aloud; it was the barest transgression.

"He thinks I could be a model," said Goldie. "Can you imagine it? He wants to take some pictures."

"I can imagine it."

A boy in his class had asked Paul if he'd ever seen his mother nude, and if so could he pick out a crayon that best matched the shade of her bush.

"He's bringing his camera over tonight. He's going to take some shots and show them to the manager at McFee's. They need merchandise models. Can you see that? McFee's today, *Vogue* tomorrow. That brings me to truth two."

"*Numero dos*," said Paul.

"Good boy. *Dos. Dos* is that even though your pops was a louse—"

"You didn't say louse. You said fraud and dud."

He wanted to know his father because it might tell him what was inside himself. He suspected some wrongness had been bred into him, and that only by knowing it fully could he stand a chance of escaping it. *Fraud, dud, louse.* He'd carry these words forever; all his life he'd hold them up to his experiences, one by one, as a person holds a paint sampler to a wall, seeking a match. At ten his instinct was simply to collect the words. At ten he thought: I was born from my mother's head! He had learned in a book about Athena. He pictured his mother, bulging eyes, bloody brain, his fetal body slipping naked from her cranium onto the kitchen linoleum. Oh he wasn't stupid. He knew about ovaries and all, just liked this idea better.

He couldn't picture his father's face. Supposedly he'd been a man whose modest handsomeness he drank away with Old Grand-Dad. But tonight Paul learned that he'd carved things from soap. It unsettled the account; it made a decent man of the figure scooping Fluff with his fingers.

Dud, fraud, louse.

His mother said, "I'm trying to tell you something here. You want to listen?"

"Wait," Paul said. "What's a louse?"

"Like a bug." He could tell she was getting impatient.

"What kind of bug?"

"I don't know," Goldie said. "Like a roach, how's that?"

"I like roaches."

"I know you do, Paul. I'm not sure why."

"I don't like Beetles," he said. This was a joke; Beetle was the name of their town.

"It doesn't matter. Your father behaved like a bug. But my whole drift is that even though he's a louse, and you're his flesh and blood, you are not a louse. You need to remember that."

"I wouldn't mind being a roach. They live for millions of years. Their shells are armor. They can get into anywhere. I opened a box of cereal once and there was a roach inside. The box wasn't even opened. How did it do that?"

"Oh they creep me out. Please stop."

"Some have wings," he said.

"Clover used to be an exterminator. He's been lots of things. He was once a housepainter and a guitar teacher. Now he's an artist, a photographer." She pressed her tongue against the rim of her glass. "I have a model's face, maybe, but my hips are too big. That's truth number—what number am I on? Three. These hips are too big. Do you know what they call these things?" She put down her cup, patted her flanks.

"What?"

"Mama hips." She laughed brightly, and looked at her watch, and stopped laughing. "He's late. I did my hair and all. He's bringing his camera. I made this cake."

Paul stared at the cake, his cake.

"The car is mine, right? It's not Mister Clover's birthday."

"I told you ten times."

She had cleaned the house for the occasion. She had baked the cake and shaved her legs to the thighs. The cake looked good, her legs were smooth, but the house looked exactly the same. It was collapsing in its slow, powdery way, outside and in, bricks crumbling, foundation rotting, the roof patched with tar paper. In gaps between splintering floorboards was the dust and dirt from five years of their life here, this mulchy cottage, just the two of them. The floorboard nails had loosened, rose up, caught sometimes on their socks. She paid Paul a dime for each one he hammered down again. He was good with tools, had a certain grace with a hammer—an innate confidence. Women weren't born good with tools, she didn't care what Gloria

Steinem said. It's easy to have an opinion when you look like Sophia Loren.

The place was tucked into a wooded area at the east end of town. Once it had been the guest cottage of a stately manor, but when its owners fell on hard times they burned the big house to the ground for the insurance money. This was decades ago. The cottage, by luck of wind, managed to be spared the flames. Its meager charm derived from a stone fireplace, a claw-foot tub, and a massive door knocker in the shape of an owl.

"My face is perfect for McFee's," she said, and touched the wave in her hair to make sure it hadn't faded.

"I'm hungry."

"Don't whine."

He said it again in a deeper, even voice.

In the tiny dining room, a thin robin's-egg cloth covered the card table. A shelf in the corner held their mismatched dishes, silverware propped in a mug. She had swept each room, scrubbed the kitchen's peeling linoleum, plucked cobwebs from corners. She had even bleached the bathtub, her favorite place, where she spent hours reading magazines, napping, or writing letters she would never post to the boy's father. She'd swept and scrubbed, and Paul had hammered errant nails back into place, but even so the cottage looked the same.

"Truth number five," she said. She poured the last of the gin.

"You're on four."

"Four? Fine. Truth four."

He did not like it when she drank. When Goldie was sober she talked, she talked quite a lot actually, but not like this. Her chest took on a lacy flush, and she ran her index finger back and forth along her clavicle. The local boys wanted to know what was inside her underpants. Their fathers wanted to know what was in her underpants. Paul kicked Mike Fitzpatrick in the kneecap and was suspended for three days when Mike said he'd like to put a dollar in his mother's underpants.

"Truth four: Mister Clover is the real deal. He's a gentle soul. He just might turn out to be the white horse. You have to keep an open mind. Can you do that?"

"I'm hungry," he said.

"There's applesauce. Or olives."

"I'm hungry for cake."

Goldie wanted a perfect evening. Mister Clover would see that they'd waited. He was bringing his camera. He had spoken about a portfolio. Her face could bare her soul, he'd predicted. He had spoken about cheekbones and the brightness of eyes and he used the word *incandescence*. In his presence she was nervous and quiet, like an animal stunned by a superior beast.

"Another truth," Goldie said. "We're poor."

"Number five," Paul said.

"Number five and six and seven, honey."

Goldie had one hundred and seventy-eight dollars in the bank. She was a grocery clerk at McCauley's and sometimes babysat a pair of toddler twins and sometimes weeded the garden of the spinster across the road. There was a bowling alley half an hour away; once in a while she helped out there, spraying Lysol into shoes and laughing at the owner's dirty jokes.

"Get yourself some applesauce."

The boy obeyed, trudged into the kitchen. He was wearing pale blue pajamas, the broad-lapelled sort worn by old men, and plush slippers resembling baseball mitts.

They were poor and she was pretty, and there had to be a

way to capitalize on beauty that didn't involve the weary, circular articulation of one's hips as one stood on a slippery bar above a throng of men in white T-shirts. Pretty people didn't need to suffer the way she was suffering. Mister Clover had told her so.

2

A Peeping Tom named Tom.

He was Thomas Grant, thirty-nine years old, plain, clean-shaven, a face people tended to ignore or trust unthinkingly. He carried himself like a can collector in a windstorm, luckless and determined. His graying, buzzed hair grew into a widow's peak. He was a nurse, a "male nurse" as they say (this drove him crazy), at an abortion clinic. His job was to sit with the waiting girls and to make sure they understood the procedure. He would prick their fingers, measure their blood pressure, and, afterward, take their vitals and give them apple juice and animal crackers. To work he wore pale blue scrubs which made him feel feminine, and so on weekends he wore plaid flannel, jeans, and steel-toed boots.

His apartment complex overlooked the strip mall. He was

raising his child, Jade, by himself, her mother having departed when the child was four. Now the girl was nine. By all accounts he was law-abiding, decent. He was writing a children's book about a talking milk bottle. He gave money to the lame and the blind, volunteered to run the bake sale at Jade's school, and never abandoned shopping carts in the grocery lot. He was a tender, accepting presence at the abortion clinic. In all respects save one, he was a good guy.

Goldie was his undoing. She alone could bring on such urges. He told himself he wasn't crazy or sick or obsessed, but merely in love. But not *merely*! Love was the thing. The hardest. The noblest. Though, since he did not feel noble, perhaps it was not love. Perhaps it was awe? He was decidedly in awe, which may be an even more sublime state, he reasoned, more difficult, more demanding. Only Goldie could compel him to telephone the old woman next door, beg her for the third time in a week to watch his child, and to kiss Jade good night in a hurry, to throw on his scarf and gloves, to run the half mile to the cottage where she lived with her son, so he could watch—breathing into his hands so as not to fog the glass—a woman he had never spoken to and never would.

Goldie! What could he possibly have said? The world did not offer the words. Language was a net with holes too big to catch what he could say to her.

He watched their sad domestic life unfold. He watched her primp and putter and snip at the boy who sat before her in uneasy docility, like a member of a corrupt court. She was regal—that was a word he could use. He was in awe, yes, and also terrified of her. He wanted only to watch, not to touch, not to be seen, not to enter. When he watched he could smell distinctly the layers of pine and mud in the air, a bristling underground scent that made him feel dirty and thirsty and also righteous, like coming home from a long hard hike. Here he could have an erection without needing to fondle it, without the gratification of touch. He was only his eyes. Her beauty was sudden and trenchant, an illness one must succumb to.

"Good night, baby," he whispered to his girl. He drew the blanket to her chin. Her hair was the light red of certain small apples, her nose faintly freckled. Supine in her bed, she could have been advertising cough syrup, stirring hearts. Her round face and muted expression lent her an aspect of sleepy convalescence. She asked him to sing to her, and he did, but the lullaby was fast and far from soothing and all the while his heart raced. His heart was a judge's gavel, pounding *guilty, guilty, guilty*, and so he was, and so he let himself run away.

He promised the woman next door, her breath fierce with bourbon, that he'd be back by ten.

She shrugged, said, "Take all the time you need."

He jogged, taking a shortcut through the woods to avoid the town center, loving so much the snap of twigs beneath his feet, loving the sense of himself, of his running self, like an inviolable creature, as deserving of these woods, this pace—as deserving of the instincts that propelled him—as the animals crouched beyond his sight. The moon was a dull blade. The stars were incidental and always had been. All that mattered was that he could run, that he had located this awe inside of him, like a rare coin in a pile of pennies. He ran full of lust and authority, ran faster, feeling no doubt, the path slippery with pine needles and rotting leaves. Occasionally a pair of yellow eyes. Occasionally an owl's hollow bleat, which he might, if he felt bold, mimic.

3

" Are you ready for another truth?"

He knew that her truths were not truths—or they were true but not Truths. She was making them up as they went. She was trying to distract him, soften him by way of disclosures. She had not bought him a proper gift and so delivered these statements in the manner of a gift, as if her candor were itself a gift. What he wanted was the opposite of candor. He wanted the lie of silence and cake. He wanted a serene smile, and for her to take him into her arms, and to feel she had no other need, and for her mouth to stop, just for tonight, his birthday.

"The next truth is that now is the time, Paul. Now, little man, and only now."

"Time for what?"

"I'm losing my looks," she said. "Maybe not yet. But I will, and soon. Now is the time to model, if it's going to happen. Now is the time to find a—"

She was going to say *husband*, but the word broke apart. It was like a stone that, prodded, turns into sand.

He wanted to lick the frosting from the undercarriage.

"A man," she said. "That's all. Just a man. I don't want to spend my golden years cooped up here alone. I don't want to be one of those ladies with a book of puzzles." Her eyes shone, and she bit down on her thumb. She did not want to cry. Her mascara would run. Paul would look at her with his turned-off face, his strange, calm, priestly face. His stillness was masterful, not entirely of this world. She respected it even as it sent waves of fear along her spine. He was not her; he could do what she could not do: he could preserve the boundary between his little self and the world. Why couldn't she do that? Her own self was bigger, she reasoned, so its boundary harder to manage. But she felt strongly that Paul would never lose this capacity. It was a gift, and she didn't have it, and her son did. Had she helped him have it? She hoped so. It seemed the greatest of gifts, even though she was dumb to its origins and frightened in its presence. She had borne a child who possessed the ability to shut her out. It was miraculous and sad and right.

"I want a companion," she said gently, and averted her eyes. "When I get old."

"But I'll be here." He realized as he said it that it wasn't true. For just a second he'd forgotten that boys leave. When he remembered, he said, "I'll live down the street."

"You'll be in Hong Kong. You'll be in Hawaii. I met a guy who was once a pimp on Oahu. Most *pliant* women—that's the word he used." She snorted. "No, you'll be putting out fires or pimping or painting houses or catching fish, whatever boys like you do when the mood strikes."

He asked what pimping was and she thought for a moment. "A pimp is a person who sells to lonely people what other people get for free."

"I don't think I want to be a fisherman."

"Good for you."

"Maybe a fireman."

"Fishermen die young and sleep around. Trust me."

"A fireman. Here in Beetle."

"There aren't any fires in Beetle."

He gestured out the window, to where the big house once stood.

"There's nothing worth saving, that's what I mean. Let it burn."

He would not look at the cake.

"You'll be out making your fortune. You'll be far away. You'll be searching for whatever ring-a-ding captures you. Maybe there'll be a war, honey. Maybe you'll be out killing whoever we see fit to kill. Maybe you'll be our hero."

He wished for a war and often told her so.

"A war with China," he guessed now.

She examined the tops of her hands.

"I don't think China. Not China."

"India?"

She yawned. "They say hands give away a woman's age better than anything else. I'd say the neck, the upper chest."

She looked at her watch.

"Paul, my little man. Be nice to Mama. Be nice to Mister Clover is what I mean. When you look at Mister Clover, pretend you're looking at me. What we have here is what's called a window. That's an important truth."

"What number is that?"

"Be nice to Mister Clover. You can make or break this thing. Years from now, I don't want to be sitting at this table all alone. I don't want to be sitting at this table while you're out screwing some little tart. Men are never alone. I don't want to be sitting here waiting for you to come to the door with a bundle of joy. You shouldn't expect that of me."

"I don't."

"You don't know it yet, but it's what you expect. And that's fine—it's what you're supposed to expect. But we've been through a lot together. Be nice to Mister Clover. This is the least you can do."

He nodded gravely. He said nothing. He did not look at the cake, or ask for the cake. His feet grew hot in their slippers.

"Happy Birthday," she said. "I mean that."

He bowed his head at these words, as if at a blessing. A few minutes passed. They listened for Clover. For a moment they heard a rustling, and Goldie tilted her ear toward the noise, but it stopped. It was not Clover.

Paul felt a tickle on the back of his neck, a faint shiver, a signal that something in the room had changed. He looked around. Nothing had changed.

His mother said it again, louder: "Happy Birthday!"

Nothing had changed, but he felt they were being observed.

One time, maybe a year ago, he'd woken to noise from his mother's room. What began as a mild whimper became louder, strident—her voice, then someone else's—louder, urgent, not pained exactly, not right either. The sounds overlapped; he could tell there were more than two people in her room. Paul rose, crept into the hall, and saw her door halfway open. His mother was in bed with Chuck. He knew Chuck—Chuck the Schmuck, his mother said—but there was another man there too, a man he didn't recognize, a man kneeling at the foot of the bed, hair to his shoulders, elbows on the covers, his back to Paul.

A scarf over her lampshade lent the room a deep, plummy cast. Her dress lay on the floor. Her shoes. Her underwear. Chuck, with a grunting laugh, pulled the covers over his head. Now all Paul could see was his mother's torso, her head propped on two pillows. Her face was flat, unthinking; she might have been watching TV; she might have been waiting for the dryer to finish at the laundromat. Under the covers Chuck became a bobbing lump. His mother hummed. They watched. Meaning everyone. Chuck, hidden, doing whatever he was doing, that was a kind of watching. The man at the end of the bed, he watched while he squeezed her foot through the blanket, while he murmured, "That's the music, that's the music, honey, keep singin' that song." And Paul, behind them all, watched. Then Paul saw that the stranger, the kneeling man, lifted a hand and touched, lightly, the back of his own neck. He ran his hand up and down the nape. It was as if the man had felt a shiver, as if his body knew that he, too, was being watched. Paul took a breath, prepared to flee, sure he'd be found out—but the stranger did not turn around. His mother's noises changed, came now through her teeth, like a child mimicking a train, *chugachugachugachug.* Paul wanted to turn around but could not. Her sounds rose and fell. *Chugachuga.* Then her face was no longer a TV-watching face, a waiting-for-the-dryer face. Now it was the face of someone in pain, or, no, someone preparing for pain—a face as a needle comes at your arm. At once Paul's own neck tingled; at once he knew that there was someone else, someone behind him, also watching. But he didn't turn. No one turned. No one moved. In this way, necks tingling, he imagined a train of people watching his mother, one after the next, each sensing the other's presence but not willing to look, not wanting to confirm the feeling, because to confirm it would be to take their eyes off Goldie, and who would do that? Goldie arched her body, threw back her head, the skin of her throat purple in the light. Her soft locomotive chugging rose in volume, picked up speed, until it exploded—until it was the whistle that warns of a crossing—I'm coming, save yourself—the good municipal scream—the stay away, stay away.

He ran back to his room. He felt sick and dumb, wanted to puke, to stop the thudding of his heart and stop the hotness in his stomach. He was wearing footed pajamas. How he despised them, their stupid feet, their long zipper! He'd never wear them again.

"My birthday boy," Goldie said. "Where does the time go?"

He said he didn't know.

"Ten years. A whole bleeping decade. Can you tell me where it goes?"

She was wrong about time. It went too slow and headed nowhere. Time was a commercial on repeat, a loop of advertising, buy this or that or this or that, it doesn't matter what, buy something and be glad for it. His childhood would never end. He would be ten forever. He would never eat the cake. He would never have a toothpick in his penis or a virgin bride. He would always be Paul.

He said, "Time is dead."

Goldie laughed, "My wise guy!"

He never saw those men again, not Chuck or the stranger at the foot of the bed. Still, ever since that night he sensed eyes everywhere. The woods were eyes. The kids at school had eyes under their eyes. Soon enough his mother was dating Freddy Marino, one of the God crew, on whose pocketknife handle was etched *Be sure your sin will find you out,* so for a while everything was on the up-and-up.

4

Thomas watched. He did not peep. Peep implied furtive glances, an eye against a crack in the wall, implied perversion and greed and contempt. He told himself: *This is not peeping.* This is one human being in awe of another, and could awe be criminal? Only if it was not real awe. Only if it was need or disdain disguised as awe. He needed nothing from her. He felt toward her only a throaty tenderness. So he gazed at this woman and her son, this family, as it were, in an open, reverent manner, damp-eyed, curious, but always, he told himself, with reverence that obliterated prurience. He looked at them through the bottom corner of a large, uncurtained window, not some crack in the wall, not some secret camera. It was looking, just that, no tools, no greed, no need for reciprocity, no touching of the body. He made sure his breath was slow, his back straight, as if to demonstrate his decency. If he'd come upon a true peeper he would have beat him up. He would have genuinely felt like he was defending her honor.

He first saw Goldie in a diner. He and Janice had been sitting in a booth, negotiating the end of their relationship. Of course he hadn't known that then—he thought it was just another argument and they'd fuck it off. They ate steak and eggs, fought with the ketchup bottle. It was dusk, one of those sad places that serve breakfast all day.

Goldie, in the company of a toddler, sat at a booth toward the back, in his line of sight but behind Janice. He watched Goldie eat a slice of pie, watched her chew in a slow, wincing way. The sign over the counter declared OUR PIES VOTED BEST EAST OF THE MISSISSIPPI. Voted by whom? What was pie like on the other side of that great river? Thomas had never seen the river, never been west of it, let alone tasted Western pie. The diner was stuffy, wood-paneled, a stag head above the cigarette machine, a baseball player's photo, autographed in grandiose loops, framed above the counter. There was a little jukebox circled in pink neon affixed to the wall of the booth, and Goldie shuffled though its offerings absently. She drank a lot of coffee. She wore many silver rings and an electric blue shirt with buttons in the shape of diamonds. Her eyes were elsewhere. Even when she talked to the kid, even ordering more coffee, even moving her lips faintly as she read song titles, her eyes were elsewhere. Every now and then she'd come to for a moment, startle back into herself; then she'd hastily minister to the kid, wipe crumbs from his face, offer a spoonful of whipped cream. Her tenderness was compensation. The kid was strapped into a high chair. His feet in green sneakers hung heavily. His face had the full, polished redness of an old man at the beach, blunted by decades of sunlight. The kid, too, seemed elsewhere, would startle when he noticed a spoon aimed at his mouth or when his mother's hand, in that impulsive instant, smoothed his hair.

Her face was round and rouged. The wide mouth winced as she ate. Her hair was big, wavy. She clearly was not satisfied with the pie, not satisfied with anything.

Thomas wondered if he could change that. How? He didn't know.

Now, eight years later, the face of the son was more artfully, vigilantly blank. A balloon tied to the back of his chair, a cake waiting between them, while she talked and drank and ran a finger along her clavicle. She was talking to pass the time. Thomas could not hear all the words, but he could watch her mouth move. He could tell she was talking just for talking's sake, but the kid was listening. Of course that's what kids did, listened to everything, took it all in. They heard their mothers say *louse* and *dud* and *fraud*. They heard their mothers say *This child is killing me*. It went beyond hearing; it went straight to the gut.

Eight years ago, Janice had said, "The way you eat your eggs has always struck me as weird."

"Nixon uses ketchup."

"If you care about having a relationship with my mother, you'll resign." Janice's mother, born-again, could not abide his work. "You take the tiniest bites."

"Jesus Christ."

"There are openings at the hospital. Marnie told me. And don't do that. You did that to spite her."

"Did what?"

"They're looking for nurses."

"Jesus Cripes. Better?"

He saw that she wanted to say something but was afraid. "Marnie said it's great over there. Good benefits."

"I like my job."

Janice said she truly didn't care what the hell he did, didn't care how many babies got butchered—perhaps they wouldn't be in this jam if she herself had paid a visit there—but yesterday her mother agreed to provide free day care for Jade on the condition that he quit.

"But you don't work. You're home all day, Janice. Why do we need free day care?"

She shot him a look of wounded hatred; she could manage that beautifully, join woundedness to any aggression, so that you felt pity despite yourself.

"I am dying in that apartment. I am not cut out to stay home all day with a—" She paused. "I'm sad," she said finally. "I want my mother's help. Maybe I'll take an art class."

"Yes, take an art class. We'll pay for a babysitter. We don't need your mother dictating our lives."

"She'll give us money!"

"I don't want it."

"We need it."

"Not on that condition."

"She's got a point. It's dangerous at the clinic. Weekly threats. Bombs and all that bullshit—you said so yourself. That note on the doctor's windshield? Marnie said the hospital's great. Nice people. Good benefits. Doughnuts on Friday sort of thing."

"Doughnuts?"

"And flexible hours."

"I don't like doughnuts."

"You like crullers."

He shrugged. It was true.

"That note was terrible. —What are you looking at?" She turned. "Her?"

"I'm looking at you."

He looked at his wife's face, hard, to prove it.

"You're looking at her. You've been looking at her since we sat down."

"Please do yourself a favor and take a breath."

She said, "She's got a fat face."

"Don't do that."

"I'm sad."

"Sad how?"

"Sad I want to run the fuck away. Sad I want my mother to love us."

He knew it was the wrong question. "Where do you want to go?"

"I don't know. How should I know?" She frowned. "Chicago? Toledo? Orlando? It doesn't matter. You see?"

He sighed.

"She's a cow." She jabbed her thumb over her shoulder. "I'm miserable. Can you help me?"

He didn't know and said so.

"Look at you. Look at you looking at her. My mother is right. You murder things."

They sat at the table for a long time.

Now he wanted nothing. He did not desire entrance. He was not a father or a husband or a nurse or a son at these moments. The woods moved around him. He kept himself in shadows, his face close to the glass. His mind swung like a bell between his women.

5

At last Clover arrived, shaggy-haired, in fatigue pants and a white dress shirt, Birkenstocks, a camera case slung across his body, a special copper bracelet on his wrist meant to obliterate aches and summon inner peace. His neck was reedy, eyebrows raised. He apologized for being late. The life of an artist, he said, and wound his finger around his ear a few times to mean *crazy, crazy, a crazy life*. Goldie murmured deferentially. He ruffled Paul's hair, sat down with them at the table, tapped his fingers on its edge. He said he loved the place, its cavelike quality. He said it felt like a dark, quiet aquarium. She offered him a drink, gin, beer, bourbon, but he accepted some water.

"I've made a cake," Goldie said. "It's Paul's tenth birthday."

Again he ruffled Paul's hair. "Well well," said Clover. "The big one-oh. You feel different today, man?"

"Not much," said Paul.

Goldie clapped her hands.

Clover leaned back in his chair, rubbed his gut as if sated. "I'm afraid I can't partake of the cake. I don't do refined sugar."

"It's just got regular sugar," Goldie said.

"Sugar, dairy, empty carbohydrates, booze. They cloud the mind," Clover said. "Plug the bowels. You ever had a colonic?"

Goldie shook her head.

"Best thing in the world. You'd love it. Rids the body of all toxins." He gestured to the cake.

"Interesting," Goldie said. The cake now struck her as rude—she felt ashamed, as if she'd told an off-color joke.

"Woman over in Munroe does 'em. Calls herself 'Sunny.' Sunny put my testimonial on the front of her brochure. You'd be amazed at how good you feel afterwards. Like taking a long swim in an ocean. That kind of pure, open clean."

"It sounds just fantastic," she said, but she didn't really know what a colonic was. She had a vague sense it had something to do with the asshole, but probably not, because why would he be talking about his asshole on a first date? She had to remind herself it wasn't officially a date. The date was to come. In the meantime, she would learn about colonics. In the meantime, she would remove the cake. It seemed dumb now, sitting there coated in sugar, an emblem of her ignorance. Goldie stood, gave Paul a warning look, and picked up the cake. She carried it into the kitchen and placed it on top of the refrigerator. When she returned she held three oranges. She set them on the table, said, a little shyly, "Do you do oranges?"

"Oranges I do. Oh yes sir," and he took a bite straight into one, through the peel. Chewing, the corners of his mouth glistening with juice, he extolled the virtues of orange peel, of bitter foods in general, rose hips, certain medicinal weeds, and then moved on to the pleasure of jumping freight trains (here he turned to Paul and warned him to wait a couple years), nude beaches, and Mapplethorpe, a viciously nasty photographer, and by nasty he meant exceptional.

"Speaking of Mapplethorpe," he said, "you ready to say a little cheese?" He patted his camera case.

She had been ready forever. She touched her hair. "Do you like what I'm wearing? I can change. I have a black dress, too. Or something different."

He squinted at her dress, frowned, but said, "You're perfect."

"The necklace?"

"The necklace we could do without."

She unhooked the clasp and it fell onto her lap.

It's starting, she told herself. She stood up. Her head felt slow, heavy, but her heart was going fast. Clover was dashing—it was an old-fashioned word but felt exactly right. He had a kind of vigor and carefree quality she'd never known in a man. Paul's father had been slow. His lazy body with its paunch and bulges never moved like Clover's, never with such fast, confident surges. She'd never known a man to use words like Clover, or one who paid attention to his insides or to weeds or art. She wanted badly to kiss him. She felt slow next to him, and had the sense that a kiss might slow him down, or speed her up, somehow even them out a little.

Clover winked at Paul, who sat in his chair, watching as Clover took his mother's picture, first against the white wall, like a mug shot, just to get going, and then propped on her elbows on the floor in front of the fireplace, then collapsed on the couch, then fully clothed in the empty bathtub. He was an artist. This is what artists did: shots of people wearing clothing in the bathtub, shots of pretty women making ugly faces ("Uglier," he commanded, "no, uglier"), shots with her hands covering her face, shots of her knees, several of her feet, toenails, which she was glad she'd painted.

"Top-notch," he whispered, camera flashing, "top, top-notch." She liked his splayed elbows, wide stance, liked even his remonstrations, which made him seem serious: "Quit the pouting" and "We're not going for Miss America here, Goldie."

When he asked her to lift up the skirt of her dress and sit on the toilet she said, "Really?"

He began to talk about the duty of the subject, the strangeness of real art and the tyranny of received ideas, but then he interrupted himself, sighed, said, "No, not really."

She liked it very much when, between rolls of film, he commented on the cleanliness of the house. She thanked him. But then he said, "I can smell the cleaner you used today, Goldie. Ammonia, bleach, both are serious health risks. Bad for the kid and bad for the earth. I'll give you some literature on the subject."

After a while he stopped taking pictures. He drank a glass of water, wiped his mouth with the back of his hand. He promised he would show the photos to the manager at McFee's.

"Do you think he'll like them?"

"If he has a dot of sense. What do you think, Paul? You think your ma looks hot?"

Paul said that he did. Yes, sure, pretty.

"Hot," Clover corrected.

"Hot," Paul said.

"Incendiary," said Clover, and slapped his thigh.

But what Paul thought was that his mother looked strange, startled, and that her face, which could be so nice, did not look nice now, looked buggy, red, and her neck was tilted unnaturally. Paul thought that Clover said mean things, and said things having nothing to do with his mother but which she took as compliments. For example he said, "They say the eyes are the window to the soul, but I say it's the mouth," and Goldie said "Thank you," her voice very soft. Then Clover said, "This isn't some porn now, Goldie," and she laughed as if flattered. Clover said he'd like to get some shots of her out in the world, among people, with music playing, maybe at that new club over in Milltown? Would she like that? Would she like to go out there with him? She got her coat. She kissed the tip of her son's nose. She whispered he could go ahead with the cake now. She knew, after their talk, he would understand.

6

He had written Janice's name in his margins. He had studied each letter, each little workaday letter, which, placed together in this peculiar arrangement, as if by some enchantment, became her name, became *her*. On their second date she gave him a round piece of sea glass, the wave-polished bottom of a bottle, pale, watery green, a color he could find speckling her irises if he looked hard enough. He looked hard. He prayed that she'd stay, that she'd soften, become nicer, over time. He was willing to give it time.

When she found out she was pregnant she'd threatened to hurt herself.

He said, "You don't have to have it."

"My mother would kill me!"

"She wouldn't have to know."

"It'd be all over me. She'd know. She'd read it on me. She'd *know.*"

Her mother was magic, omniscient, cruel, and also the only one Janice could turn to to recover from the world's cruelty. It was her paradox. She wore olive eye shadow, heavy foundation, magenta lipstick—makeup so deeply and evenly applied, so opaque, it reminded him of a coroner's work. It was as though she was already dead and therefore could never leave them— another paradox.

"I want to hurt myself," she whispered. "I do."

"No, baby," he said.

"No baby," she said.

It was an irony, he thought, that she who so desperately relied on her mother, who knew so well the savage connection to one's mother, would one day abandon her own child. She couldn't herself bear being one, couldn't bear holding the mother's power, for Janice herself wanted no power. She wanted only whim. She wanted only a few naked Polaroids of her mole-speckled body to admire, those cute juice glasses, some Zeppelin to crow along with.

Thomas watched Goldie walk toward the car with the photographer. He was a tall hippie guy. Somewhere on his body was a bell, maybe attached to the strap of his sandal, so he jingled faintly as he moved. All those guys wore bells, little signs of their lightheartedness. He deserved to be punched. Seeing them, seeing the guy's easy loping strides and Goldie's careful, high-heeled totter, the guy's primer-gray car with the feather on its antenna, Thomas wanted to spit. She could do infinitely better! From behind a clot of shrubbery, he watched her gasp a little in the night air, her shoulders rising. He heard her admire the creep's ramshackle car, saw her wait for him to open the door for her, and then open it herself, and climb in. The car puttered down the gravel road. She was gone. She left the kid. She could do so much better.

He moved back to the window. If he couldn't watch Goldie he could watch the boy. It wasn't the same, not at all, but there was still a satisfaction in watching the kid. He held certain clues. It was like getting a look into her medicine cabinet. The boy remained at the table. One of his huge slippers had fallen off. Still his face was blank, his head slightly tilted, like a ventriloquist's doll on a hook at night.

"I'll have it," Janice had said. "I'll have to have it. I will."

"You'll be a good mother."

She winced. "Please don't talk like that. I didn't say I'd be a mother. I'll have it, okay? Can we just leave it at that?"

He didn't know what she meant, where they were leaving it.

Her face was pale. He loved her with unbending passion. He said so. He uttered a few more sentiments, and then she went to the bathroom to be sick again.

7

They drove along Route 22. On the radio a voice was saying: *The Lord our Savior won't accept excuses. The Lord our Savior doesn't care a lick if the babysitter's got a rack like a*—and he turned the station dial until he found banjo music, cheery bluegrass, and then leaned back, nodding along. "That's sure some strumming." He whistled through his teeth, darkly, like a cowboy.

"I appreciate this," she said.

"No need. It's a pleasure. Though I feel kind of bad about your kid."

"Oh, he'll be fine. He'll put himself to bed. Like I said, he's an independent boy. He likes to be on his own."

"Good thing to be, independent. There's no better talent."

"He's wise beyond his years."

"Yeah?"

"Plus his math skills. He's been asked to be a tutor for another boy—a boy who happens to be in the grade above him."

"Well now."

"His scores are very high."

"People used to say that about me—wise beyond my years. Can't say it's always great fun. I mean it can be a burden. No question it pays off, but wisdom's tough for a kid."

"They said it about me, too," she said, but this wasn't exactly true. What they'd said was: *You're too big for your britches, Goldie. You keep up this way and you'll be knocked up at fourteen.* She knew it wasn't the same as wise beyond one's years, but it was the version girls got sometimes.

The banjo slowed. Now someone plucked the sort of tender, sleepy melody she associated with against-the-odds weddings. It felt like a gift, that this sweet song should find this car out here on this road, should find this radio, them—that they were a *them* tonight was itself a gift and a surprise. How, after everything, did she end up in a car with an artist? His wasn't a pickup, or a red Camaro swamped by musky pine deodorizer. It was a piece of shit and it didn't matter; he didn't need a good car to stand for his manliness. Inside it smelled stale, a bit like body odor if she was honest, and it needed paint. He didn't care about paint. His was a life of the mind. A life of the camera. A life of the beauty underneath the beauty, he said. He had called this incandescence. All of it, the ugly car, his words, the tiny bell, made her feel nearly certain that life could find a way to redeem anyone who was remotely decent.

Inside of her she carried, in a small tough nut, her days at the Lady Parade and a few other bad things she'd done. But this nut was small. And around it was everything else: her good smile, her devotion to her child, her style, her hope. Mister Clover had seen these other things. More than that: he'd wanted to take their picture.

The slow, sweet song was winding down. It would end soon. Its slowness had the opposite effect on her body: she became revved up, impatient, her feet tapped a little, her knees shook. She felt a kind of thrumming in her stomach, like having drunk some milk that had begun to turn. She stole a few glimpses of his profile as he drove—he was handsome, if a little pretty. He had a girl's round, pink mouth, but the rest of his face absorbed its femininity—the dark and jutting brow, the fuzzy underchin, the big ears. His hair was uncombed and coarse, gray-brown, long enough to tuck behind his ears.

"Tell me about yourself, Goldie," he said.

It caught her off guard. She shrugged. "I have a simple life. You saw it."

"I saw it," he agreed. "But what's underneath it all?"

"Well, my parents."

"Yeah, I imagined something like that."

A misty rain had begun and his wipers squeaked across the windshield. She was silent for a moment. Her father's buddies had called him "Dappy." He was an electrician who drank alone in the attic most nights, who occasionally came downstairs to hold both of her hands in one of his huge, dry hands and warn her about the ills of the world. But she couldn't really say this, could she? Neither did it seem right to say that her mother, praised always for her vivaciousness, for her ass-length hair and fine, rippling laugh, died when her car left the road in the July of Goldie's eleventh year. The car was found days later at the bottom of a gully. It would be off-putting, certainly, to say this, or to say that for years she thought her mother faked her death, that one day Goldie would come upon her at a bus station or on a busy avenue in some city, would come upon a nervous woman with dyed hair and big sunglasses, and they'd embrace in spite of themselves. She should not say these things, right? But as it turned out she didn't need to say anything, because he started talking again, and this was an enormous relief, for she knew it was basically impossible to say anything about your parents without flattening them out to their saddest parts, without showing the part of you that's just the same.

He said, "My old mum is a playwright. The Valley Players are putting on her show next month. It's called *Winter: A Death in Three Acts*. You should go—it's really tremendous. I helped her edit it. First-rate."

She said, "Yes, I'll have to check it out," wondering if this might be a date.

8

He didn't want the cake anymore. Now that he could have it, now that it was his and no one else's, he didn't want it, not the cake, not the matchbox car, they had no meaning. No— they had new meaning. They meant: *If you eat you'll become that Fluff-devouring guy on the kitchen floor.* Or they meant: *You'll become him anyway, but faster if you eat.*

That wasn't true either. They meant: *Who are you kidding, kid? You're him already. You were born him.*

He sat at the table wishing he were somewhere else.

Three years before, his mother had taken him into the city. She wanted to eat a special kind of sandwich and bring him to a shop that sold famous pickles. She wanted to buy them each a new pair of shoes. But what did he care about shoes? The city was magnificent and filthy. Poo spit breath pee yeast. Being

there was like entering someone's body—it made him think of a
movie where the heroes get miniaturized and injected into a
human bloodstream and travel around in a special submarine,
dodging vessels and cells. How could he try on a pair of shoes?
How could he be expected to care about his feet? He'd let go of
her hand and gotten lost.

Fifteen hours later he'd gotten found.

He wasn't allowed to play baseball or see any kids for a month
after that, no dessert either, or TV, though the TV part lasted
only a few days. Without TV he was always hanging around her,
tapping her elbows, interrupting her magazine time and bath
time with jokes he'd invented and numerical equations. It was a
lonely month. She kept saying, "You've fried my nerves, Paul . . .
You've fried me all up," and she did look fried for a while after
that, fidgety, tense, always chewing the inside of her cheek so
her mouth looked twisted and old. "That was the very worst
night of my whole life," she said, and he saw that she meant it.

He was sorry, he was, but it wasn't the worst night of his life.
He hadn't meant to get lost. He'd been just seven years old, a
little kid, fascinated still by sewer sludge and bottle caps, by the
faces in kneecaps. He couldn't be blamed. The city was loud and
pure. It was itself the way a body is itself; it had no say in the
matter. He couldn't avoid the windows full of radios and robots,
the shuttering subway grates, the jolt that rose splendidly into
his loins when a train passed underneath—*underneath*—him,
and the rows of phone booths, all those phones with their rigid
silver cords like the tails of the rats of the future. There was a
man whose beard was a squirrel. There was a beach ball in the
gutter, fully inflated, floating along in the wind made by traffic.
But these were not the things that took him from his mother.
They just held him back a little, and then she would turn and

grab him, tug his wrist for a while, until she herself got distracted and would loosen her grip again.

After walking for a long time, they came upon a park. They turned a corner and there it was, endless, full of yellow flowers and squirrels and birds, everything fluttering. A shirtless man on roller skates flew by them, by Paul and his mother, and she turned to watch, cried "Speed demon! Hot potata!" and this is when she let go of Paul's hand for the last time.

The park smelled of grease and melon, a picnic air. Free of his mother's grasp, he was drawn to a stream where a pale red fish whipped itself in circles around a beer bottle. He was drawn to a tangle of barbwire. He found a yo-yo without its string. He found an unopened can of RC Cola. The place was full of traps, bitty snares, harmless and perfect mysteries, a pile of athletic socks here, a trumpet case there, more and more yellow flowers the deeper in you went, orange newts. But it wasn't nature that interested him, it was how ruined nature was, how full of metal and glass and plastic, and he understood that in some essential way nature really was best when it was spoiled, you could know it better like this, could see it for what it was, though you weren't allowed to say so or you were a litterer and unlawful. He didn't want to litter; he just enjoyed the effect. When did he realize he'd lost sight of his mother? It dawned on him slowly. He let himself pretend it wasn't true. He turned in a few circles. He called for her. He retraced his steps, then surged forward on the path. But she was nowhere.

Before he could panic he heard a voice say, "Looking for something?" It was a lady pushing a shopping cart and dragging four old dogs. She wore two leashes around each wrist.

"My mother," he said.

She shook her arms, releasing the animals. They approached

him shyly, nuzzled his armpits and belly. Coffee cans, bags of dog food, newspapers, and tangled clothing filled the shopping cart. Her hair was long and coarse, like an Indian's.

"My mother," he said again. "I can't find her."

She gave him a glinting, easy smile. "You can't, can you?" She nodded. "That's *the* problem, isn't it? Can't find her anywhere. But look." She motioned to the stream and the trees and the purplish sky—it was dusk by now.

She offered to help him look. They walked the great park in many wide loops. They passed many mothers, none his. She took him into the park's nooks, its snarls of trash and overgrowth, and never did he feel afraid. He felt shaky from hunger and exertion, and feared the punishment coming when he saw his mother again, but he knew he was safe with this lady, that she would help. She pushed her cart, grunting sometimes as they went uphill, exuding calm. She sang a song in a different language and now and then yelled out to the dogs, who heeded her. It grew dark, so she brought him to her house, which was a tiny shed like a cave, four walls of particle board and a tin roof tucked into a stand of poplars. She promised they'd look again tomorrow. She gave him graham crackers and a piece of chocolate from a padlocked box (she made him close his eyes while she entered the combination). Then she told him the story of the three bears. Its familiarity was a relief and a disappointment. She was a kindly monster. If she ate him she would eat him with tenderness. As he lay on the dogs' beanbag, sleep approaching, an unexpected calm settled over him. It was like he'd come home, like this was the place that was meant for him. He knew that was silly but felt it anyhow. The dog called Shelby curled around him. For a few moments, until guilt overwhelmed him, he pretended she was his mother. A rain began, like a barrage of bullets on the tin roof, but he was safe.

He woke up early and knew for sure his mother would be angry and crying black tears. He left quietly. The old woman did not stir when he stood up, nor when he took one last graham cracker from the box. Three dogs were asleep; one watched him. He smiled at it, then hurried away. The sun was just rising, the park more ordinary today, uglier in the new light. Litter, today, was more like litter. He walked toward traffic noise, certain someone would see him and help him find his way to being found, which is just what happened. An old man brought him to a police officer on a horse, who to Paul's disappointment did not put Paul on the horse but instead called another police officer, who put him in a car, not even a cop car, an ordinary car, and buckled him in.

Paul often wondered what that lady was doing now. Was she as lonely as he was, in her cold shed? Or had they gathered her up long ago and put her someplace? He was not stupid. He knew something was wrong with her. But he couldn't help it: sometimes he wished he hadn't left. Why do some people get what they want and others don't? He sat at the table with these thoughts. They were too familiar to be distressing. But then something that *was* distressing began to happen. It started in his throat—a flickering, flitting sensation—and all at once he wanted to do something mean. The feeling in his throat became a commotion in his whole body, a fluttering in his stomach, then his groin, his thighs, knees, soon filling him from head to feet. It urged him to hurt something, it was the force of badness rippling through him. It was in his body but did not belong to him, not yet, and he wanted to get it out. Could he get it out? He rose from the table, shook out his hands. He stamped his feet. It didn't help.

He clutched his hammer and, one by one, loosened the floorboard nails. Then he pounded them back into place. This didn't help either. It wasn't a real chore. He had no work to do, no duty except to stay, to listen, to wait. The cake was toxic, like Clover said, and Paul thought about pounding the cake with his hammer, making a mess of it, but what would that accomplish? He felt terrible, crimpy, fluttering and hot, his body no longer his body. The strange sensation radiated lengthwise, like a twisting ribbon. It found even his toes and made them tingle. He took off his slippers. His feet were pink and ugly and blockish. With his fingernails he pinched his toes. He started with all of them but felt the pull of a single place, the skin between the big toe and the one next to it, that webbing on his right foot. He pinched harder, there.

The sensation stopped. His heart calmed. He breathed. His mother was decent, his father irrelevant, the lady in the park a harmless ghost. He breathed some more. But then, as soon as he released the webbing, the feeling returned. He pinched again—it stopped again. Let go—it returned. He could not pinch himself for the rest of his life. Panic.

With the hammer he pried a nail from a floorboard in the corner and held it between his thumb and forefinger. He pressed the point of the nail to the web between his toes. He inhaled, raised the hammer, and struck. The nail pierced the skin and entered the floorboards.

"Ma," he said, but that wouldn't get him anywhere. So he called: "Oh God," and this is when he saw the man watching him through the window.

9

They pushed through a crowd of people to get in. The new club was red and black, a checkered floor, velvet booths along the walls, flat faces looking daringly at hers. It was like walking into a playing card. She held on to Mister Clover's wrist; he yanked her though the throng to the back where it was less crowded, where they found a nook and stood, bobbing to the thrumming—you couldn't quite call it a song. The band was four chubby guys on a vaulted stage, long hair, wristbands, the singer's words impossible to make out though you could tell from the veins in his neck he meant them something awful.

They watched the crowd. A few girls had kicked off their shoes. One was applying lipstick to a man's mouth. People danced sloppily, bravely. It was a new club, with newfangled décor, but it smelled like every club she'd ever been to, the same

smoke and sweat and beer. You couldn't hide that. You couldn't
cover that up with paint or heart decals. The music quieted a
moment, and in the lull she thanked Clover again, and told him
how much she liked him.

"You're so—" For a moment she couldn't think of the word.
"So different." It wasn't the word she meant, wasn't a good word,
for what did *different* mean? Nothing. It only had meaning when
you explained what he was different from, and she wasn't about
to do that. She wanted to say something else. She told him that
she found him handsome.

"Quit with the Clover, yeah? You should call me Joel."

"I didn't know that's your name."

"Yes," he said. "It is."

The music picked up again.

Clover—Joel, but the name did not suit him—placed a glass
of something in her hand. She drank it. Then a different man put
a bottle of beer in her hand, and she drank that too. Everyone
was laughing. Clover held the camera up to his face. She smiled;
she raised her glass to the camera. She smiled and pictured them
living together, far from her cottage, in his clean apartment that
would have plush carpet, houseplants, a long-haired cat. He'd
make fresh-squeezed juice. He'd make pancakes. He'd take pictures of them, Paul too. Paul liked to see pictures of himself.

"Stop with the smiling—I want to see Dark Goldie. I want to
see Goldie Without Her Locks."

She stopped smiling.

"That's right. Yes. I want Goldie Who Knows."

She tried to make her face know.

"I like you a lot," she said.

"Raise your arms now, yeah? Put your hands behind your
head."

She did. His camera flashed.

She said, "A lot."

"Look over that way—what a beauty. Yes, raise your chin."

She did.

"Close your eyes a little, like you're sleepy."

She did, she was.

"I'd like to be alone with you." She wasn't sure he heard, so she said it again.

"You're a true beauty," he said in return. "The rarest sort."

Next he snapped her at a table of men in cowboy hats; they were game—they played the doe-eyed fools, mouths gaping, she the queen, pious among them, chin high, arms over the backs of the chairs at her sides. "That's it, that's it, yes sir!" Clover, squatting, froggy, captured it from many angles. Afterwards the men returned to their taut, upright bodies, while she collapsed more deeply into herself, shoulders slumping.

Then he wanted her to lie on top of the bar, provided the bartender approved. Would she be up for that? A rose or at least a carnation between her teeth?

"I don't know," she said.

"You'll look like Marilyn Monroe," he shouted, and walked off.

One of the cowboy hats was talking to her, his hand touching her waist, pulling her toward him. She kept trying to turn and find Clover. She didn't want to lie on the bar but had told Clover she was up for anything. She wanted to please him. She wanted to be in McFee's catalog, to model their merchandise, wanted for people to see her glossy and proper.

"You want to take a look at her?" the guy in the cowboy hat was saying. He was talking about a car. She kept turning to find Clover—for a moment he was lost in the crowd—but there he was, right there, standing next to the bar and talking to a man in rubber pants, and she saw that they were touching each other's lower backs, and that the man's hand was sliding down onto Clover's ass, and that Clover laughed. Then they kissed each other. The kiss started out like a joke, a goof, but it didn't end that way.

The guy in the cowboy hat was hovering, still talking. When Goldie turned to leave he grabbed her arm, but she yanked it away, freed herself from his grip with a quick jerk, the way you tear off a Band-Aid.

The bathroom was red: lightbulbs, floor, stalls, even the toilets. It gave the women young, febrile skin, which they admired in the mirror as if it were really theirs. She sat on a toilet and blew into her hands. She reminded herself that she was smarter now. *Remember that, Goldie*. She'd come through a war. All those rooms, that slippery bar, Paul's dud of a father, all of it was a war. But she'd come through. *You need to think of it like that, Goldie: you're smart now.* Smart meant patient. Smart meant careful. She knew better than to get into that car. She knew better than to lie on a bar. And didn't she know better than to do anything for anyone's camera? At once she felt sober, composed. Her lips were gummy, and she wiped her lipstick off with toilet paper. How would she get home? She didn't want to see Clover again. The only person she cared to see right now was Paul. She could call a cab. That would be smart. That was what a person does who has come through a war. She calls a cab. She finds an anonymous person who will do what she wants without question, who will protect her not because she is she but because the rules say so.

10

Thomas was being watched. At first it was not unlike coming to work at the clinic and pushing through a throng of protesters. They carried their signs and sang their songs and imagined that these acts connected them to God. But it was easy to make a sign. It was easy to stand in the cold and sing. What did that require, really? What Thomas did was harder. He took the pulses. He handed those girls their animal crackers. He saw the stuff. Sometimes he assuaged their doubt, even though he wasn't supposed to. He knew the things to say, and usually they thanked him.

He arrived each day in his scrubs, his face newly shaven, ready for his work, a cup of coffee in hand. The protesters called him names, *murderer, Hitler, coward*, on and on, *fascist, killer, evildoer*, and sometimes even his own name, Thomas, *Save Yourself,*

Thomas. They watched him carefully. Their words were not careful but their eyes were. They watched his steps, they watched his eyes, they watched his throat and hands and shoes and even the steam from his coffee.

He liked to turn to them. He liked to give them a better view of his face, liked for them to see that there was exactly no doubt in it.

The boy in Goldie's living room had a hammer in his hand and a bloody foot, and he was looking at Thomas.

Thomas was being watched.

He and the boy looked at each other. Blood rushed from the kid's foot. For a moment Thomas's heart knocked in that easy, familiar way, but then it began to race. On the boy's face Thomas saw reflected, very clearly, his own doubt. The boy's face was not a face anymore but a mirror for Thomas's doubt.

"Shit," Thomas said.

The boy's eyes widened.

A vision flashed through Thomas's brain. He saw someone with a ladder propped against his apartment building. He saw a stranger peering at his daughter, indifferent to her sheets and toys and sheaths of glossy hair, no doubt, no love, Jade caught beneath this gaze like an orphan. It came so fast, Jade asleep and observed by a stranger who would never comprehend his indecency.

Blood puddled on the floor. What had the kid done? The nurse in him felt the urge to staunch the bleeding; the nurse wondered about a tetanus booster. But the nurse in him was small tonight. The nurse was all but gone. Thomas cursed. The boy read his lips; the boy cursed back.

Thomas ran. The woods smelled crisply rank, like rotten mulch. Beneath him his feet moved fast, faster. He felt like a boy sprinting from his angry father, that acid rush of stupidity and sickness and helplessness, the way a child knows he'll have to stop sometime, knows he'll get caught, must get caught!, but maintains the belief anyway, while he's running, while he runs, the crazy belief that maybe he can run forever. Maybe? He ran, his lungs burning, snot dripping, the kid's blood bright in his mind.

Why did the kid do that? Who was it meant for? It was like a performance, but Thomas didn't know who the audience was supposed to be. Him? He didn't think so. The kid smashed a nail into his foot, and he did it with a kind of swift, flat, total certitude. His face was empty. Where had he gotten that kind of face? Or maybe the kid was retarded? Mongoloid, as Janice's mother would have said. Maybe there was something wrong with him? All of Thomas's certitude was gone.

He ran as if chased, nearly fell several times, branches and twigs slapping his skin. "Shit," he said over and over, until he lost his breath.

Janice's conviction had baffled him. No, more than baffled awed him. He had not the faintest understanding how she could pack a bag, kiss the baby's head (but not him), simply walk away from their sparse life, away from those gossip magazines, from the Polaroids in the sock drawer, the juice cups, their bed. How on earth could she be so *certain*? It seemed a rare, even a noble thing. Yes, he begged. Yes, part of him begged—clasped her sinewy arm and begged, wept, said all the things you're supposed to say: *Think about the child! I'll quit my job! I'll do anything!*— even while another part, a smaller part, stood back and watched the spectacle, studied Janice's face, its complete and hideous peace. She was doing the wrong thing but doing it so *surely*. She was doing it with perfection. In this she escaped morality. In this she made of submission—submission to yourself, to your wicked-est needs—an art. She was far away now. Orlando? Toledo? He had no idea. All he knew was that she had become herself. Of this he had no doubt; in his mind she had become freely and fully and ecstatically herself, as only criminals and saints can be.

Janice's absence had licensed him to spy on Goldie. That's what he'd told himself. It was his retaliation. Was this not a way to connect with Janice? Was it not a message to her, wherever she was? But now he only felt disgusting.

He ran toward his daughter, sick with his ugliness, a pain burning his side.

"How much do I owe you?" he said to the babysitter in Jan-ice's armchair. She'd been sleeping. Her gummy eyes and dap-pled bosom rose whenever money was mentioned.

She looked at her watch. "Fifteen."

She saw through him. She knew what he was up to. When he gave her a twenty, when he said "Keep the change," this con-firmed her suspicions. She nodded to herself. He saw her touch the filigree cross at her neck.

"Jade wake up?" he asked.

"No, no. That girl is out cold."

11

After the guy ran off, Paul picked up the phone to call the police. But he was a smart kid, and before he dialed it dawned on him that he could not report the pervert in the window without revealing that he was home alone, that his mother had left her ten-year-old boy home alone on his birthday while she went to a nightclub. He knew what happened to kids whose mothers got drunk and left them alone at night. They ended up like Eddie VanSay, sleeping in a basement and tied up with fancy scarves by the foster mother who was considered a saint for taking such trouble into her blessed home. Rick Malone didn't fare better: he got a bunch of black eyes before being shipped off to an institution for kids who make adults do that kind of thing. It was not a wise choice to call the police. He put the phone down. The kids at school, his absent father, Clover, this coward. Perverts filled the world, and he understood that chances were he would become a pervert too.

There was no rubbing alcohol, so he poured gin on his foot. When it stung, he blew on it as his mother would have. He touched a Q-tip to the wound because this seemed a medical thing to do. Then he found gauze among the clutter under the sink, wrapped it around his foot, and put on two socks, all while a pounding heat crept up his leg. He would limp, but not enough to draw attention. He would skip tomorrow's baseball game. He would hide the bloody socks under his bed. His foot hurt, but not too badly. It beat along with his heart. Finally he was calm. He was proud for the first time. Those other times he thought he'd felt pride, they were not the same thing.

PART 2

LEONORA

What a day! What a day! Not sunny but wickedly bright, the sky white as snow and silver at the horizon, the tree's bare branches suggesting the arms of a rich, emaciated matron, all elbows and knuckles, the bark like cashmere. The birds hovered but did not land. Leonora tried to breathe deep, to inhale the silvery air, but its coldness was the cold of a coin placed firmly in your palm while you're waiting for a bus in the heart of winter. She looked for a long time at that tree. Every other day she'd seen it as any-old-tree, but today it struck her as alive, beautiful, and she wished it were summer and she could climb it. She wished she were the kind of girl who climbed trees. Mostly she read books. She was learning to play bridge, and she knew she'd spend the summer reading and drinking lemonade at the card table with her nana, not up this tree, not up any tree.

She knew herself, accepted who she was, but sometimes, it was true, she envied tomboys in bandannas who scrambled up trees, girls with scraped knees who didn't apply ointment or Band-Aids. This was the tree she'd climb, if she were that girl.

She was freezing, despite her mittens, despite the yellow scarf wound round her neck, despite her boots lined with sheepskin from New Zealand. She tried to breathe deep, to take the air fully inside her head, but she had the start of a cold, a stuffy nose. She walked past the tree, let her mittened hand lightly touch the hump at its base. She and her brother were on their way to school. It was a Tuesday in February.

Her father called this season "showstopping winter." He was always cold. Like a woman! Women shivered, huddled over coffee, complained about the weather. But in her home, it was her father who took hot baths and wore the afghan like a shawl and was forever cranking up the thermostat against her mother's protests. It was her father who did the laundry and her mother who paid the bills. Which was funny, wasn't it? Funny because he was an economist. An economist who doesn't pay his own bills! He pontificated on the debt of nations while his wife wrote the checks. He loved the cost of things: highways, banks, dams, rails, turbines, aqueducts. Other stuff too, stuff most people didn't think had a cost, like places, like diseases, like future events that hadn't even happened yet but might, and what then? As for what they paid for potatoes, as for the price of their dry cleaning, for her allowance, he couldn't be bothered. He loved newspapers and old books and not shaving. Crumbs in the pockets of his cardigan. Wet brown eyes, a pink nose, fingernails his wife reminded him to clip. In certain ways he called to mind a puppy. He worked late, often missed dinner, missed the children's bedtimes, and so established a tradition of waking Leonora in the morning. At 6 a.m. he'd creep in softly, open her shades, pull the milking stool to her bed, and read. She woke to his voice each day except Sunday, when everybody slept late.

These days he was reading a long story about a guy who wakes up as a bug. He read her a little every morning. She was glad about it, meaning glad this was a morning ritual—she wouldn't want to hear that stuff at night. They were at the part where the bug's mother swats him with a broom. Her father had said, "I've been waiting forever to read you things like this. For so long your favorite book was *Jenny Has a Bellyache*. Remember that drivel? Oh, I didn't blame you, of course I didn't. You were a child. Books like that teach empathy. But how many times did we read it? Hundreds. Thousands. Now you're a big girl. We can do the masters, can't we, honey?"

The Magnificent Ambersons. Sister Carrie. Shakespeare's sonnets. He took such joy in this ritual, sitting on that little pink stool with his elbows on his knees, holding a tattered paperback in faintly trembling hands. These were grown-up books, important books, and yet he read slowly, grandly, as for a child, just as he'd read *Jenny Has a Bellyache*. She was unnerved by this new story, by the plight of that hapless, greasy man-bug, but maybe she was more unnerved by the bright and bursting quality of her father's voice. It was a dark, sad story. That was the point. Why try to disguise it? Her father was a smart man, but he didn't always understand what she liked. There was a book on his shelf called *Know Your Own Daughter*. It made her happy to see it there, touched her, though she wondered if he'd ever read it.

Now in the cold February air they walked to school, Leonora and her brother. She was in the sixth grade, he the third. He wore snow pants and sneakers. His too-big parka, unzipped, framed a Mets T-shirt. His hat was jammed in his pocket. She said his name but he didn't respond, just sniffed the air harshly. She pointed to his hat.

"You'll catch a cold," she warned.

He shrugged, made an exaggerated pout, said, "I never get sick."

"That's a lie."

"I like to get sick."

He spit on the ground, paused to admire the spittle.

"You like being spoiled and watching TV. That's what you like."

Sometimes she spoke to him as a mother does—not their mother but the starchy, coiffed kind from television long ago. She employed the faintest British accent. They always walked to school together. Sometimes they sang a song—the boy hated to sing but also hated when she pestered him. The song was always the same, something she'd learned at school. It was from the Underground Railroad. It went: *Somebody's knocking at my door. Somebody's knocking at my door.* She sang a line, then the boy. Their voices overlapped in a round. Then, together: *Oh sinner! Why don't you answer? Somebody's knocking at my door.* Her voice was clear, tender, and flat. The boy had a finer voice but swallowed the words. It was Black History Month.

"*Sounds like the Lord,*" she sang now.

"*Sounds like the Lord,*" he sang halfheartedly.

The boy was forever making snowmen and fake boogers of rubber cement. He carried its scent on him—a gluey, bitter smell. It didn't alarm her; most boys smelled this way, until they smelled like their father's cologne or body odor.

"Sing nicely." She was that mother again. Her posture was too good; some of the girls found it suspicious.

But instead the boy wandered off. They were supposed to

stay together but he was always wandering off. Boys. They were programmed to mindlessly collect, to yell about what they found, to scream their good fortune and then forget it a second later. She had never met a different kind and didn't expect to. Today her brother discovered a big plastic owl poking out of a garbage can. She called his name but her throat hurt, her toes were numb, so she didn't protest too much when he ran off. She wanted to get to school, to settle into her overwarm classroom where the radiators hissed and where her own pastel portrait of Frances Perkins hung over the social studies shelf. Mr. Broom would give her a piece of toffee candy when she submitted her math homework.

Oh sinner.

The fresh icy air, the great white open sky, all this felt scarily at odds with the dim and humid world in the book. She wanted it to stop, the bug story, but her father was so sweet, perched on her stool in his old blue robe, his morning breath, sleep in his eyes, he loved so much reading his favorites to her. Anyway, that was the point—wasn't it? Creepiness? To let creepy things menace the perimeter? Otherwise you were an ignorant girl. Otherwise you were naïve, oblivious, sheltered. Then *you* became the ghost—then *you* became the thing at the perimeter. Or so it seemed to her.

Gregor was the name of the bug. Once he'd been a regular guy, a middle manager, her father said, and then suddenly he was a roach, the basest thing, despised, forlorn, disgusting, and ancient. She was interested in literary transformations but usually liked them to go the other way.

She sang under her breath. *Sounds like the Lord.* The song made her happy. Was it supposed to make her happy? Probably not. It was a song from a horrific period in American history.

Even so, she liked to think about the Underground Railroad, a tunnel deep in the earth, deeper than the subways, with rail tracks made of bone, candles dripping gloomy wax, cockroaches galore, all manner of person humping along, filthy, shoeless, and babies tied to backs, everyone singing this sad, hopeful, feverish song, and of course afros and mites and rats and pee. She knew there was not really a railroad or even a hole in the ground, knew it was a metaphor, but clung to the image of a train of people, a mournful conga line, voices merging and echoing, the whole world, over and under, dark and messy, mud. What did it say about her that she took pleasure from such a scene? Was she a racist? All people are racists, her mother told her, in some secret part of themselves. You can't avoid it. You too? Leonora had asked, aghast. Me too, her mother said. Why else would I devote my life to helping black people?

In the distance she saw her brother holding the plastic owl over his head and running down the street. A smaller boy in red earmuffs trotted after him.

She would have opened her door to slaves or Jews. Which is why when the man appeared, which is why when he said, "Could I bother you a moment, miss?" which is why when she saw he wore glasses with fingerprint smudges on them, a nick from shaving on his cheek, when she saw he had the same tartan plaid scarf as her father, she stopped. It was her instinct; she didn't think twice. He wore a scarf like her father's.

She hadn't seen where he came from. He was a regular-seeming guy, a middle manager, newspaper under his arm, briefcase with shining gold hinges.

"Hello," she said.

Her brother was gone.

"You seem like you're in a hurry," he said.

She didn't know how to respond.

"Well, I guess."

"I'd love just a moment of your time."

She did not think, *Who is he? What does he want? Is he safe?* This is what she was supposed to be thinking—in the thoughts under her thoughts there was: *Why aren't you thinking what you're supposed to be thinking?* For her real, uppermost thoughts were these: *I'm pretty. He stopped me because I'm pretty.* She wished it were not so. She wished he'd stopped her for some other reason. Girls aren't supposed to know they're pretty. They're supposed to be oblivious, to believe that beauty is an accident, irrelevant, a trick, but of course no one is oblivious. Girls know where they stand right from the start. When the man looked at Leonora, when she saw him looking down at her face, her coat, her boots, her face again, when he blinked—was he blinking maybe more slowly than was normal?—even though he gave no impression of indecency, even though he seemed harmless, ordinary, even embarrassed for himself—well, it didn't matter. She was sure he thought she was pretty, that this is why he stopped her, and she knew it to be true, knew she was pretty, and so she was ashamed for them both.

He said, "So. Let's see. How should I say this?"

He swallowed, setting in motion a massive Adam's apple. She watched the mechanics of his swallow, watched how his throat moved and felt the same thing she felt when she watched a machine do something ordinary and miraculous, like sort change.

"On your way to school, I imagine," he said.

"I am." She was staunch, confident.

"Maybe fifth grade? Sixth?"

She hesitated; he blinked; she confirmed the latter.

"I have a proposition." He swallowed again. It was so elaborate, that swallow—casual, wondrous.

She said, "What kind of proposition?"

"It means I'd like your help; it means I have an idea to run by
you."

She was mildly offended. "I know what it means."

"It won't take long. It would—it would make a world of
difference."

She was supposed to run and she did not. She prepared herself to run, she knew the risks, but now, face-to-face with him (a
notorious Him, a textbook stranger), her instinct was merely to
listen. She said, "What can I do for you?" and was surprised by
the rote, disinterested way it came out, like the voice of a tired
waitress.

1

S am's girl wasn't pretty. You couldn't call her that, but he didn't mind. He liked her long neck, like a dancer's, pale clean hair to her shoulder blades. She was gangly, wide-hipped, big feet. It didn't matter. He liked everything: her shirts a size too big, her sagging kneesocks. She went without a bra but not in a wild way, not like Mimi McKendrick who wore beads and black nail polish and let her little breasts knock about. His girl crossed her arms over her chest, drew attention to her own embarrassment, her shock at having wound up, one day, today, for no reason except dull destiny, a woman. Her eyes were clay-colored, her fingernails bitten to the quick. He admired everything about her. In her presence he was all clenched fists and thubbing heart.

"Helen."

It brought to mind his grandmother (who wasn't a Helen but of the age when women were Helens) and a wooden horse and also a cat with half a tail he'd known as a small boy. The name was many things, belonged to people and animals and some cities, but it was hers first and hers foremost. It had a formality, he thought, a sanctity. It was proper. His first-grade teacher was Mrs. Helen. It could be a surname or a pet's name or a myth, but now that it was her, this girl, that's all it would ever be.

"Helen!"

There was nothing to do but shout it.

"Keep your voice down," she said. "Hush."

She said things like that—*hush*. She was just sixteen but spoke like a mother already, in a weary, vaguely amused voice.

"Helen," more softly.

"That's better, yes."

They were sitting on her bed and kissing. It was nearly dusk on a Tuesday in early spring. Her room was a child's room: pink walls, braided pastel rug, shelf of dolls in church dresses and straw hats, a ribbon tacked to the back of the door, which was closed. The door was closed and they were sitting on her bed and they had been kissing. It was kissing, yes, but it wasn't what he had imagined. It was kissing in name only: lips brushing dryly, no exchange of saliva, idle tongues, hands on their own laps. Still, he would take it.

The ribbon behind the door said *Runner-Up* in gold letters. A pink ribbon with gold letters, and at once he saw her as the runner-up, a too-tall girl pulling herself from the pool, out of breath, bloodshot eyes, a scrape on her knee, downy fuzz in her armpits. The sky would have been overcast, her mother frowning— "There'll be more races"—and handing her a towel which her sister had already used.

"I have a paper to write," she was saying. "It's due Wednesday. The War of 1812."

"I know about that war."

He knew nothing.

He loved her as the Swimmer. She pretended not to mind being runner-up. She hated her mother, hated the girl who'd won the race. She loved the color of sky, like bone, and the chlorine burn in her eyes. Her face didn't show anything. She rode home in the back of the station wagon, arms and legs goosepimpled, lips blue. She hung that ribbon up out of defiance. I will not care. I am not this ribbon. He saw everything with precision: her blue lips, bloodshot eyes, her cold and healthy heart. He was making it all up. He didn't know about the ribbon. He didn't know about her heart. He barely knew her. "Helen," he sighed.

"They'll be home by seven." She was talking about her parents. "I need to get dinner ready; they'll want to eat when they get back."

On the wall was a piece of framed needlepoint, a peach-colored baby face and, in needlepoint script: *Babies are such a nice way to start people.* Beneath this was the date of her birth. But he couldn't believe she was ever a baby. It was impossible to imagine her without this particular gravity, this restraint.

"Helen." He was careful not to yell.

"Yes?"

But he didn't know what to say.

"Oh, Sam." She patted her hands on her lap.

He said, "I need you is what I think I'm trying to express."

Express? Why did he talk this way?

But she said, "Need?"

They were silent.

"You're something else, Helen. I want. No. Everything."

"You mean intercourse, right? That's what you mean by *everything*?"

His hands and feet and neck burned.

"Sam." She said this, too, like a mother. "Is that what you mean by everything? Intercourse?"

"Don't call it that."

"Why not?"

"It sounds medical."

"I want to," she said. "I *do* want to." Her voice was light, cool, a little mean.

He was terribly afraid. "Maybe we're not ready. No, we're not ready."

"I want to," she said. "Listen to me."

He was listening.

"Helen. Helen." He said her name the first time to remind them both of the girl she was supposed to be, and then said it again, louder, to celebrate the departure of that girl. He meant to speak to both Helens at once. A wonderful thought occurred to him: She was two Helens. He didn't need to choose.

It was six-thirty. Soon her parents would return.

They agreed to meet in the woods by the river, the next day after school.

They went outside and stood on her front stoop. The trees, newly budded, cast long shadows on the lawn.

"Don't tell anyone," he said.

"Who would I tell?"

"Patricia?" This was her slit-eyed best friend.

She laughed. "You don't really know me."

His throat tightened. "Of course I do."

"Is the girl you know the kind of girl who wants to have sex with you in the woods tomorrow?"

The answer was a terrible, blessed no.

He walked down the street. Daffodils aimed their cyclopic heads at him. The dusk sky was yellowish, speckled with dim clouds. He walked until he was out of her sight and then ran. His mouth wanted to make a sound but he was afraid to let it. He clamped down on his bottom lip. What could he do between now and then? He couldn't go home yet. He couldn't run forever. Finally he let his mouth do what it wanted and it made a small, breathless gasp like cresting the Ferris wheel for the first time.

He ran until he came to Marco's, a dilapidated sundry at the corner of Maple and Eve, chimes on the door, old Marco with his cigarette behind the counter humming some dead song from his youth. It was rumored that Marco hired a woman to bathe him once a week though he was perfectly able to take care of himself. Sam wasn't supposed to be here; his Aunt Constance didn't approve of the place. There was a faint panic and pleasure in disobeying her. He looked through the selection of rude greeting cards, old ladies on the toilet, buxom nurses. One card was just some naked guy wearing one of those plastic Groucho Marx disguises on his penis. *Incocknito,* it said inside. He touched animal figurines, boxes of candy cigarettes. Everything was dusty. A stuffed frog. A squirt gun. A pencil that played the New Year's Eve song when you pressed a button where the eraser should be. Nothing was right. He couldn't present Helen with some trash.

"For a girl? I can tell." Marco flashed his orangey teeth.

"No girl," said Sam.

"Sorry. A *woman*? You got your hands on one of those, I bet."

"I don't think there's anything here," Sam said. "But thanks for letting me look."

"You know who's one swank doll? Mrs. Marcusi, that's who. She's a tall drinka."

Mrs. Marcusi, in kilts and flesh-colored knee-highs, shelved books at the library.

Sam moved for the door.

Marco called, "Hey! Hold on. You own the world and have no idea. I know what you want. You want a present for a real woman, right? I envy you. Come back here a second. I have the perfect thing."

Marco fumbled below the counter, lifted a small bundle wrapped in brown paper. Slowly, tenderly, as one removes the dressing from an injury, he peeled back the paper. It was not what Sam expected to see. A mug. A large, beige coffee mug encircled by a ring of giraffes. These giraffes were engaged in an act of—well, it was intercourse.

"Orgy," Marco declared. "Orgy of the animal kingdom." Giraffe heads in giraffe crotches and rears and ears. They were linked, lapping and caressing and humping, tails entwined, necks and ears and hooves and tongues.

"Erotic safari," Marco said. "Shows a wild side. Women want that, trust me."

A wild side? They were children. They needed a pass to use the bathroom. They drank milk from tiny cartons. He couldn't give that mug to Helen. It was disgusting. He would never give it to Helen.

He paid.

He was supposed to be dead, was supposed to feel that he deserved nothing, not happiness or home or peace or Helen. He was supposed to feel that his life was borrowed. He was an orphan and therefore his life was not the puzzle everyone else's was. It was just a clean, flat surface, and he would one day slide off. His death would be a kind of catching up. He had to remember that. He ran home, holding the paper bag to his chest. He would keep the mug in the back of his sock drawer. His Aunt Constance could never see it; she would have cried at a mug like that. But he had to have it. It was the first disgusting thing he owned, and it felt like a start.

2

Constance's life began with another woman's death. That was its true start. It began not when she was born, or finished school, or left her mother's home. Her life began, finally, when Louise packed her family into their station wagon, put on her sunglasses, turned the ignition, and drove into a train.

At the time, Constance was secretly pregnant by Louise's brother. Their wedding was the last time Constance saw Louise. A wedding! With guests and an organ player and a minister whose habit of rubbing his paunch made Constance sure he knew her secret condition and was taunting her. She could hardly believe it was happening to her, so resigned had she been to a life in her mother's house, to growing old alone. Yet here she was, in this awkward dress, wearing mascara for the first time. After the ceremony, they descended into the church basement.

The windows were high, small, and covered with ochre linen that muddied the light.

Constance's mother pulled her aside, hugged her shoulders, and said, "I hope I've prepared you." They stood in the alcove that held the coatrack and the framed picture of Jesus with a shag haircut. "I mean for tonight. I mean for"—she waved her hands—"for the rigmarole."

"I'm prepared, yes," said Constance.

"I wasn't," her mother said. "I was not at all prepared. Oh, but I'm afraid I was supposed to give you more advice. Did I give you enough advice? Is there anything you want to know? Ask me! It will hurt some. What else?"

Constance was the only daughter, the youngest. Her father, her three brothers, were long gone. She looked at her mother, saw her mother's mouth moving, heard her mother's too-late ministrations, and felt nothing but freedom. She was married.

"I know enough." She sounded unlike herself—so serene, so effortless. How did she manage that? Such poise! This was not what she expected. She was supposed to quake, to weep. Or maybe she was supposed to confess that she already knew what it was like, that she was already pregnant. She was certainly supposed to feel guilt. But she did not. She was tall and plain and resolved. A wife. Oilcloth covered the plywood tabletops. A buttercream cake and small pile of gifts did not come close to filling the table in the corner. It was a simple, ordinary affair. The music was sappy, the food plentiful, mayonnaisey salads, melon balls, a gravy tureen filled with jelly beans, for it was just after Easter. But forget the food. The food wasn't what mattered. What mattered was that she was pregnant and married and couldn't stop looking at her husband's sister.

Louise in a cranberry taffeta dress, black eyeliner.

Louise whose lips were oddly pale.

Pale lips, sucking a ball of honeydew.

Louise, drinking punch from a Styrofoam cup. Louise, when the punch was gone, taking a bite from the rim of the cup, spitting a crescent of Styrofoam into her palm, doing this again and again, until there was no more cup, until the cup was just a pile of pieces in her hand. And later, in public view, adjusting the top of her dress, cupping a hand around each breast and heaving it upward. Later dancing too closely with the pharmacist. Later, by herself, reading a wall plaque, on her face a quizzical expression, an expression of confused awe, of mouth-gaping wonder, so striking that Constance felt compelled to see what the plaque said, was surprised to find it was merely a list of some people who'd helped to plant the garden out back.

Finally, toward the end of the reception, Louise caught Constance's eye and gave her that smile. The smile! It was a prize ribbon. It was coffee before dawn. It was a bathtub, no, a bed. It was—what else? It was a bird on a railing in sunlight, a precarious, utterly-itself thing. She had been waiting for the smile, which could say different things. Now what it said was this: *You're as good as gone, my girl, but at least we're in it together.*

They were in it together. They were sisters-in-law. It was a good day.

That night, during her first sanctioned lovemaking with Joe, Constance could not stop picturing her sister-in-law's hips pressed against the pharmacist. Her own hips, beneath Joe's, were still. She willed them to move a little, left to right, and then in a tiny circle. Joe, into her neck, said, "Whoa boy—okay now," and it was over.

Dear Joe, solid old Joe, had none of his sister's drama. He had no private smile, no secret gaze, and this is precisely what Constance loved. He was easy to read. He was good. He was like a simple tool—it does the job, goes back on the pegboard when the work is done. So few people are as settled into themselves, she thought; so few people have such simplicity of purpose. Dear Joe. Dear boy. She married him. She was secretly pregnant. That he had a sister who wore swirling skirts, and swore, and drank beer, and had two children yet seemed wholly unpossessed of any maternal spirit, and wicked hips—this was a bonus. Someone to watch, to study—someone as from a foreign country whose customs she could observe close-up, whose ways she could inspect—at leisure.

But as it turned out there was no leisure.

The next day she and Joe left for their honeymoon, four days at the Falls. They stayed at a motor lodge called *Splash!* The view from their window was a busy road, a hamburger joint. They couldn't afford a place with a view of the water, nor would she have wanted one. It turned out to be awful, a screaming gash in the earth. It did something to the pressure in her left ear. Why are people compelled to gather at the most violent places? Constance's stomach tumbled as she looked over the rail, the whole world reduced to this cavernous monstrosity. She blinked, turned away. She understood why people might put themselves in barrels.

Her life began now. Here. An ordinary moment, the evening of the second day of the honeymoon. They were in their rented room. Joe, sitting on the edge of the bed, kept his eyes on the muted television, on a horse running through a field. What was he thinking? She could not guess. She had just washed her face, and was drying it with a towel, thinking that she very much liked the smell of the miniature soaps that came with the room, that perhaps she should ask for a few bars to bring home with her.

She sniffed the towel and her palms. A strident floral scent. An optimistic smell. No, not flowers. This smell was to flowers as—

There was a knock at the door. Together, they looked up. A voice: "Uh—Joe? Joe Griffin?" It was as if the Falls itself had paused—wasn't there a law that said you were anonymous in your motel room; that your name would go unuttered; that you would not be disturbed; that perhaps, for a spell, you did not exist? She had hung the placard on the knob! (Hung it with not a little shame: this demand for privacy seemed, perversely and precisely, an invitation for others to imagine unspeakable deeds.) And now a knock, despite the placard. Now, following this knock, a name, *his* name. She shivered.

It was the manager, a tool belt around his waist, empty except for a hammer. He said, "Sorry to bother you folks. Call for you. Family emergency, I'm afraid." He wore the striped hat of a train engineer and a silver ring on his pinky. He led them to the office. On the table was an ashtray crammed with cigarette butts, a can of beer, and the phone, receiver on its side. Joe hesitated a moment, then picked it up. He said, "Hello?" So casually, as if answering the phone at his own house. She watched his broad, heavy-lidded face absorb the news. His eyes narrowed momentarily; he pressed his lips together. That was all. His face returned to itself.

The honeymoon was over. It was not appropriate to ask for the soaps. They left immediately. A light rain had begun and the road threw off an oily, opalescent sheen. Louise had been crossing the train tracks. She had tried to outrun the light, had ignored the bells, and now she was dead, and her husband was dead, and the baby. But they weren't going back for the dead. They were going back for Sam, the older boy; he'd survived. Constance shook. That calm, that poise—they were gone, had never existed.

She was heading back to Ringdale, the town of her birth, but now she was married, now she had a husband, a new house, a nephew whom she would raise as her son, a baby in her belly. She had a family and she had a family tragedy, when before she had nothing but her bedroom, her shelf of mysteries, and her mother. This new life unfurled before her the way a flower opens. It was a flower opening in a time-lapse film, revealing too fast its private, dewy innards, the yawn of its petals reduced to a flash, everything soft made stark.

"We'll take him in," Joe said. "Won't we? Of course we will. Right?"

She said, "Of course we will."

Of course, she said, but inside her was a pulling sensation— the same thing she'd felt at the Falls. The words *look away* flashed in her head, just like when she'd gazed down at that terrible feat of water, but now there was nothing to look away from. There was just the windshield, the empty road. Look away from what? She allowed herself a vicious, utterly incomprehensible thought: She did not want to bear this child growing in her gut. She did not want to have a child at all. My goodness! She almost wanted to laugh, for she had no idea a person could become such a surprise to herself. Then the thought disappeared, pushed out by other, horrible thoughts, images of Louise, dead, of her body, their bodies, in the yellow weeds by the tracks, buttercups.

Later that night a burly cop who stunk of garlic thrust Sam into her arms. He was four years old, pale, chubby. He wore pajamas that were too short for him, moccasins, a fringed leather vest. His fingernails were overgrown and dirty.

"I'm an Indian," he said flatly. In one hand he held a homemade headdress—a single indigo feather attached to a strip of construction paper.

What was she supposed to say? "Very nice." She did not know how to be around children.

He came to them with a little scratch on his left nostril, just the tiniest thing, a wisp of red thread. It was all the accident had done to him. How could that be? A locomotive tore the car in two and that was all he got. Only after it healed did she admit to herself that she'd been carrying a certain irrational fear: that he was an angel, or some kind of saint, or perhaps a monster. (It was hard to know the difference.) That he survived out of magic and would bring that awful power into her home. But it healed. He was just a lucky boy. But: lucky? On more than one occasion this was said of Sam, "lucky boy," and always Constance inwardly cringed.

On the second night she gave him a bath. She placed him in the tub, handed him a pot and a ladle to play with. She said, "Honey, do you know how to wash your hair?" but he didn't answer. She was unprepared. Did a four-year-old know how to shampoo himself? To rinse thoroughly? To wipe his rear end? He sat in the sudsy water. His face was round, owlish. His bangs needed trimming. She saw that his stomach appeared bloated, hard, and that his navel was a greenish-blue, protruding pock, not unlike a grape. She noticed his penis, that it was the same pale color of his cheek, and that it was erect. She turned away.

Louise was dead but in those early days her presence emerged, somehow more vivid, more intense, than when she'd been alive. Constance would find herself thinking: *What would Louise say about that? What would Louise do here?* When she was scared to hold Sam on her lap, for fear of the erection, or for fear of his tenderness, or—which was worse?—lack of it, she imagined Louise laughing, imagined Louise's knowing, secret gaze, and then Constance was no longer afraid. They were in it together, as it were. As she moved around the kitchen, as she tended to her husband and nephew, cooked and cleaned, paired their socks, made their beds, she imagined she was in Louise's body, or Louise in hers, tried to move the way Louise moved, with that easy glide, with that same haughtiness in the hips, the same elongated neck. A few weeks later, when she miscarried, she somehow felt this was Louise's doing. Not that Louise, from the other side, beckoned her unborn child forth—nothing like that. Rather Constance felt that these mutinous thoughts were not really her own but belonged to her dead sister-in-law. In this way Constance could observe herself without culpability. In this way she could sit on the toilet, a clump of bloody toilet paper in her hand, a spasm of pain radiating from her midsection, and the word that could appear in her mouth was: *good*. She whispered it. She wondered how that word could appear in her mouth but not her brain. It belonged simply to her body. *Good. Good.* It was as if it had been whispered by Louise, by the dead, who were allowed to say unspeakable things because no one heard them.

It crossed her mind that they'd switched children. Here she was raising Sam—was Louise perhaps, in some dim afterworld, tending to Constance's miscarried child? She didn't allow herself to linger on this idea. It was hard to imagine, after all, Louise hand in hand with—what? A dark syrup, an absence of form. She didn't dwell. They had chores to do, things to purchase. They bought Sam school supplies, shoes, clothes, a goldfish called Dingo who lived for one month. How could they have been so stupid to buy the new orphan such a fragile creature? She would never forget coming upon the boy as he stood over the bowl, that fish floating on the water's surface, Sam's face blank, without grief or surprise.

Gradually their lives settled down, assumed an ordinary routine. His photograph on their television set, a thin, gamine child in a pressed plaid shirt. Long neck, sober eyes, a certain pinchedness in his face that drew attention to his cheekbones. He grew into a well-mannered boy, thoughtful and polite, and, she had to admit it, somewhat plain. There was nothing monstrous or saintly about him. He was a kid who did his chores and oiled the chain on his bike and, on her birthday, wrote to Constance in a homemade greeting card: *I'll always be grateful to you.* He was sincere, earnest, so much like her in this respect she actually found it disappointing. Louise was nowhere on him. After a while, her presence in Constance vanished, too.

Years of peace. Homemade sweaters on Christmas morning. Kite flying. When Joe was made manager of the hardware store, they celebrated with yellow cake and fizzy wine. Respectable report cards got lasagna and chocolate milk. Basketball in the driveway. The chore chart. Their life together felt inevitable, circumscribed, marked by a restrained tenderness. They were not affectionate so much as devoted to their rhythms, which was a way to say to each other: *See? Of course I love you. It goes without saying.* They did not speak of the past. The past was gone. Who was Louise? She had been a woman, but now, like many women, she was dead. That was how vague the whole thing felt, how removed. Oatmeal in the morning. "You'll be late!" New socks. Television after dinner. Bed by nine-thirty. No one was late. It went without saying, all of it, anything. She was grateful, and, after a time, stopped feeling guilty about this. Years of quiet. Years of order. Had she earned it? She didn't think in these terms.

But the dead do not always remain so.

Louise came back on a Tuesday in Sam's sixteenth year. It was the early spring, a day of chittering birds, mud, a hubcap sun. As always Constance was the first in the house to wake. On the hook inside the closet door hung her housecoat. She put it on, and then her terrycloth slippers, and went to the kitchen, pleased by its spotlessness. Was there a nicer feeling than waking to a kitchen of gleaming appliances and countertops, all the dishes washed, all the silverware in their proper troughs? She noted the polished faucet. She noted the felt potholders—made by Sam in the third grade—hanging evenly on a set of china hooks above the stove, and the magnet in the shape of a banana securing Sam's school photo to the clean face of the refrigerator, and the pink sponge in its heart-shaped glass dish to the left of the sink, a sponge which she'd boiled the night before, as she did every week, before she replaced it at the end of the month. Her kitchen! She stood back to admire it. Into her body came a simmering elation. Her pleasure had a sexual edge; it was a seizing kind of contentment, a full-bodied rush. A kitchen such as this one, clean and ordered and knowable, was like a gift to herself. It *was* herself. She put on her apron. She made a pot of coffee, started the oatmeal, the bacon, tidied up as she went.

At six forty-five it was time to wake Sam. As always, she gave a quick knock, then opened the door, poked her head inside. His was a tiny room with white walls, bare except for a magazine picture of a negro guitarist. Tucked into his mirror was a small photograph of his parents on their wedding day, a gauzy veil lending Louise's face not so much a romantic as a dusty, unwashed aspect—but Constance did not look at this now.

What she looked at was Sam. She looked and looked and then could not unlook, could not unsee. He was sleeping on his back, the blanket caught under his left side so that it exposed, very clearly, his pale blue boxer shorts. Something was wrong with his shorts. She looked. She did not stop looking. There was nothing to stop her from looking. Then, still asleep, making a series of dreamy vowel sounds, he rolled over, pulling the blanket with him.

She cleared her throat. She said, "Time to get up."

Sam: "Uhhm."

She said his name, but he didn't hear.

What was wrong was not his shorts but the capacity of his shorts to hold their contents. His penis had emerged and was pointing at the wall like the arm of a sundial.

She returned to her kitchen. How had she missed the spot of dried milk next to the toaster oven? A scattering of coffee grounds on the counter. The bacon fat hissed in its pan, which was now dirty, and the sizzling fat made the stove dirty. That was the thing: as soon as you cooked something, the kitchen got dirty again. There were moments when she scorned her own hunger, for sating herself meant soiling a dish. When no one was around, she ate out of her hand.

She swept the coffee from the counter to the wastebasket. She rubbed away the dried milk. She turned off the burner under the bacon. He was no longer a child. It was bigger than when he'd been a little boy. That was not surprising. But it was bigger now than her husband's. Her husband, a grown man, six foot two, broad and dense, mature, for God's sake a *man* . . . how could his skinny teenage nephew, that downy boy who barely came to his uncle's shoulders, possess a penis that so dwarfed Joe's? She poured herself a cup of coffee, added a little cream, two cubes of sugar, embarrassed by her wobbly hand.

She sat down at the table, gripped the mug between her palms. It was at this moment that Louise returned. It was Louise's voice she heard, Louise's firm, slightly mannish voice, the words from Louise's pretty mouth, and they were these: "He's not your son."

Constance straightened in her chair.

"Sleep well?" Joe stood in the doorway, stretching. He grabbed his hands together behind his back, raised his shoulders—she heard a cracking sound.

She rose, kissed him. She pointed to the stove: "I made oatmeal. Bacon."

"Perfect. Heaven. Hey, do you know where my brown belt is?"

He was shirtless, wearing the pants she'd ironed for him the night before. A thin trail of hair climbed up past his navel, ended below his sternum, fanning there, like a fern.

She told him where the belt was. She poured him a cup of coffee.

She knew where his belt was. She knew where his car keys were, and his spare keys, and the flashlight, the spare flashlight, the extra soap, the measuring tape. She knew everything in the house, where everything belonged, had created for them an immaculate, unimpeachable order. When this order was in any way threatened, it was as if she herself was threatened. It was like hearing footsteps behind her in the darkness, so bodily was the sensation of menace.

"I might play hooky this afternoon, day like this. Supposed to hit seventy-three by noon. Maybe shoot a little pool with Rich, maybe go down to the river? Little early for shad, but what the hell. Wet the line. Breathe it in. I'll be home by dinner, yeah? Sound good?"

"Sure thing." She worked on a smile. "It's spaghetti night."

"You mind if Rich comes? He's crazy for your meat sauce."

She said she didn't mind.

He swallowed his coffee, moaned with pleasure. Then he

poured some syrup into his bowl of oatmeal, crumbled a piece of bacon on top. Who ate like that? She felt the urge to chide him.

"Little early for shad, but stranger things have happened, right?"

She agreed.

Louise in a dress that was too tight in the bosom. Louise dancing with that pharmacist, swaying her pelvis, whispering something into the pharmacist's ear that made him pull away, startled, then laugh. Louise eating honeydew. Louise putting a key in the ignition, sunlight flying off the windshield in a million directions, the baby fussing, the husband cracking a bad joke, everyone doomed but the boy in the backseat. Louise in a hospital, legs spread, pushing him out, this Lucky Boy who was not lucky.

Here was the boy. He kissed her cheek. He had gotten dressed, wore jeans and a white T-shirt, high-tops, a wristwatch with a fraying strap. (On a piece of paper in her wallet, Constance had written: *Birthday ideas: new watch strap.*) Upper lip pink from shaving. Knapsack slung over one shoulder.

"Morning, CC. Morning, Joe." He was breathless. "Gotta run."

"Breakfast first?" She pointed to the oatmeal. Sam hesitated, then went to the stove, spooned some into a bowl, stood over the counter to eat. Why was he in such a hurry? He failed to make his customary appreciative eating sounds. He was flushed. Knapsack on his shoulder. Usually he sat with her, ate heartily, chatted, took his time. Now, leaning over the counter, he swallowed two, three bites and then dumped the remaining oatmeal down the drain.

Had he been feigning sleep?

Louise: "He knows."

Her laugh, plangent and bold, a cascade, a cold waterfall, filled the kitchen.

Louise: "He *wanted* you to see."

He was wiping his mouth with a napkin. He was rinsing the bowl in the sink.

Don't be absurd, Constance, she told herself. *Don't be ridiculous. He is my son. Of course he is my son. The penis is a penis. A fact of biology. So I looked—so what?* And this remonstration seemed to succeed, because for a moment she felt herself again, calm, hungry, sure of the ordinary order of things. The dead were dead, again and always.

"Have a good day!" she said, but the false brightness she heard in her voice—a singsongness, a fluttering against the walls of her throat like the wing of a minuscule bird—immediately restored her doubt. Something was deeply wrong with her.

The door slammed behind him. He was gone.

Joe was chewing with his mouth open.

She felt, for the first time in many, many years—what was the word that meant you were alone in a dirty room and a bulb is flickering overhead and there are fingerprints on the windows and no one comes when you call them, no one, because all of it—the love, the order, the calm—has been a trick of your imagination?

Joe said, of the oatmeal, "Holy shit this is good."

Terror.

3

It was a gorgeous spring day, and Judith was gone. No note. No explanation, no reassurance, nothing. Her room was empty. She had not made her bed, or raised the curtains, or done anything except leave them, an act more pure and unhindered than anything Grace, her mother, had ever performed.

Grace went to the girl's closet. What was missing? The pink duffel bag with the ballerina appliqué on its side. Her yellow dress. Her blue dress. Anything that showed her tits.

Her dim room retained the close, sweetish smell of sleep. The dresser had been cleared of its nail polish bottles and necklaces. Gone was the postcard of the guy propping a ladder up to the moon, *I want, I want* in black letters along its bottom edge. Gone the tin of strawberry lip balm. Gone even the chipped saucer that held her tweezers, thumbtacks, buttons. Even the mismatched buttons in the saucer! Why had she taken those? What use were they to her? The girl couldn't sew. She'd replace lost buttons with safety pins before she'd sew. The girl was impatient and immodest and bored and sixteen, and now she was a runaway; it was impossible to imagine her threading a needle.

Only the ugly pairs of underwear remained in the top drawer, the ones with stains, stretched waistbands. She'd taken her favorite jeans, and that mothy tan sweater, and the red scarf she sometimes wound around her neck and which lent her a decapitated appearance.

A bowl of dried-up ravioli on the nightstand.

"Judith?" As if she were hiding under the bed. Then, absurdly, Grace lifted the dust ruffle and looked.

Hank was in the shed, trying in vain to repair the Weed Wacker.

"She left."

"Who?" A smear of grease on his cheek. Then: "She'll be back."

"I don't think so."

Hank straightened up, wiped his palms on his thighs. He was a bartender: broad, cool, mock-begrudging smile, perennial five o'clock shadow, a man for whom the smallest gesture—a wink, a lift of the chin—communicated everything.

Now his mouth turned up slightly at the corner. He said, "She's probably at Shelly's."

"I have a feeling." She was surprised by the force in her voice. "A mother's intuition."

Hank tilted his head, squinted warily, and he was right: she was not a woman who believed in intuition, not a mother who believed she possessed any special sensory connection to her child. She was cynical about such mothers. She was suspicious about such women just as she was suspicious about people who read their horoscopes or went to church. Yet she knew. It was unlike her, but it couldn't be denied.

She said, "I'll call the police, I think."

"You're overreacting." At the beginning, he was the sober, practical one. "They won't take you seriously. You're crying wolf, honey."

"Wolf? No."

She saw a road winding through thorny woods, saw their daughter on this road walking in her swaying, confident way, the waitressy swish of her butt. The teeth of a wolf flashed like mica in the darkness. Tick of claws on rock.

She was sixteen, that was all.

Hank said, "She's testing us. She wants to make sure we respect her freedom. When she knows we do, she'll come home again."

It was not true and she said so. The fear, the reality, was the opposite: this had nothing to do with them.

He went back to his work.

He was right—they should wait on the police. To go to the police was to confirm a crime.

A day passed. Grace spent it sitting on the grass in front of the house in her lawn chair, smoking, looking out over the fields.

"Judith!"

A breath.

"Judith!"

On and on like that she called to the air.

Next to her a glass lay on its side, a line of ants along its mouth. A ladybug moved from her calf to her knee. It lifted its wings but did not fly away. Was it true, that the number of spots on a ladybug's back indicated its age? She had been told this in her youth, by another child. Of course it wasn't true, but it had stayed with her. In the distance, a tractor. She could make out Judith's old elementary school, and the roof of the supermarket, the small pond where they sometimes swam on hot days, drifted in inner tubes. Soon these buds would be leaves and the view would be lost.

The next morning she said to Hank, "We have to do something. We need to see Shelly."

He sighed, exasperated. But then, after a beat, as if she was the passive one, he said, "You know, let's talk to Shelly."

She was Judith's only female friend, a chubby, pug-nosed girl famous for having a brother who skipped town years before with another man's pregnant wife. Otherwise Shelly was no one. Her mother cleaned motel rooms; her father had been gone forever. She lived on an overgrown dead-end, in a house whose white siding had long ago turned a mottled, mushroomy gray. Grace and Hank drove there before sundown. They walked toward the door, past a wheelbarrow missing its wheel, past a birdbath slicked with algae, past a rusted lounge chair, and the seat of a swing, the head of a hammer, a broken plastic pail. Grace reached for the door knocker, sensed it would come off in her hand, so rapped instead on the frame.

Shelly answered right away, nodding as if expecting them. Inside wasn't as bad. Fresh white walls, industrial carpet, neat stacks of magazines. On the top of a bookshelf they saw a tableau, three pictures in matching frames: a toddler Shelly, a teenage Shelly, and, between them, a boy whose snarly grin, even at fifteen, told you he was planning to cuckold a father-to-be.

Hank and Grace sat side by side on the love seat in a room that smelled faintly of pot and less faintly of citrus deodorizer.

Shelly flopped into a tartan plaid recliner, put up her feet. You could see her nipples through her shirt. Grace saw the nipples, saw Hank see them, saw Hank try to figure out where to keep his eyes. Shelly appeared to see this too. She wore a leather band on each wrist. Her hair, a dark blunt bob, met her jawbone with razor edges.

"I don't know where she is," she said coldly. Then, friendlier: "You guys must be worried and all."

"Should we be worried?" Hank sat on the edge of his seat. "Do you know something? Did she say anything? You can be frank. Anything?"

Something in his rush of words disturbed Grace, embarrassed her, almost. Shelly seemed to be holding back a smile. Calmly Grace said, "Did she give you any idea where she was going?"

The girl shrugged. "Oh you know Judy. California, Alaska. Someplace far. It was just talk, I thought. It busts me up. I loaned her fifty bucks a few days ago. Fifty. Five-oh. That's a big chunk of change."

"What about boys?" Hank, winded, grabbed at his knees. "Was she dating anyone? Could she have gone off to meet someone?"

"A handful. Judy was—oh, how do you say it politely? *Experienced,* I guess that's how."

Grace would not be moved. She was here to gather information. She said, "Who does she like the most?"

Shelly thought for a moment. "I don't know his real name. I had a nickname for him that's not something I'm comfortable saying in the presence of adults. Everyone else called him 'Q-Ball.'"

"This boy, he goes to Copper Junction?"

"He's not from around here—and he's not a *boy.* He's a man, sort of. Or not a man but definitely not a boy. Something in between. I don't know much about him. He likes to rhyme. He wrote her rhymes."

Grace saw a kid in a jean jacket gripping a pool cue, shaved head, a seam of stitches on his temple like a baseball.

"Listen, I'm Judy's friend," Shelly said. "I care about her all right. But that dough—it's a lot of dough is all. She told me she'd pay me back."

"We need your help now," Hank said. "Tell us everything you can about this guy, okay?"

"You'll give me the money?" She looked off for a moment, rubbed her fingers together like she was feeling cloth.

He only had twenty on him but promised he'd come back with the rest.

"Everyone just calls him Q-Ball 'cause he's got this ugly little beard that comes down at an angle. It curves to the right, like a Q's tail. The letter Q?" She drew a slanting line on her own chin. "Who knows why he grows it like that. Probably to show the world how unusual he is. He just appeared one day outside the pharmacy. I don't remember seeing his car. I didn't get the license plate number, if that's what you want. I'm no private eye. I think he's a creep and I told her so."

"Q-Ball," said Hank.

Shelly nodded.

It embarrassed Grace to hear this name. It made their daughter a stranger. Of course she was already a stranger, had always been a stranger, even before she left. But this name, like a badge one must defer to, made it absolute.

He cleared his throat, said, "Anything else? Anything at all?"

Shelly straightened up. She said, "Judy got warts from him. Down there."

Hank never returned with the money.

Next they went to the police, made their report. "Q-Ball," she said to the cop, who rubbed his chin, said, "He got a last name?"

She had never felt smaller in her life.

The cop said, "Hey, I feel for you. We'll check it against our lists of known aliases, but I can't promise much." He wrote something in his notepad, said, "Kids these days . . ." It wasn't clear whether he meant Judith or Q-Ball. "What else? You got a physical description?"

Hank described the facial hair. Then he said, "He may have a transmittable disease."

The cop's pen hovered above his notepad. "Like the flu?"

"Like—warts," Hank said.

"Warts?"

"Private warts."

The cop stared at them. Then he wrote it down.

She returned to the lawn chair. She was briefly, irrationally hopeful—had a vision of some hulking cop leading the girl up the walkway by her ear, as if she'd been merely loitering behind the bowling alley—but nothing happened. Ants on the lip of her glass. Woodsmoke on a thin breeze. She found herself thinking about her girlhood back in Ringdale, her awful silk shirts, her own desire to flee, to hitchhike to some harbor, to be the stowaway, cold-eyed, witness to everything, a sketchbook in a beatup saddlebag. Except in Grace's case there had been no man—no desire for sex. Her own hope had been to flee from the burden of sex, to earn some kind of reprieve. Yet sex, it seemed, was just what the girl was after. What were they supposed to do now? She had the uncanny sensation that the last sixteen years had been a figment, and this was her real life, alone, hers and Hank's, that she'd gone through with the abortion. She didn't want to cry but couldn't help it. From her perch on the hill she could see the roof of the bar. It was still called Floyd's Well after Hank's uncle. Down there, men were drinking, elbowing, tossing back rye whiskey and beer chasers, throwing darts. Briny, inebriated, breathing this same spring air, they could not be stopped from anything. Grace was totally and completely sure that Judith was holding the hand of a convicted felon, a man rife with all manner of VD, that they were cruising the country in a wreck and sleeping beneath highway underpasses, sharing warm beer, and she was giving him head on demand.

Judith!

Couldn't she have at least left a note? Something small for her mother to hold? How could they have raised such a heartless thing? No note. No clue. No quick phone call. Was the tiniest reassurance too much to ask for? She was selfish, just as Grace had been selfish. Except Grace had come to her senses! Grace had done what she was supposed to do, which was marry the sanctioned boy and say her vows before a room of credulous people, and assume, mostly in earnest, a steady, ignorant life.

4

Sam had to make sure that no one took this feeling away from him. He had to be sure, too, that no one *saw* the feeling, for he sensed that its observation by another would spell its loss. So he ate his oatmeal fast and dumped the rest. He wanted to flee, could not bear this kitchen that seemed, in its order and familiarity, to challenge his ardent heart, to threaten to tame the chaos at the core of him. He would not be tamed. He would not allow anything to come between himself and his gluttony. That's how he felt upon waking: gluttonous. Not for food, not for his aunt's sticky oatmeal. He stood at the sink, forced himself to swallow a few bites. Helen's face remained in his mind the way sunlight stays in your eyes when you come into a dark room—it expanded hotly, everything else made vague in its swollen presence. He wished he'd dreamed about her so that he could say, simply, "I dreamed about you." He wanted badly to say romantic things and for them to be true.

Finally he was out the door. It was starting. In his knapsack was a condom that had been given to him, more than six months before, by the pharmacist's son. Sam walked down Main Street, past weathered houses in their tidy lots. As he approached the school, saw its brick face, its quivering flag, its principal standing on the front steps, he wanted to cry with relief and terror. Now he was afforded a sharp, unsparing kind of vision. He saw things like the principal's plastic belt and his phony smile, and the chalky red berries on the bushes, the greenish hue of the granite steps, a girl's penny loafers fitted with dimes. He steadied himself, closed and opened his eyes. He scanned the crowd of students but didn't see her. A bell rang. The principal waved his hands like a traffic cop.

All his life Sam had been working. He worked on his grades and his manners and on being good to his aunt and uncle and, today, at last, worked on preparing himself for Helen. He thought this would be easy but it turned out to be work. It turned out to be letting a little furnace of desire warm his belly, letting the heat circulate, run a little up his throat, a little into his loins, but not too much, too much and you gave it away, too much and Mr. Waters saw your face and then you were clapping erasers after school, too much and they would know, the boys, the girls, they could see these things, they were dying to see. The waiting was not pleasure but work, an exhilarated and mammoth labor, and it took all his restraint to focus on his teachers' voices, to answer when called on, to keep his body in order. He was like a man on a horse—*steady, steady,* through gritted teeth. At lunchtime he splashed his face with water. He managed to eat half a sandwich.

"You wanna shoot a little pool after school?" Kip asked.

"I've got plans." Sam looked away, aware that if he said any more he'd give it up.

He didn't see Helen all day, was starting to believe that she'd stayed home sick, succumbed to second thoughts, when there she was at the water fountain, leaning down to sip, one hand on the fountain's handle, the other holding back her hair, exposing the skin of her nape. She was wearing a pink dress, its hem loose in back. The whole thing felt so tenuous, so alarmingly fragile. It occurred to him that perhaps he should pray. But what did God care? God didn't step in to make sure boys got their rocks off. Later his math teacher touched his cheek with the back of her hand, said he looked flushed. He busied himself with his equations, trying to keep his face calm while his tongue scrambled the roof of his mouth.

Finally the day ended. The bell shot him into a new life. His pace was quick; he feared Kip might approach him, or the pharmacist's kid, and so he walked like he had an appointment, which was true, he did. He practiced things he might say if someone interrupted him. *I have a toothache. I have to run an errand for my aunt.* The worst part was having to pass the hardware store. If Joe was out front washing the windows, or greeting customers by the door . . . He feared his uncle would spot him, pull him inside, request he cut some lumber or sweep the storeroom, which was part of their arrangement; his allowance depended on Joe's odd jobs. But the store was dim, quiet. No one out front. And—look! There was a sign taped on the door, in Joe's ragged scrawl: *Closed Early—Sorry for Inconvenience.* So it was true. So it would happen. He was free. No one could stop him. Destiny, that boomerang, hit his gut, took his breath, spun away again.

It was a sunny day. The air felt clean. He breathed it in. *I have to run an errand for my aunt. I have a toothache.* His thoughts were moving too fast. *Settle down. Settle down.* And there it was, that collection of trees, that palace of new green, where inside would be the river, and would be Helen, and would be too, he realized, a new version of himself. He saw himself in those woods as if he were there already, saw a faint, blurry-edged Sam, a translucent form sitting by the river, flicking sticks into its gentle current. Then he saw his ordinary, opaque body approach this spectral one, saw the two of them join, as if one body were sewn into the other. He reasoned this was what love meant—a merger between one part of you that's been waiting for the other part. He stood on the cusp of the woods. *Settle down. Settle down.*

When he was sick to his stomach, Aunt Constance poured him ginger ale and stirred the carbonation out of it. She would do it now, if she saw that the bridge of his nose and his cheeks were flushed, that he was sweating, she would pour him a cup of ginger ale, stir. He could hear the song of the spoon on glass. And she would place three saltines on a plate and she would touch his forehead, and maybe rummage in the cupboard for the thermometer. But if she knew what he was doing? That he was standing on the edge of the woods, standing on the edge of the woods and about to have sex with Helen. The Swimmer. He would see her breasts. He would marry her. Helen at the altar, awkward Helen in a big dress that hid her breasts and knees, her face restrained, her dress swallowing her up in heirloom froth. No one would know about this afternoon in the woods, no one in that church or anywhere would know. No one but he would know that the restrained face was not her real face, that it was a veil over her desire.

Sam's parents were dead. His baby brother was dead. He had

been saved, miraculously, by God or whomever, from a terrible, bloody death by train. His life was meantime. He had suffered. He had suffered but quietly. He had asked no one to join him in his suffering. He showed the world a fine boy. Helen was the reward. Love was the reward, and he would have it, he would not squander it. He took a step into the woods.

5

Wait. Before she submitted to sex, before she married, before she gave birth, before she raised a daughter, before that daughter ran away without so much as a note—Grace was a girl.

Let her be a girl. Let her avoid her vegetables. Look at her sure, arrogant face. She clips her nails to the quick. She doesn't try to tame her cowlick. She doesn't care, not a bit, about boys. She never wants to touch a naked man. She never wants to get married, or wear an apron, or do the thousand things you're supposed to do in order to don the mantle of womanhood. Womanhood is, for all intents and purposes, a slog—oven mitts, sweet potato casserole, a dresser top spread with potions, endless frenzied ministering to the man. But you have to hide the frenzy. Frenzy can't been seen in a woman, though of course it's there.

Is girlhood any better? No. Girlhood is waiting, is frenzied waiting, is needing permission, is the rude smacking of gum, always,
in her ear. Grace wants to be neither girl nor woman. She wants
to be an eye, an observer. She wants to notice and wander. She
wants to take many trips on many boats to places where she can
lie nude in the sunshine.

Grace was sixteen then. Good grief, where did she get her
ideas? Nowhere. Or: everywhere. Vague, indestructible images:
a woman in a yellow bathing suit lying on the deck of a boat in
an advertisement for menthol cigarettes. The gentle sea. The
flat, effortlessly pretty face of the reclining woman. Grace
absorbed it all. Not the message about the cigarettes (smoke
these for a glamorous, seafaring life), which she understood was
a fiction. The real message was: *Go far away.* The message was:
Is there a man in sight? There is not.

Maybe she would be a biologist. Or maybe art school. Maybe
Paris, where she would drink black coffee and sell her work on
the street. She would wander the catacombs. She would scorn
her old life, the whole town of Ringdale, all the faces that looked
at her face, all the busywork and good manners and girls who
made a list of the best boys at her school, the top ten, she would
scorn especially those ten vaunted boys.

Hank Phelps was always number one.

Wait. She hasn't married him yet. Let her be sixteen a little
longer. Let her paint stag beetles and Black-Eyed Susans. Let
her fantasize about Paris, the Galápagos, Jakarta, Berlin. See
the books she reads: Amelia Earhart, Emily Dickinson, detective stories meant for prepubescent boys. She is so young. She is
so wrong about herself. Give her the gift of false convictions,
just a little longer, a paragraph.

At Ringdale High School, at the end of the 1960s, Grace was

considered an oddball and a lesbian. Did she care? No. Oddball, lesbian, snob, teacher's pet, strange dresser. She wore boy's trousers and old silk blouses her mother didn't want anymore. She wasn't a lesbian; she wasn't one way or the other. She thought of herself as immune to love. She'd never had a crush, not boy or girl or teacher or uncle, no one, not a flicker. What a gift, to be spared love and its frivolous, chatty reverberations, to be spared the note-passing and bathroom-crying and awkward dancing. Grace would not be ruined by love. She would be asexual. Yes. The idea was so ennobling, so bracing, she mentioned it to her mother, who chuckled and said, "We'll see."

Her mother was right, of course. Within a year Grace would be married and pregnant. She would marry the most popular boy at her school. They would have a daughter, and the daughter would grow, and one day the daughter would skillfully raise her brow and look at Grace as if to say: *Why did the cosmos curse me with such a dull mother?* and Grace would want to throttle the girl.

But Grace said, at sixteen, to her own mother, "I'll never, ever marry."

Her mother smiled. "I thought the same thing. Did you know that? I wanted to be a—"

"No!" Grace cried, because her mother had wanted nothing else than this house and her father and Grace. That was how it had to remain.

A few weeks later came the encounter that would mean the undoing of Grace's plan. It was her senior year. So close to the end; she had nearly made it out. But walking home from school one day she passed Hank Phelps and his best friend Joe the Lug sharing a cigarette on the stone wall that girded the cemetery. They were an odd pair: crow-haired Hank, the breezy, worshipped idol of the school; Joe, aloof, sheepish, in his eyes the dull, affable gleam of the middle-aged.

Hank raised a hand, said, "Hey there, Gracie." He had a jocular sneer and the solid haunches of a cowboy. Everyone knew he did two hundred sit-ups each night before bed.

Joe the Lug just offered his abashed half-smile.

A certain feeling rose into her body, began at her feet, traveled up her shins, into her thighs, into—

"Don't call me 'Gracie,'" she snapped.

She knew what it meant instantly.

"Sure thing," Hank said. "Righto. How's the world treating you today, *Grace*?"

His cocky, mocking tone, his cheekbones, his shiny boots with their two-inch heels. No one wore boots like that! He sauntered down the hallway. He once kissed the French teacher on the hand and didn't get in trouble.

"I'm fine," Grace said. She aimed for disdain but heard a throaty creak behind her words, like a boy trying to disguise his changing voice.

She would not want Hank. Hank was too obvious. Hank was wrong on so many levels. But she couldn't deny the feeling; it was like a long, high, quivering note held inside her body. It rang. It lasted. It made her shaky, woozy, sentimental. It made her want to hug her mother and nap and sneak into her father's basement workshop to page through the dirty magazine he hid in the bottom drawer beneath a tangle of extension cords. So if the feeling couldn't be denied, and if it was too unbearable to attach to Hank, she would attach it to the other person in whose presence she'd been when it first showed itself: Joe the Lug.

Joe no longer the Lug. All right then. If she had to have one, she'd have a strange crush. She knew from other girls that you were supposed to collect details, everything, even the most mundane, so she willed herself to watch him. Joe, of all people. He wore a plaid shirt in Christmas colors, fraying at the wrists. His hands were huge, hairless, with nails opaque as piano keys. A broad face, a softening in the jaw that presaged jowls. Small, sweet mouth, thin upper lip. Somehow he'd befriended Hank, the most popular kid at school; he wore the strangeness of this fact on him, a faint sadness in the eyes, like premature nostalgia, like he knew his luck couldn't hold. At lunch he'd pull an apple out of a brown bag, bite into it daintily, like a woman trying to preserve her lipstick. Two cartons of milk. Hunk of salami. Sugar cookies saved for last.

Grace watched, she studied, but really wasn't moved. She suspected it was the act of watching—not the subject being watched—that intrigued her. Finally she had to tell someone. This was the next part. First, you collect details about the boy. Then, breathless, slightly frantic, you confess all in the bathroom. Though she had never joined in, Grace witnessed this many times before. When one day she came upon Dee Lutz fixing her bangs in the bathroom mirror, she knew it was time. They greeted each other. Grace washed her hands, dried them. She looked in the mirror, pretended to pick something from the corner of her eye. She straightened her collar. Finally, aiming to sound breezy, her heart picking up, she said, "If I tell you something, promise you won't laugh?"

Dee gave the assurance, but as it turned out she did laugh. "Joe's a nice enough kid," she said when she'd gathered herself. "But I just can't see you two together. I heard Constance Griffin has her heart set on him."

"Constance?"

"It's pretty widely understood."

"Oh."

"We're all rooting for her, poor girl."

Dee was looking at Grace with curiosity.

"Well," Grace said, trying to sound unbothered, "Constance does seem to make a lot more sense for Joe."

Dee nodded pityingly. "But you'll find someone else," she promised. "You just need to keep your eyes open. He'll show up. Your prince. He's around here somewhere." And she swept her hand before her, across the bathroom, as if her future boy might be hiding in a stall.

Grace thanked Dee for her encouragement. She wanted to leave the bathroom now, but Dee had begun to talk. She had taken Grace's admission as an invitation to speak about her own crush, a boy named William Timpokin who was famous for his impersonations of their flabbergasted principal. Had Grace noticed that William's pimples had recently cleared up? And was she aware that he could run a mile in six minutes flat and had a cousin who was a real albino?

Grace was not aware.

As Dee spoke she applied lipstick, blotted it with a square of toilet paper, applied more, blotted, applied. Finally, stepping back, she frowned, wiped her mouth clean, and began the process again. Grace watched in irritated awe. All the silly, wholehearted machinations of love. All the *work*. Was there anything more unflattering than frosted lipstick? And yet Grace felt for the first time a flutter of pity, and she knew that she, too, was done for.

A month later Grace found herself in Hank's attic bedroom, a wood-paneled cavity with sloping ceilings, pennants on the walls, magazines about radio-making and car repair in tall piles. A mattress lay on the floor against the wall, no bed frame, no box spring, just this mattress on the splintering floor. It was like a monk's bed. She could tell he'd sprayed something lemony in the air, which endeared him to her a little. *Oh Hank.* He was practically illiterate, yet he had a miraculous confidence. He was a poor student but his teachers loved him. He touched Grace like he knew how but also like he'd never touched a girl before. How did he manage that? She knew for a fact that he'd touched several girls. She wanted to be a scientist, detached, disinterested, she wanted to be mean and brilliant, but in his little bed the scientist in her fell away. She didn't even care. There was no data to analyze, no hypothesis to prove or disprove, just his heart whose knocking she felt on her breasts. His legs were long, lean. His penis was what the girls called a gasper.

At the end of their senior year Hank was offered a deal. His Uncle Clyde owned a bar in a farming town called Copper Junction, a sleepy place a couple hours north. This uncle had no children of his own and saw in Hank's fine bones and bad jokes the boy he'd always wished for. Ready to retire, to free himself from darts and drunks and aching feet, he asked Hank to take over the bar so he could decamp to Florida with a woman called Betty-Lynn. Hank, in turn, got down on one knee and extended a bunch of flowering weeds (this was like him—he was fond of half-considered romantic gestures, and of gestures that put him on the level of her crotch), and asked Grace in a panting voice to marry him, to move with him to this bumfuck town, be the wife of the town's new bartender. They'd get a house, too—that was part of the uncle's deal, a small house on a hill with a view of some strawberry fields. So what did she say? Would she marry him and whelp his pups and make him the gladdest son-of-a-biscuit on this sad old earth?

She could not think.

She looked down at his handsome face, his eyes which had widened like a child's, the blades of his cheekbones, the pulse in his neck.

The Eiffel Tower and the Seine receded.

"Well? What do you say?"

More than anything she was amazed: how swiftly things change—how wickedly little control she possessed over herself— how only yesterday she'd been so convinced of the golden, inward, directionless course of her life.

Her mouth was empty of words.

She allowed herself to imagine the Galápagos, dazzling white light, silent ambling tortoises.

A good, simple life, he promised. They'd get a dog—whatever kind she wanted, though he was partial to shepherds. He'd learn to make a gimlet. A sidecar. Polish punch. The jukebox would be *theirs*. Think about it. No parents. No curfew. They could stay up all night whenever they wanted.

Now she felt her face perform a new expression.

Is that a yes? Does that mean yes?

It did. A yes, a yes.

They married. The house turned out to be little more than a shack, and the bar was a terrible place with a ceiling the uncle had painted black, a nudie calendar, a couple finicky pinball machines. "It's an adventure," Hank kept saying. At first this soothed her, but then she started hearing the word *adventure* as *crime*. His handsomeness had become incidental. Did she love him? The scientist returned. She began to see everything in exacting detail. The floors in the house weren't level; anything you spilled ran west. The kitchen window had a feed bag for a curtain. A toilet plunger with no handle. A toilet that flushed by lifting a damp chain in the back.

It was not a place she could bear to call home. Still, they fixed it up as best they could. Her parents gave her a little money, enough for a few gallons of paint, a sofa, a set of curtains with pom-poms dangling from the hem. But even after these improvements, Grace had the uneasy feeling that she'd been kidnapped, carried away against her will, and that by staying, fixing the place up, it was like she was an accomplice—like she'd relinquished the right to cry to be rescued. When, a few months later, she got pregnant, these feelings overwhelmed her.

She heard there was a doctor in Beetle who could help.

She hitchhiked there one day while Hank was at work, brought all their money, took Hank's stash of bills from the coffee can hidden in the attic crawl space. The doctor, an old man, looked over his glasses at her. He said he could help her, said he believed in personal freedom and self-determination, but his expression was one of barely concealed disdain. He took her pulse with cold fingers. He palpated her stomach so roughly she found herself thinking: *He'll hurt the baby!* Once she thought such a thing, once that nascent protective impulse went off in her, she couldn't go through with it anymore. It was as if the doctor's cold, vigorous hands brought the baby to life and tamped out her own.

She had never felt more defeated. What had happened? She had left herself just long enough to get caught in a life. She pictured Darwin, his broomish beard. She was not a scientist but some dumb-to-itself thing a scientist studies. She was a subject. A girl won over by a boy. The doctor described the procedure in a rote voice. Next to him, a nurse nodded along. When the doctor left to get his tools, Grace said, "I've changed my mind."

"Oh, honey," the nurse said, "don't cry." She handed her a tissue. Grace wasn't crying, hadn't felt like crying, but once the tissue was in her hand a sob rose in her throat.

She returned home, returned the cash to its hiding spot, ate an orange, a banana, a can of peas without heating them, a package of Twinkies, and vomited. The baby was born seven months later. They gave her a name—Judith—that turned out not to suit her. It was the wrong name but it couldn't be taken back. Nothing could be taken back. That seemed to be the lesson of Grace's life.

She would raise the baby and make their meals and three afternoons a week tutor high school kids, the Continental Congress, *The Old Man and the Sea,* basic algebra. She would enter full womanhood, submit to it, and find it wasn't as bad as she'd anticipated. It held certain unexpected comforts. Such as the pleasure of a sleeping companion. Such as the immense contentedness that overcame her while watching her child throw her corkscrew body into and out of the sprinkler. Such as knowing you had arrived at yourself—that, yes, there was a whole wide world out there, a world of sex and science and complicated, meaningful art, but you weren't required to do anything but stay where you were, and dress your child, once in a while stick her in the tub, and generally make sure life ticked along. Parenthood, it turned out, wasn't so hard. She found its rhythms. She sang its songs. There was a trick to being a mother, she realized: you just had to use a light hand. Her daughter called her "Grace," and called her father "Hank." Why not? Who cared what the neighbors thought? Why adhere to the old, tired conventions? Sometimes she drew insects, flowers, but not with the same urgency as before. She smoked cigarettes, and, in summertime, lay in the sun with a sheet of aluminum foil under her chin. She wanted very little.

But then her daughter turned fourteen, and their life suddenly became tenuous, tense, strange. Judith morphed, nearly overnight, from a compliant, sprinkler-jumping girl into—

what? Into a creature wry and impatient. Dour. Also her back-side rounded. Her chest grew large, and her legs long, and somehow she got hold of an antique cigarette holder, which she chewed or wore behind her ear. Late for curfew. Missing from bed in the morning. And she didn't insult them—which, after all, might be construed as some inside-out kind of love—so much as ignore them. Day by day, she grew more indifferent, more imperious, absent. Boys in beat-up cars who honked but never came to the door. Packages in the mail with no return address. Even when she was home, at the dinner table, moving food across her plate, she wore a tight, withdrawn expression.

"Ah, she'll grow out of it," Hank said in bed one night.

"She seems . . ." What was the word? What was the new thing? "Heartless," Grace tried, which wasn't quite it, but came close.

"Sure, she's heartless. She's a teenager. What heart did you have back then? None, if I recall."

"That's not true."

"I gave you your heart," Hank said matter-of-factly. "I opened you up and popped it in." He made a clucking sound with his tongue.

Was he right? Possibly. She placed her palm on her chest, felt for that old drumming.

In the meantime, they decided, they would give the girl more freedom. It was a kind of reverse psychology. You want to break your curfew? Fine. Now you have no curfew. You want to steal our booze? No. We'll give it to you. Relinquishing her power made Grace feel powerful. She felt sad and powerful, and the power mostly overwhelmed the sadness, and so she waited patiently for her daughter to return to herself, and to them.

But this did not happen. Instead, in her sixteenth year, Judith ran away.

No note. No explanation. Not even the barest reassurance, which would have been only decent. Her room was empty. She was thorough in her packing—took even the loose buttons on her dresser—and yet failed to leave a note.

She'd been gone a week. Shelly knew nothing. The cops knew nothing. The phone didn't ring.

All Grace could do was sit in her lawn chair and smoke. She imagined the boyfriend, Q, imagined his busy pelvis—sunburnt chest—unclipped fingernails—yellow callused palms. These body parts flashed at her like images in a television commercial, teasers, inciting a riot in her heart. Meanwhile the spring air mocked her. The smell of barbecues mocked her. The laugh track of sitcoms, the sun, the trees, the earth, the glossy sky, anything hopeful or routine or blue or green mocked her, until she thought she could not take it, could not take a moment more, thought maybe she'd scream and scream and not stop until they came and straitjacketed her, and she was ready for this, ready to submit, and then Hank called out from the house. "Grace? Gracie? C'mere for a sec?" like it was an ordinary day.

She found him in the kitchen. He was hanging from the pull-up bar, wearing tight jeans with bleach spots on the thighs. He said, "You want to make something to eat?"

She didn't respond. They looked at one another. Their child was gone. Maybe she was dead.

Then, in a mild, ruminating voice, the sort of voice he might use to say what he wanted for lunch, Hank said, "I'm going to kill him."

His eyes moved to the pantry that held, on its uppermost shelf, in a shoebox and wrapped in a floral dishcloth, his handgun.

At once they both had the same thought: The gun would be

gone. How had they not considered it? They blinked. Let her have taken the gun. It rose like smoke in between them, this hope: Let her have taken the gun. Let her have pointed it at whatever asshole tried to do whatever they did these days to girls from small towns who don't know any better. Of course what boys do to small-town girls was the same now as it always was. So let her have the gun. Let her have the gun and the guts to use it, if it came to that. Neither spoke. Hank got the step-stool. He retrieved the box. But there it was, still nestled in its home, a dumb thing, gleaming and useless, a beetle on its back.

"I'll kill him," Hank said. "I'll do the balloon trick with his balls." He could make two things out of balloons: a monkey and a parrot.

"There's no one to kill," she said gently.

"I will."

"There's no one."

The phone rang.

Hank froze.

It rang again.

Hank said: "I'm going to kill whoever's on the other goddamn end of that phone," and it was her.

6

He stood on the cusp of the woods, and then took a step. He could already smell the silt of the river. The woods made the lowest noise, a flickering of insects and leaves. In the distance, the froggish song of a bird. A single cloud blotted the sun. A breeze, and the woods cracked, the one cloud broke in two, elongated, fused again. He opened and closed his hands. His hands. *His.* He could do what he wanted with them. The immensity of his freedom stuck him with the roiling abruptness of a fever. He lifted a foot, thought: *I will kiss each fingernail. I will kiss between her toes. I will do everything. I will say everything.* It was the first time in his life he felt unembarrassed by need—his desire was faultless, elemental; it might make a mess but it was legitimate, like blood, no one could say a word to the contrary.

He took another step. A dozen black birds hovered, alighted on the tree above his head. *Run,* he thought. *Hurry.*

A voice from behind him: "Sam."

It was his uncle's voice.

They knew. Of course. It was no surprise. It was impossible to have a private desire, impossible to be a boy and want something without the whole world seeing it. He could hear the sniggering birds. He could smell the water. Heavy footsteps behind him. *Run.*

"Sam."

She was waiting under a canopy of green ecstasy.

"Sam! Hey!"

He couldn't run.

Helen was in there, sitting by the river, her bare feet in the water, and even though his whole body shook with desire and fear, even though his future was being peeled from him as a woman peels the skin from an apple (each time his uncle said his name it was a turn of her wrist), he could not ignore the man who saved him. A hand found his shoulder. He turned. He saw his uncle's broad, bearded face, lumberjack jaw, thick lips. A kind, unattractive face that compelled pure devotion. You couldn't refuse him a crumb. This was the tyranny of the good man, and the lust of an adolescent boy was no match for it.

"Hi, Uncle Joe." It seemed a great shame, a failure of love, that he could offer this simple greeting.

"Thank God I found you, thank God." Joe's upper lip curled a little, not a snarl but a softening, a shivering twitch. "Kip said he saw you come this way. Man alive, Sam. We're in a fix here. A state of *emergency*." The word was cast crisply into the air, clean as a siren. But it was the wrong word.

Now Sam was walking the other way, away from the woods, away from Helen. He didn't mean to be walking. His uncle walked and he followed. His uncle talked, gasping between words, saliva gathering in the corners of his mouth, and Sam listened. The woods fell away. The woods were gone. They had never existed.

"I'll tell you what's going on, Sam, and I'll tell you why I need your help. Say what you will about equal rights. When push comes to shove, women need protecting."

Sam cried, "Did something happen to Constance?"

"No, Sam." They neared the car, its engine humming. "We're going to the city."

"*Why?*"

Now Joe turned, looked Sam square in the face. His frown was so fierce, so amplified and practiced, that it resembled nothing more than a smile.

"A girl's in trouble. We're going to protect her. All sorts of awful things happened, but we're on our way now. I'm talking about your cousin Judith here," and there was impatience in his voice, a flicker of irritation, as though Sam should have known.

He was so relieved it was not Constance, that he had not lost another mother, so relieved they were talking about Judith, whom he detested, that he said, dumbly, "She's not my cousin." He was so relieved it was not Constance that when Joe said, next, "Get in the car," Sam got in.

Joe released the emergency brake.

"She's a girl and she's in trouble. The nature of the relation seems beside the point." Joe pulled a piece of paper from his pocket. The paper, the hand, shook. "It's a *hotel,* of all places. Gone. Didn't call for a week. Maybe she ran away. Maybe she was kidnapped. They can't tell for sure. Poor Hank. Can you imagine? Today the phone rings and she's *here*"—he waved the paper—"she's here and says she needs to be retrieved as soon as possible."

Joe relayed the plan: since they were closer to the city than her parents and could get there sooner, and since time was of the essence, they—that is, he and Sam—would find the girl, bring her back to their house. Hank would be there by midnight. Hank, Joe's old best friend, like blood brothers. But even if they hadn't been blood brothers—even if a total stranger had called, sobbing, his girl gone off and Lord knows what, himself too far away to get there by nightfall—of course Joe would step up. This is what men do.

Sam hadn't seen Judith for a couple years. She was one of those noisily sighing girls who steals cigarettes and rolls her skirts at the waist to make them shorter, one of those girls always announcing her boredom, scrunching her nose at the cheese plate his aunt offers (the cheese plate Constance spent an hour cutting and arranging), smirking at Constance's overlarge disappointment. Judith: even her name, its snootiness, the puckered little *o* it made of your mouth, disturbed him. He remembered, the last time he saw her, how she drank her father's beer, just lifted the nearly full bottle from his hand and finished it herself. Hank had said, "Say please, honey," but this was a joke—she wasn't required to say please.

"I need you with me, Sam."

"I guess," Sam said. "But—I don't know."

"You *guess*? A girl's in trouble."

Her trouble was not his trouble. The trouble, now, was Helen's, but Sam couldn't say this, could he? Helen who was in the woods, who'd think he'd abandoned her, who'd think he'd succumbed to second thoughts or changed his mind or found someone else. He was leaving her on the bank of a river and he wouldn't be able to have her again.

"I was supposed to meet someone," he said simply.

"This is an emergency," Joe replied. "This is one of those moments . . ." And it was clear, in the way his chest rose, in the way he gripped at the wheel, that he'd been quietly hoping for one of these moments all his days. "Hank and I were boyhood friends. You do anything for a friend like that." He drove toward the highway ramp. "If we make good time we'll be there by nightfall."

Sam needed to get out of the car.

He said, "See, I was supposed to meet a girl."

The spell of the crisis, for a moment, seemed to break. His uncle said, "Well now." But then he shook his head. "This is the kind of thing you do to *earn* the girl, Sam. To earn the right to a girl."

The interstate transformed a specific place to an unspecific one. Sam's disappointment was bodily; he felt it in his testicles, a diffusion of stings. He felt it in his his thighs and even, somehow, in his buttocks. But then it was gone. All at once, those sensations of longing left his loins and moved up into his stomach, and he was hungry. How could he be hungry? His stomach made a familiar wheedling sound while she waited in those woods, caught in a future that wouldn't ever happen.

"You're a good boy, Sam. You're a good boy for coming. Apple in the glove box if you're hungry."

Sam reached for the glove box, then decided against it. He should not reward his hunger. He would not eat the apple and this would be an act of faithfulness to Helen.

7

They were going to forgive her. It was decided. It had always been decided, even before the girl ran, even before she was born. You forgive your child. You are always forgiving them, always, every moment, every breath. It's the work of parenthood.

The call came. Grace wanted a drink but there wasn't time for a drink. Hank tapped his watch.

They would forgive her for everything. Even her meanness, even her beauty. She had been like a house of cards, brilliantly poised, edges upon edges, but now she had fallen. It was bound to happen. She had fallen, and now they were in a hurry to gather her up.

Grace readied her face. She stood in the bathroom and applied silvery eye shadow, lipstick, a sweep of blush for each cheek. She wanted some protection, the feeling of a mask.

Hank said, "Let's go."

"She'll leave again. You're aware of this?"

"She called. She asked to come back."

Grace allowed him to lead her by the elbow out of the house. He backed their yellow Valiant down the driveway, his mother's paste pearl necklace shuddering from the rearview mirror. The road lay empty before them.

It was what she wanted. They were getting her back. Yet as soon as the call came in, as soon as she'd heard Judith's unnerving, slow, even voice on the bedroom extension, Grace had been filled with dread. What had happened to her daughter? What injury or shame was great enough to propel her back to them, when she'd made it so far? She wanted her girl back, yet as soon as the phone rang she was startled by a feeling so close to fear she didn't know what else to call it.

She was not wearing shoes. She sat in the passenger seat, barefoot, the plastic floor mat beneath her feet covered with sand and receipts, candy wrappers.

Grace said, "I'm just trying to prepare you for the inevitable."

"Nothing is inevitable," he replied. "Prepare *yourself*."

"She'll break your heart. That's what I mean. I have to look after your heart."

"My heart. My heart." He lifted a hand off the wheel, made it into a mouth that would not stop talking. "What do I care about that blood balloon? It's hers to break."

The world was blurring by. They rose to the crest of a hill, saw cows chewing up a field in the distance, the whole sky empty as a palm.

"You'll get a ticket," she warned.

"She can have my heart," he continued. "My kidney. My liver. When you have a kid you give that stuff up."

When she was six, Judith had said to her, "Mama, what do you want to be when you grow up?"

"I am grown up."

"No, I mean when you grow *up* up."

What was she getting at? Grace's own mother, from her earliest memories, had seemed intractably, hopelessly old. Did Judith not perceive Grace with the same distortion?

Grace said, hazily, "Maybe I'll be a firefighter."

"Boys are firefighters."

"A doctor?"

"A mother," corrected the girl. "You want to be a mother."

"I already am a mother," Grace said, touching the girl's chin. "To you."

The girl looked annoyed. "I'm going to catch sharks. I'm going to live in Florida. I'm going to wear a necklace of shark teeth and everyone will be frightened when I walk into a room."

"Where will I be, when you're in Florida?"

"You'll be here," Judith said brightly. "You'll have another little girl. Her name will be Karina Marie. You'll be old."

The child spoke with a light, insouciant sort of authority. She spoke as if it were true, as if saying it made it so. And Grace had thought: *No. I am the one who gets to go to Florida. I am the one with a shark-tooth necklace.* She imagined herself on a folksy homemade raft like in *The African Queen*. She thought: *I am the one getting out of here; Judith is the one who'll be stuck with a baby.*

It was the only time during Judith's childhood when Grace recalled feeling the need to escape, the only time she felt the whims of her adolescence return. She had the urge to say: *Your father had a vasectomy!*

Now Hank stepped on the gas.

"Maybe we should set up some ground rules," he was saying.

"Like we get to meet her friends. We get to say yea or nay. And she needs to be home by—what's reasonable? Eleven?"

It was too late to start again, and Grace said so.

"It's never too late!"

His fervid optimism, his hope. But Judith was not theirs anymore.

"She's always ours," Hank said. "Don't let her tell you otherwise. She's a con man. You have to think of her like a con man. We love her but we can't trust her. That's the new plan. Eleven o'clock sharp. And we get to meet the boys. We'll have them over for supper. I want to look them in the eyes. I'm a bartender," he said. "I can see inside their heads."

8

Helen was waiting. Her dress came over her knees, pale pink cotton, cinched at the waist with a belt like a shoelace. It was ill-fitting, tight at the bust and loose at the waist, shorter than it was meant to be. She was such a tall girl; it was hard to find clothes. Practically, primly, in the manner of a houseguest undressing for bed, she removed her shoes, her knee-socks. She placed the shoes next to each other, heels against the base of a tree. She balled the socks, tucked them into one of the shoes. She waited.

He stood behind a pine, hidden in shadow. Despite his best intentions, he could not speak or move. It had become impossible to do anything except study her ankles, her feet which were long, narrow, and white. He saw that she squeezed her toes, clenched them into the muddy ground, and released them. He imagined putting his mouth on the ball of her ankle. He imagined how fantastically cool the mud must feel on her feet, how that sensation of gripping freshness would rise up her body, jolt upward, enter her loins—he imagined this because he knew that sensation, because he was feeling it himself. He wanted to go to her, to apologize, to make amends, to bite the bone of her ankle, but he couldn't. For the life of him he didn't know how to move. He was pinned cheekwise to this sticky bark, while not fifty feet away on the mossy riverbank she gazed at the water. Her skin echoed the sky in its faint, peculiar green. The water was black and sequined, its surface winking like the sides of a fish. And now what was she doing? What she was doing was the thing he'd been imagining all day, and yet *how* she did it shocked him: with grace and speed, as a magician snaps the square of silk from his hat, she took the bottom hem of that prissy dress and, in one motion, whipped it over her head. It was off. It was gone. For a moment she held the dress above her. Now it wasn't a dress anymore—it was a flag. No, it was *the* flag, the flag that declares the beginning of a new country. His heart, his stomach, surged. *Good God. Good grief. Holy mother of.* She wasn't wearing underwear of any kind. And while she'd set down her shoes so neatly, while she'd balled her socks and tucked them tidily away, the dress she merely tossed aside—it landed in a heap on a jumble of rotting logs. It was part of the wilderness now. She stood there for a moment, lifted her chin, appeared to examine the tops of the trees, all those buds and brambles, a roof of incipient green, a radiating veil, a green and shivering heat. He could not hear the birds anymore. He could not hear the water. He was only his eyes. He could only look. Calves, thighs, rear. He stared. Wrist. Wrist. Shoulder blade, blade. He could not move, could not speak. The neck like a dancer's, the knobby knees. The breasts which were bigger than he thought they'd be, loose and low. And then she did something that terrified him. She smiled. She smiled, yes, but it wasn't a smile he knew—it wasn't a smile he'd ever seen on Helen or anyone else for that matter. How, then, could it feel so familiar? The smile was cold. It was, in its toothiness and absoluteness and calm certainty, death itself. She offered this smile to the sky, to the river, and then turned and—could she see him?—leveled it right at him. It was a weapon. He could not turn from it. He could not speak, could not offer anything in return except his dumb staring face, except his clodhopper lust. *Baby,* he tried to say. He said it. Again. *Baby*: but the word emerged as if from the mouth of a child, high and plaintive, a whine. Did she hear him? He couldn't tell. She didn't respond. She simply walked into the river. He heard her call out slightly at the cold, heard her make a whimpering sound like any ordinary girl would make. For now she was an ordinary girl again, shivering, rubbing her arms, bobbing slightly up and down. Then she vanished beneath the surface like a trick, the water sealing itself above her, clean and cold as ice.

She didn't come up again.

Between her legs there had been a patch of hair the color of wet straw, and that was gone too.

He opened his eyes. They were on the highway. On the radio someone was complaining about a sports team. Those perennial bums. Lazy, overpaid sissies. Good for nothing. Fat, too, said a fat-sounding voice.

It was a dream, but in every part of his body he felt it was not a dream. He thought: *Helen's dead. She's drowned.* "I need to make a phone call," he said to his uncle. He realized he was out of breath.

Joe turned off the radio. "Huh? Who'd you need to call?"

It was a good point. Who would he call? The police? Her parents? And say—what? I had a premonition that your daughter drowned? She and I were supposed to have intercourse in the woods and I think she's there now and drowned in three feet of slow water? It made no sense.

"Forget it," he said, but his heart was pounding. "It doesn't matter."

It made no sense but he saw her just the same, the corpse of her, vein-marbled skin, dead mouth, dead nipples, saw a team of people in uniforms dragging her from the water back to the mossy bank. He saw flashbulbs. He saw someone use a pair of tongs to lift that pink dress, slide it into a plastic bag.

Joe said, "What's on your mind?"

No, it was a scene from a movie. That was all. It was fake. *You're no psychic,* he told himself. *You're just a horndog. If you can't have her you'll kill her,* that sort of thing. He needed to clear his head. He rolled down the window. Cool, polleny air rushed his face. "I'm fine," said Sam. "Hungry."

"Apple in the glove box."

It was over. It was a dream. *Just eat the apple. Just eat the apple.*

Soon they arrived in the city. Or—no. They didn't *arrive;* one couldn't drive to such a place. It was as if the city simply appeared, rose up from the plain world to take issue with everything you've ever said or thought. They got closer, closer, and at last entered its heart. The city was scabrous, dingy, humid. It was a buzzing of flies and fluorescence. Its smell, too, buzzed in the air, trash and pizza and fried things, a woven odor that prickled the skin at the back of your neck like a light touch. The skyscrapers inspired a funny kind of queasiness in him, buildings so vividly erect, stern, they were like signs of a future species. They drove past tenements, past glass storefronts full of shoes and books and dresses, a whole window of bright yellow dresses the color of a kitchen sponge, and then down a cross street past a kid who kicked their bumper. Joe pulled over and bought two rubbery hot dogs from a sidewalk vendor. There was a hissing in the air, a weak crackling charge, like the moment just after fireworks conclude. At one intersection a man with a kerchief over his mouth tried to wash their windshield.

"What do you think?" Joe asked.

Sam didn't like it here at all.

It had a kind of hoary glamour, brought to mind those cartoons in adult magazines where the devil is not evil but rather a gentleman sophisticate, puffing on a long cigarette, surrounded by women and books and fire. The devil walked among them. It was almost like a party. It had all the fiendish, permissible cheer of Halloween. Sam's heart was racing; he wanted to throw open the door.

But then, at the next stoplight, everything changed. He'd been seeing it wrong. At the corner, waiting to cross, stood a regular woman wearing a tweed coat and those lace-up shoes with little heels. His aunt wore shoes like that. She was holding the hand of a small boy. They were ordinary people living in a very big town, waiting to cross.

Finally, on a dim side street paved with cobblestone, the car jerked and bounced, then stopped before a low concrete building. Joe grunted, put the car in park. Somewhat grandly, like a person sitting down to a feast, he rubbed his hands together. "We made it, Sam." There was some pride and surprise in his voice, as if their very arrival had been in question, as if landing here were itself the feat. He turned off the engine, said, "What a dump, huh?"

Chrome letters spelled *The Wickman* across the building's face. A bird's nest sat in the crook of the *k*, and a green-and-white-striped awning, splattered with bird shit, hung over the front door. Otherwise it seemed perfectly fine, but Sam said, "A dump, yeah." His heart picked up again. She was in there— tedious, limb-flinging Judith was in there waiting for them, probably drunk or high. He wanted to get this over with. The sun was setting.

"We'll be nice to her," Joe said. "No questions. No disapproval."

"I got it."

"You follow my lead. No sudden moves. We get her to the car and drive to our house. Her parents meet us there and take her home. Simple."

"Simple."

"You might not want to look her in the eye."

"Okay."

"And you might want to avoid touching her. No handshakes. No pats on the back."

Sam agreed.

"And she'll be crying, Sam." He thought for a moment, brows knitted. "You get yourself ready for that, too. She won't be the girl you remember. Put on a soldier's face. And be yourself."

They got out of the car with the inflated authority of police officers, slammed their doors. They were like cops. They were like soldiers. Inside was a girl whom together they could save. Joe's shoulders, chest, rose. He set his jaw. Joe held the door for Sam. The lobby smelled of smoke and cat piss. Mustard-colored wallpaper shone like old corduroy, separating at the seams. A natty orange cat slept in the middle of the lobby, its tail twitching. Behind a counter, his feet up on a couple milk crates, a man was reading a magazine. A glowing green UFO on its cover: *Last Days of Peace!* The guy looked up briefly, said something like "Hep ho," turned a page. His beard was the same color as the cat. They walked briskly through the lobby. In the elevator, Joe said, "What a place, huh?" Sam agreed. "In and out," Joe said, but the place distorted these words. Crimes happened here. Sex happened here. Every room had a girl like Judith in it. The quiet itself felt like a crime. "Breathe through your mouth," Joe said, but Sam didn't need telling.

9

Hank had been swearing like a sailor all afternoon but now he said, "Oh cripes." Grace turned and saw the flashing lights behind them.

The cop's barrel chest appeared at the driver's side window. At first Hank did what he was supposed to do, handed over the documents, nodded sheepishly. But when the cop said, "You know how fast you were going?" she saw Hank tense, saw that his shoulders rose, and he replied, "As a matter of fact I do, yes."

Grace dipped down in her seat so she could get a look at the cop. His badge said *M. Kully.* Twenty-something, with sandy hair that cascaded over his forehead in a composed wave, a square jaw, one of these delicate rosebud mouths like babies have. His complexion was dewy pale, a blush that hadn't yet become ruddiness. She knew they were in trouble. The cop was more handsome than Hank.

"As a matter of fact," Hank continued, "I'm in the middle of an emergency here. I'm in the middle of what you could call a crisis."

"Yeah?" Officer Kully put his hands on his hips. "What sort?"

"The sort that involves a child—"

She touched Hank's thigh. "Just do what he says."

"—the sort that involves a teenage girl who's been taken. My daughter. We're on our way to—rescue her."

It was the wrong word: *rescue.* It suggested intrigue. As if Judith had done something other than get very bored and let— *ask*—some cocksure guy to take her to the city for a few days.

"I clocked you at ninety-seven. You realize those back tires are almost bald?"

Hank's face had reddened; his legs shook.

"It's an emergency here. My girl is waiting. I'm telling you greater harm will befall her if I'm late."

Rescue. Befall. He had convinced himself of these terms. He was racing, as if the child truly needed their help. But it was *Joe* who was going to the city. They were merely driving to Joe and Constance's house—Hank was speeding, and for what? So they could sit and wait with Constance.

The officer sighed deeply, said, "Sorry you're having trouble with your kid. Sounds rough, sure does. But you're probably thinking, *Hey, this bumfreck village. Just a bunch of farms. Chickens. Hicks.* Probably thinking whatever you've got going on matters more than abiding some backwoods *laws.* Am I right?"

"I respect you and your laws and your chickens," Hank said.

He paused. "I've got a daughter. You got one? Of course you don't. You got a sister? Pretend it's your sister. I don't need some lecture here. Either write me a ticket or give me a warning, but let me go."

Kully was staring at Hank, the smallest movement in his jaw.

"Sir, you think a person can speed anytime he's got a personal issue? What would happen to the roads if every driver adopted such a policy?"

"An issue! Oh man. Oh shit. A *personal* issue. Did you even hear what I said? This is a crisis. Can you get your head around that?"

"How many drinks have you had today, sir?"

"Drop the sir, all right? I'll take a ticket. I'll slow down."

"How many drinks, sir?"

"Sir! Sir!"

"Please step out of the car."

"No drinks. Zero. Nada."

"I'm going to ask you again to step out of the vehicle."

Hank made a steeple with his fingers, held them over his mouth. Now his voice was low, full of a hushed, coiled intensity: "Let me clarify. I promise I'll slow down. I agree I was going too fast. I agree your laws matter. But, see, the thing is that I need to *go*. My girl." His voice broke at *girl*.

Again Grace put her hand on Hank's thigh, but it was the wrong thing, the worst thing, for Hank responded as if the *cop* had put a hand on his thigh. He swatted her hand away, smashed his own fist on the seat between them, and then raised his other hand to the kid's face, open-palmed, and held it there.

Sunset. Pink sky. Crickets bounding the fields. One second of calm. One last moment of intactness. A breath trapped in her throat, Hank's palm to the kid's face, her own hands resting on her lap as if waiting for lashes. Finally an authority—finally someone to draw the line. It was the closest they'd come to grace. In the next instant the cop had Hank's wrist in his hand, was twisting it, twisting the arm behind Hank's body, so that her husband arched his back in pain, cried out, and then collapsed on the passenger seat, his head forced onto Grace's lap.

"You're kidding me," Hank said, into his wife's crotch. She looked down at his head, his black hair, the shining skin of his scalp. The cop still held his wrist.

"You've got the wrong idea." But Hank's voice was fading, lacked surety. His tears wet her lap.

"My baby," Grace whispered, and touched his ear.

From this point on Hank complied. He allowed himself to be handcuffed; he ducked into the squad car.

"You get her," he said to Grace through the window. "You hold her. Tell her Daddy loves her. Please say that."

He had not been Daddy since Judith was two.

The cop slammed the door, drove off. They were gone. Her husband had been swept away by the law. She stood on the dusty shoulder, heard the whirring of insects, saw a spray of lavender by her feet, Queen Anne's lace white as a dinner plate, an assortment of scabby bushes, weeds, things she could not name.

For some reason she said, to no one, "Wait!"

Wait for what?

Grace got in the driver's side, the seat still warm from Hank's body. She had the irrational feeling that he was gone forever and fully, that he would never return, so that sitting where he had been sitting moments before, feeling the warmth his body made, it was like being touched lightly by a ghost. She thought: *It's happened. It's happened.* The moment was like the answer to a riddle— it provided, like a riddle, a very brief and blunted satisfaction.

Something plain and inevitable had been confirmed. What she felt was that she had never been more alone.

She could retrieve her child. She could bail out her husband. Or she could do both. Or she could do neither.

She had given Judith a name that meant freedom. This had annoyed Grace's parents, who'd wanted some reference to them, or those before them—Mildred, Clarice, Mary—who'd wanted a name that carried their past. But Grace would not comply. Judith was made for the future. Grace knew it the first time she'd seen her screaming face.

10

They were carried upstairs in a tiny, shuddering elevator, its inspection record defaced by a naked woman rendered in felt-tipped pen. A naked woman with a tail! Sam kept his eyes from this drawing—just a glimpse told him that he should look no longer at the bulbous breasts, stars for nipples, or the opaque triangle between her legs, or the tail concluding in a triple curlicue. He should not look. Why did this casual doodle strike him as more dangerous—more violent—than the real-life naked women he saw in photographs at Marco's store? The doors opened. They stepped into a dark hall, thick tan carpeting rutted by years of footfalls. They walked slowly, preparing their faces, found the door, paused. Joe swallowed; he knocked. No answer, so he called, "Hello? Judith? It's Joe. It's Sam, too." They heard a little noise from inside.

She wore a butter-yellow dress, metal bangles on each wrist. Her feet were bare. She met them with a bald scowl. They saw a flicker of relief pass over her face, then nothing. Joe exhaled her name. She said, "So they say."

It was a small room, a sink bolted to its wall, one window with its plastic shade drawn. On the dresser sat a gilt-edged Bible and a plastic cup of water. A pink duffel bag waited by the door. The smell belonged to a basement, though they were on the fourth floor. Judith sat down in the middle of the bed, on a blanket the color and texture of peat moss. She leaned back on her elbows, crossed her legs at the ankles, tilted her chin upward like a sunbather.

Joe said, "Thank God you're all right."

Her voice was calm. "Who said I was all right?"

Joe moved toward the bed, stood before her. "We're here to pick you up."

She frowned. She looked at Sam. She said, "Hey."

To his surprise he said "Hey" back, casually, coolly, like they were two kids passing in the hallway at school.

"The car's outside. You have everything in that bag?"

Judith shrugged. "More or less."

"Let's go then."

She just yawned, sighed heavily. To whom it was not clear, she said, "It's a bad, bad life."

"Huh?"

"I'm going to get myself a wife."

"Let's go home." Joe spoke loudly now, with great care. "I bet you're hungry. We'll get you a milkshake."

"I cut off my lord's lord with a knife."

"Honey?"

"Not so good. I don't have the knack. I spent the last week

with a songwriter," she said. "He liked to talk in rhyme. Once I balked and then he beat me within an inch of my life, tried to make me his wife, but luckily I got my hands on a knife."

Joe crouched in front of her. Now his face was bloodless, mouth clenched.

"Oh Uncle Joe." She shook her head. "You're more gullible than a cocker spaniel. There was no knife. Just a bad guitar player who thought he was Dylan."

Joe swallowed. "Did he hurt you?"

"His smell hurt me."

"But did he *hurt* you, Judith?"

Sam knew how much strength it took his uncle to ask this question. You could see him bracing for the worst answer, his forehead damp. Judith just waved a hand—Sam hated her casualness, her airiness, when his uncle—*his* uncle—was putting all his might into this rescue.

"He smelled, that's all," she said. "Body odor." Here she dropped her head over her right shoulder, lifted her elbow, and sniffed once at her own armpit. Then she looked up. "If he taught me one thing it's not to believe everything you hear, Joe. Especially when it rhymes."

"Stop it," Sam said. He wouldn't spend another minute in this room. "Just—stop."

She smiled. "Stop what?"

They were quiet.

Then she said, "Look, I didn't ask to be rescued."

"Yes you did."

Joe said, "The car's right outside."

"I did *not* ask to be rescued."

"You did."

"All right now, kids—"

"No," said Judith, to Sam. Her eyes were wide. "I wanted someone to see me here. That's all I wanted."

"We see you, honey," Joe said. "Now it's time to go."

He picked up her bag. He looked so strange, so pathetic, almost criminal, a big man holding a pink bag with a picture of a ballerina girl on its side.

Judith blinked—her eyes were suddenly glassy. "I can't go yet."

"Of course you can. Stand up, honey. Follow us."

She shook her head. Would she cry? Sam thought she might, but he was wrong. She laughed, a few hard, trilling notes, then said, "I want to stay here until he comes back and I want you both to tie him up."

"You're lying," Sam said. It just came out, he didn't mean it to say it. She was playing—she was teasing them. He wouldn't be teased! He had sacrificed so much for her, and here she was in this filthy room, mocking them, half dressed, uncombed, probably high . . .

"I think I should call the police. I think that's the thing to do." Joe spun around, searching for a phone, but there wasn't one. A spot in the wall looked like it might have once held a phone jack; now it was just a dark hole sprouting scorched wires.

"I'm kidding," she sighed. "Sam's right, I'm kidding." At once she appeared exhausted. "He'll never come back. He broke my heart is all. He left me. A guy, a dude, no one. I'll move on. That's the whole of it. Jesus, Uncle Joe, look at you." She rubbed her eyes with the heels of her hands, like a sleepy child. "Listen, no one's going to hurt me here. Not a soul. There's no one left to hurt me. If you want to know the truth, there's more danger out that door than in this shithole. This is the safest I've been my whole life. But you don't want the truth. Why would you? I don't blame you for it."

Joe straightened. His hands, Sam saw, were shaking. "We're leaving now," he said.

She shook her head. "I want a few more minutes. Just a little bit. Let me be alone with Sam? I can't leave right this second. I need Sam. Please. Someone my age who doesn't believe everything he hears."

"You two can talk in the car."

She untucked her legs from beneath her, slid to the edge of the bed, crossed them politely. She straightened the straps of her dress. She said, "I appreciate that you've come here, Uncle Joe. I realize it was a long drive, and I realize I've frightened you. I apologize. I haven't seen anyone or talked to anyone for days, and it's made me strange. Pardon me. I would really appreciate the opportunity to communicate with someone who's apt to understand what young people feel these days. If you could just wait outside. On the third floor there's a lounge with a candy machine and a bunch of old newspapers. A quick talk with Sam and then I'll be ready to go. Sam gets me. Sam understands, doesn't he? Better than any of us."

Joe looked at Sam. His eyes said: *A girl's in trouble.* His eyes said: *Tell me what to do.* Sam was afraid to be alone with her. He had never seen his uncle so befuddled, never seen his uncle so out of place, and seeing this was enraging and also, strangely, satisfying. He had promised Joe he would be nice, but he felt, for the first time in his life, that he could *not* be nice.

"Sure, Joe," said Sam. "I'll talk to her for a couple minutes. We'll come get you in the lounge."

Joe looked unsure, but he nodded, checked his watch. "You

can have ten minutes. That's it. Ten minutes. Then we have to go. And, Sam, if someone knocks on the door, don't let them in."

Joe closed the door; they heard him move away. Sam stood awkwardly by the bed. He inhaled stale air. Traffic moved in the distance. A siren, a toilet flushing upstairs, water—city water—chugging through the pipes around them. Everything was dirty. He had the sense that something momentous could happen here. A city siren. A city hotel. Here, too, a city girl, in a way. His heart picked up.

Judith leaned back on her elbows. "God, your poor uncle's about to have a stroke. I almost forgot what a puppy he is."

He had no idea what she wanted from him.

"You're being—an ass." He said it.

"Oh, I'm not that bad."

"He's trying to help you. We drove for hours."

She shrugged.

He said, "He's not your uncle, either."

"He's not your dad."

"Just be nice. Be nice to him or—" There was no way to finish it. He had nothing.

She smiled. "That's the spirit." Then she said, "You have the saddest story, Sam, don't you? Even sadder than mine."

"Shut up," he said.

She stared at him levelly. Her eyes were a cool gray. She blinked. He saw the remnant of a cut on the corner of her mouth. She was skinny in the way of sickness, skinny and shaking imperceptibly and ready to pounce, like a trapped animal, in this rented room. He realized something terrible had happened to her. For a moment this frightened him—what had happened? what had she seen? who had done what to her?—but it was followed by an abrupt sense of relief. Yes, something bad had happened, but it was over. She had survived it in some manner or other. He felt his face relax.

She said, "I haven't told a single lie."

"I doubt that."

"I *did* get my hands on a knife. I didn't use it, though. I held it up and told him I'd kill him. You know what he did?"

Sam didn't answer.

"He laughed. I was nothing to him. You, my dear, are what they call baggage. I feel about you as I do a head of cabbage. He said stuff like that. I wanted to do something that would leave a hell of a scar."

She looked at him carefully. Then she said, "You've got a nice mouth." It was offered with a gentleness he hadn't expected, and he didn't know what to do with it. He grabbed his lip with his teeth. Nine minutes. They kept looking at each other. Eight.

11

Constance wore her pink housecoat. In one pocket: three bobby pins. In the other: a pencil stub she considered good luck, for it was what Joe had used, those many years ago, to write down his marriage proposal. This pink housecoat was an important thing—homey, earnest, it brought to mind the kind of satisfied, efficient woman she hoped to be, content to cook and putter and smack a kiss on her husband's cheek at the workday's end. In this way it was a talisman. In this way it was a plea. Now, her hands in its deep pockets (a finger on the pencil stub), she stood in her bedroom and looked down at her bed.

A nap was a crime on a day like this. It was a glorious day, a perfect spring day, but she didn't want to be outside. Outside was hairy caterpillars and hippies, mud on your shoes, boys and girls shooting each other significant glances they were so stupid as to think no one saw. She saw. A nun could see. Heat. Halter tops. The way a jaw worked chewing gum. Outside was, to put it mildly, a mess; total rudeness. Soon Hank and Grace would show up to collect their daughter and produce dirty dishes. She had been right all along. Hadn't she? She had! It was not, she told herself, in her nature to gloat. But it was true: she'd been right. Whenever they visited that sleepy place, Hank's ram-shackle house on its weedy hill, Constance was struck by its dirtiness, by the dreadful manners of their girl. She'd feel a little pull of scorn inside her, a self-satisfied *tsk*, but then she'd tell herself—*So they're happy. So what? Don't begrudge them their hap-piness. Who are you to begrudge anyone anything? So there's a ciga-rette floating in the toilet; so the cat did its business on the welcome mat. So what?* And, diligently, she would turn the scorn inward. The *tsk* revolved. Then it was: *You're a scold, Constance. You're just jealous of their happy mess, aren't you? You wish you smoked ciga-rettes. You wish you burned incense in the butter dish and were free enough to leave a pair of underpants on the front porch.*

But she had been right all along. Her scorn was justified. She could not have been jealous, for what was there to be jealous of? Their daughter had run away, had wound up in some hotel with who knows whom, proving that clean countertops mattered. Her disdain for Hank was a secret she kept even from her hus-band. Tonight she was expected to serve them beer and cook them a hot dinner. She was expected to be sympathetic. She was expected to act as confidante to Grace, to share with her a knowing and maternal empathy, as if it could just as easily have been Sam who'd run away. She would pretend, since it was her job to pretend, but it wasn't true—Sam, her good boy, would not have run, would not have taken up with riffraff. Even so, Con-stance would pat Grace's hands, she would say something like

"Kids today" in a low, commiserating murmur, as if the era were at fault and not the ill-trained girl or her faulty trainers. And all the while Grace would look at her with those steady grayish eyes that reminded Constance of the eyes of child geniuses in movies—they looked at you too directly, or too intently, either way it was unnerving. Constance was a little scared of Grace. She had to admit it. She was also scared, maybe the smallest bit, of Judith, whose thin mouth pulled her face into meanness; whose hair she wore in a loose, glossy braid; whose eyebrows were so dark and straight they appeared slashed into her face—who resembled, all in all, thought Constance, an irritable Indian. Yes, she was scared of the girl—see? she could be honest with herself—but she wouldn't let it show.

Is this why she got back into bed? She never got back into bed. When she was up she was up, busy and bustling, until the end of the day. Yet here she was, sun shining, trying not to disturb the hospital corners, her housecoat folded on the floor next to the bed.

She would nap. She would allow herself that rare indulgence. She closed her eyes, but felt only a deeper, more heightened wakefulness. Her limbs were hot. She thought: *Grace is the kind of person who naps, not me, not me.* She wanted to hurt herself. Did she? Really? She rammed her fingernails into her palms. The need surprised her in its force and clarity. To put a safety pin into her skin, or hold her hand over a flame—some small, centralized hurt. Why? What on earth compelled this desire? No. She realized it wasn't pain that she wanted—she wanted the opposite, except the effort would be the same. Except with pain there would be no guilt, so it was the easier thing to crave.

She rolled onto her side and found her dead sister-in-law sitting on the floor by the bedside table.

Louise said, "You want to get in bed with him, don't you?" She wore black patent-leather shoes, dancing shoes, with laces of pink satin ribbon.

"What?" And: "Who?"

"Both," Louise said. "Any. All."

"That's the most absurd thing I've ever heard."

One of Louise's shoulders rose and fell.

"Stupid," Constance said. "Vile." She searched for the word that would expel this phantom and pull Constance upright, restore her to herself. From down the block she heard the squeals of children. It was wrong to nap, to *want* to nap, on this kind of day. "Outrageous. Asinine. Ludicrous." She had done well on vocabulary. "Odious," she tried.

"Maybe you want to hold him to your breast. That's what I think. You want him to—what's that word again? It's a strange word, isn't it. Suckle."

Fatigue washed over Constance's body. "Please just let me sleep." What a fool she was, what a weak woman, saying *please* to Louise—not even a ghost but a fantasy, poor man's ghost, wearing shoes Louise did not wear in life. The shoes were Constance's, from her childhood—tap shoes handed down by an older cousin. She had adored these shoes, wore them even in her bed at night, but she was a terrible dancer; finally her mother refused to pay for lessons and gave the shoes to Goodwill for a needy, less awkward girl.

Constance rolled onto her stomach. "I'm going to sleep now."

"On a day like today?"

"It's allowed."

It was true, a baby had never suckled at her breast. There were so many things she had never done. Never danced in a recital, worn a tutu, purchased a bra that contained anything but the essential materials. Never been bought a drink by a man in an impractical hat. Never read that book of erotic short stories that had been passed around town. Never kissed someone and said, afterward, "Let's just pretend that never happened."

The room was too bright for sleep, her mind too addled. She roused herself from bed.

She had allowed herself to submit once before to pleasure, or to the promise of pleasure. Nineteen, not yet married (but engaged!), they dropped the cloak of their timidity long enough to conceive, and look at the mess that followed.

She felt better when she put on the housecoat again.

She found herself in Sam's room. His bed was neatly made. A pair of corduroy slippers waited on the floor, their toes to the wall. On his dresser sat a plastic comb, a nail clipper, and a glass of water. It was like a room, she realized, in an orphanage. She understood he was going to leave soon—he was going to leave and then it would be her and Joe, alone. She would continue to cook the same meals. She would continue to buy his soap, iron his pants, spray his shoes with deodorant. Spaghetti night, taco night, oatmeal every other morning, lovemaking once a week followed by his humming sighs and a few minutes of his hand twirling her ponytail as he drifted asleep, and always the same thing for his birthday, Christmas, always his face lighting up, always "Aw! Wow!" as if she'd bought him tickets to Paris and not another three-pack of tube socks with yellow bands at the calves.

"I raised your boy," Constance said finally. "For you I did this."

"Did what?"

She gestured: *Everything*, floor to ceiling. Her hand swept the room and then returned, fisted, to her chest. She meant: the

water glass, the slippers, the food in the refrigerator, the plentiful cold cuts, the marriage to a man for whom she felt sisterly
warmth, the notebook documenting her boy's growth and grades
and vaccination schedule. The notebook was always meant for
Louise, as if someday Louise would retrieve it and find proof of
Constance's diligence, goodness: yes, he got his polio shot, yes,
he ate his broccoli, and passed math, and grew two inches in six
months, and lost his front tooth on such and such day. But Louise said, "Look, no one ever called for a sacrifice."

"You did!"

"Me?" She shook her head. "I never did anything but die."

"Go away," Constance pleaded. "Please go away."

She was gone.

Constance blinked. She needed some air. Louise had ruined
the peace of the house. As always, Louise took whatever you
cared about and laughed in its face—how had Constance ever
seen this for anything but what it was? How had she ever admired
this woman's juvenile vanity? Now she dressed, put on a high-
necked white blouse, pressed navy slacks, so in the mirror she
saw her fourth-grade self, a scrubbed openness, a tidy, sexless,
faultless being, and she felt a little better.

It was warmer than she expected. Whirring spring air; sun
like a burner. She sat in her car, unsure where to go. The lawn
was as neat as a lawn can be, edged, mulched, flowers in discrete
rows. But her tulips! She looked at her tulips, her breath growing
faster, torso dampening. They were obscene, weren't they, the
tulips? Too big! Too glossy! Tumid, bloated, veined, labial, she
had an urge to snap their necks. Oh what was wrong with her!
She felt hot, stupid, overdressed.

She went where she felt she had to go. When she pulled into
the parking lot, Louise was back. There was Louise again, buck-

led into the passenger seat, one tap-shoed foot up on the dash, the other folded under her. Louise said, "Fuck church. You might as well pray to a rooster. You might as well pray to the pebble in your shoe. Take a left."

Constance did as she was told. She drove away from church, toward the center of town, past the library, the post office. The streets were mostly empty. On the green in front of town hall she saw a few mothers and babies, old people on benches, and tulips, daffodils, in rows, in circles, everywhere neat, civic arrangements of flowers.

"Right at the light." Louise was gazing out the window, thumb hooked under her chin, on her face an expression of sleepy, mild curiosity, like a train passenger moving through any small town they'll never see again. Suddenly she turned to Constance, said, "Poor thing. I see how hard you're fighting."

"Where am I going? I have things to do."

"How much you want to like yourself."

It was unseemly. You weren't supposed to like yourself. You were supposed to respect yourself; you were supposed to regard yourself with disinterest, to notice yourself only enough to make sure you were doing right.

"Go away," Constance said.

But she hadn't really meant it.

Louise said, "I think you need a break."

"I have to buy some groceries."

"Turn here. Slow down. Good. Stop."

"A break from what?" Constance said.

The sky cloudless, vibrant blue, taut as the skin over a skull. She stopped the car.

A break.

"You want a higher power?" Louise said. "You want a church?

Open that door. Say hello to the man at the counter. The most honest god you're gonna find."

And what did Constance do? She could have done anything in the world, and what did she do? She got out of the car, inhaled a spring breeze, did not pause or think or smooth her hair. Chimes on the door. Behind the counter, a grinning old man, cigarette between his thumb and forefinger. He wore an Army-green T-shirt. Dirty fingernails, moon-round belly. Asphalt eyes, orangey teeth. The vein in his neck—greener, thicker, somehow, than it was meant to be—suggested something amphibious.

"I don't believe I've ever seen you here." A calm drag on his cigarette, then: "What a fine surprise."

She said nothing.

"Marco," he offered. "You got a name?"

She just stood there, purse to her stomach like a girl clutching her babydoll. The store was empty. Dust on the shelves. Junk. A display of farting pillows. Comic books and kazoos, party hats, a pair of sandals made of twine, toilet paper with the president's face on it.

"A name?" Louder: "Your name?"

She said it.

"She speaks. Right on. You looked so blank I thought for a second you might be deaf. I know a little sign language." He jabbed his hand in a few directions. "That means: *Welcome to my store.*" Another, grander gesture, with a wink. "That means something not polite to say in front of a lady."

"I think I'm lost."

"Take a look around. We're having a sale today. Lucky for you—half off everything in the back room."

"I only have a moment. I'm on my way somewhere."

"You and me both. You have all the time you need, Connie.

They call you Connie? Check out the back room." He tapped his cigarette into an ashtray in the shape of a person's behind. "No harm in looking, especially during a sale. Person like you must appreciate saving money. I can tell. I see it in your eyes."

She was a money-saver, it was in her eyes. A dented-can-buyer, a coupon-clipper, a penny-hoarder. She had nearly two hundred dollars in loose change stored in a cardboard box in the basement. On the side of this box she had written, in optimistic pink marker: Rainy Day Fund.

Now, when she wanted her, Louise was nowhere.

She didn't like the way Marco's eyes fixed on her, didn't like his expression, which was discomfiting not because it was smirking but because it was somehow too kind, too—what was it? It was too patient. His face had all the time in the world. She turned away, made for the back of the store, but only to escape his stare, only to escape that incongruously sympathetic, perversely steady gaze. Not because she was curious. She was not curious. There was not a door but a curtain, dusty red velvet, its raw edge touching the floor. No, she was not curious until she was, and then she was curious to her toes. She pulled aside the curtain.

"You've got the place to yourself," he called after her.

The back room, she saw, was really a large closet.

"Enjoy," she heard him call out. "Take your time." He said something else but by then the curtain had fallen back behind her and no sound could reach her, no daylight, nothing, no one. A bare orange bulb on the ceiling rendered the closet and its contents sepia, turned the experience somehow innocent, quaint, even as it was happening, even as a gasp rose up in her.

Photographs covering the walls. A row of file boxes on the floor, teeming with magazines. What was to stop her from looking? Who was to tell her not to? She allowed herself to breathe. She allowed her shoulders to relax. She looked.

Here, a woman holding a horsetail. A woman using a horsetail to whip the backside of a man whose every inch of skin was covered in tattoos.

Here, a girl who could not be more than sixteen, long hair in pigtails, cross-legged in front of a dollhouse. In her hand a doll, a little figurine. Only it wasn't a doll at all, what she was holding. Only she wasn't a girl at all.

She looked.

Photographs so stark and flat they seemed not to depict real people but rather their desperation, as if desperation were not feeling but form.

A girl—this *was* a girl—on a big bed, head thrown back, neck twisted in such a way, eyes closed, hands limp, she might have been dead. Her hair was soaked; the sheet where her head rested, you could see, was dark with water. And a fat woman whose body was covered with scars—a neat one on her belly, a raised one on her breast, over the nipple, a vertical line, so that the scar and nipple, together, made an exclamation point. Did these people exist? Where did they live? Why on earth did they do this? What did they eat for breakfast?

A tingle on Constance's neck, a shiver, and she heard someone enter behind her, heard the curtain graze the floor, saw the light change and change back. The curtain fell into place. She could feel the presence of this new person; the air shifted with the change, grew imperceptibly warmer, even darker, as if the new body absorbed light. Constance did not turn. Her heart spun. It wasn't Louise; she could tell the person behind her was real. Marco? She couldn't bear turning around. She fixed her eyes on a picture pinned to the wall before her face—but it wasn't a picture, you couldn't go so far as to call it a picture, it was just a series of images of genitals, dozens of them, like mug shots, men's and women's both, rows and rows. Like the genitals were on the lam, that's how it looked, like you would get a reward if you called a number and reported their whereabouts. Her heart unspooled like yarn, making a mess of everything, a tangle in her chest, a knot in a knot in a knot. Behind her, Marco or whoever he was breathed. Constance did not breathe.

She pictured the frozen food aisle of the supermarket. She imagined herself debating lima beans or peas under the fluorescent light of the genital-free supermarket, its gum-chewing clerks, the stacked apples, the candy bars, the sweet stink of the soap aisle.

The person behind her breathed.

The grocery store, of course, was *not* free of genitals.

The person said, "Finally I'm not the only girl."

Constance turned.

She was tall—taller than Constance. In her adult height she wore a girl's pink dress, a shoelace for a belt, and tennis shoes. She had a girl's face and a girl's shiny, lank hair, parted in the middle. She was Sam's age! Mud dotted her shoes, and the dress couldn't have fit worse.

"Good afternoon," Constance said. Shame swept through her body, taking everything decent, like a net collecting gems from a silty river. She felt her mouth twitch.

The girl crossed her arms over her chest and said, "Look at how he holds it! He's so proud!"

Constance looked, but there were so many pictures that met this description. Which one was the girl referring to? She could not ask.

The girl said, "Biology is hilarious."

Constance wanted to look calm but knew she did not.

"I mean, women have a lot to be proud of too, biologically speaking. But of course it has to be hidden. It's designed to freak you out. It's not real."

"I know," Constance said, but she did not.

"People want to be thrown for a loop. Not you, obviously. You look upset."

That was not the right word, *upset*. Constance could say nothing—her eyes stung, her face felt tight. She was so tall, this girl, too tall, in her pink dress, its hem coming down. It wasn't a flattering dress.

"It's just fine." Constance's voice shook. "It's natural—to be—natural—to be—curious."

"I think so too," the girl said. Then she smiled. The smile, toothy, sweet, unashamed—it helped to pull Constance back into herself.

The girl said, "My mother would murder me. People make such a stink. But it's just some theater. Why not? That's how I see it." She licked her lips, shrugged. She might have been talking to a guidance counselor about her plans after graduation. "I haven't done it, myself. I look, yes, but I'm not one of those girls—" She pointed to a photograph. It was a woman on her knees, wild-eyed, clasping the hairy shins of a man who stood over her, gazed down with faint disdain. The caption said: *Mr. Coventry Wants You to Beg.* "I don't feel very much like that."

Constance said, exhaling, "I've never been to a place like this before."

"Of course not."

"I was passing by. That man suggested it."

"Poor Marco, I know it. You want to, like, ease his suffering. Hey, look at this one."

The girl was holding a single magazine. Its cover said IT'S A HARD COCK LIFE.

"Oh," said Constance.

"Ignore the title," said the girl. "It's filthy. The titles are all written by men who think their stupid puns make them geniuses. It's like there's two kinds of men—the ones who want to show you their penises and the ones who want to make puns. But the puns aren't the point."

Beneath these words, a pretty teenage girl in a tattered dress, a redhead, held a mop handle between her legs.

"Orphans," the girl said.

Constance made a gasping sound, and the girl said, "Oh no, no, I'm not a lesbian. It's just—my boyfriend's an orphan." She shrugged. "I'm fascinated by them. They're my weakness." She flipped briskly through the magazine. Constance saw more teenage girls, all in tattered garb, washing windows, making beds, sweeping floors, their breasts exposed, their vaginas. The pictures portrayed hardworking, lonesome, ill-fed girls, toiling day after day, sometimes pleasuring each other with their hands or mouths. There were men, too. A warden in a suit, a young janitor, both wearing whistles and military boots. The men were displeased with the girls and found novel ways to show it. "There's something about orphans," the girl said. Then: "This is my favorite." She pointed. Constance steeled herself—but it wasn't a dirty picture.

"Sweet," said the girl. "Isn't it? That kind of longing. He wants to hurt her but can't. She wants to leave but can't. They're equal."

The picture showed a girl on her cot, flat on her back, covered by a plain sheet. Bare shoulders, hair spread around her on a pillow, dreamy face. Kneeling at the bedside was the janitor—his hands floated above her breasts but did not touch. His face was tender, worried; he bit his bottom lip. He needed a haircut. The picture didn't belong.

"Not your kind of thing, I guess."

Constance shook her head.

They looked at one another in the strange light. But at once Constance wasn't sure—was it her thing? Did she have a thing? Why did the girl presume to know? Blood warmed her face. She said, weakly, "It's natural."

"Yes," the girl replied, nodding. "Perfectly natural."

Now, with the girl's easy utterance of the word, Constance tried to understand what was natural. You could say *anything* was the way of the world. You could say that nothing was stranger than any other thing. Couldn't you? And suddenly this closet was as weird and fitting as any weird and fitting thing in the world. The girl touched Constance, lightly, on the shoulder, a reassuring pat.

The girl said, "You want to know a secret? I thought I might lose my virginity today. I had planned to."

"Today?"

"We had a plan, but he didn't show. *C'est la vie*, I guess."

"You're so young . . ."

"Sixteen." The girl shrugged. "Is that really young? I'd be married if I lived in Morocco, or the Renaissance. How old were you?"

Constance in the backseat of the car. Constance in that drop-waisted chambray dress she'd sewn by hand. Joe's big hands, his grunts, the squeak of the wipers that kept moving even though the rain had stopped. There wasn't any music: the radio was broken. She'd have liked a little music.

"Sorry," the girl said. "I shouldn't ask. This place changes everything. I'm not always like this, I swear."

"Nineteen," Constance said. "We got married."

"Yeah? I guess I'm glad we didn't do it. He's an orphan, sure, that's a plus. Anyhow, he chickened out. Poor Sam. They claim to want it, but they're scared just like girls—*other* girls, I mean. Not me, I'm not scared."

Constance felt her steady, thrumming pulse. How was it so steady? She remembered the little boy with the feather head-dress, the boy with the dead mother, remembered the feeling of his head against her chest; then remembered before all that, being in the backseat of that car, the long, quiet air of afterward, Joe's head on her chest, the wipers still moving, how he apologized over and over, as if he were the one who'd demanded it, as if it were his idea.

"I could take it personally," the girl said, "but I'm making the choice not to."

Constance meant to say goodbye and get in her car and drive to the grocery store, but instead she said, "I wasn't scared either."

"He's a sweet boy—there'd have been nothing to be scared of. I would have done it. But he never showed up. Oh well."

Constance said, "I wanted to do it." She meant to be in the frozen food aisle. Instead she was saying, "This boy, Sam, did he touch you?" The words, a thrill and a horror, left her mouth numb, as if she'd been chewing on ice.

The girl said, "Well, I gave him the opportunity. But we only kissed. Yesterday. For the first time. He's a sweet boy, a sweet kisser, but I think I'm a little advanced for him."

She meant to be paying for the lima beans but instead she was putting her arms around the girl, *Sam's girl,* and when the girl said "Oh, you're so sweet," Constance could say only, "I'm not."

They hugged and Constance felt a longing without guilt, shame, or indecency. A startled, strangled noise emerged from her throat, a noise that sounded too much—it caught her off guard—like a moan. She pulled away, coughed.

The girl coughed too.

Then Constance said she had to buy some groceries.

"Pudding," the girl said, "Lately I'm always craving pistachio pudding!"

Would Sam marry this girl? She wanted to protect them from their future.

"Wait," Constance said. "There's no hurry. Take your time."

"I guess we'll see, huh?" Her smile was faint, distracted, arrogant, as if she knew something Constance would never know, as if her very innocence supplied her with insight Constance could not possess. Constance left the child to her magazine. When she emerged, Marco grinned at her.

"You still lost?" He blew a smoke ring. She felt newly in control of herself. "No," she said. She drove to church, parked, entered, and peed. She washed her hands. Then she sat in a pew, held a sleek hymnbook, the presence of which in her palms had the same soothing power as a hot-water bottle. She felt, for the first time, safe. Louise was gone and wouldn't be back. Constance moved her lips in the shape of a prayer, and dabbed holy water on her eyelids, and then went home to prepare her secret sauce and wait for the heroes.

12

Anything can happen in ten minutes. One can cook an egg or fall in love or lose a fortune or make a pot of coffee or be born or find God or leave god or fall out of love or die. One can find the right girl or the wrong girl. One can fail to know the difference. Sam felt with the whole of his body that he would never know the difference. Ten minutes. Things happen that fast. In ten minutes you can look at a certain girl on a bed, a girl who took your Helen away. In ten minutes she can go from maniacal and mean and unforgivable—to what?

They looked at each other. She had the face of a cruel nurse, the one who's called in to tend to the intractable patients, who'll wrench an arm from its socket in order to administer a shot. "You're like a forty-year-old man in the body of a child."

He didn't have to be good. He said, "You look like a slut."

"That's Q for you."

She lifted her arm. It was slender, very pale. On the inside of her elbow were two small scabs. She said, "Teeth."

"No they're not."

"Do you want to see them all?"

He said, "Where is this guy?"

"He'll be killed soon is my hunch. He owes people all kinds of money."

Her hair was the color of cashews but her eyebrows were dark. She closed her eyes and tugged on the ends of her hair and then, eyes opening, with urgency: "Do you have any cigarettes? Please say you do."

"I don't."

She nodded, sighed. "You're a nice kid. I could stay with you here forever. You don't smoke. You're a virgin."

An intolerable silence followed. She was looking at him with clear, sad eyes.

She said, "Your mother killed your family, didn't she? I mean she did it on purpose."

He blinked.

She was waiting. She did not shrug or look away or blush or give any indication that she had just committed a crime. How was he supposed to respond? He couldn't imagine what words might be equal to the task, or what would happen after he used them. They looked at each other.

What could he do? He decided to answer.

"I can't know for sure," he said. "But I believe so."

He had never spoken such a thing. It wasn't true and it wasn't a lie. It was a feeling that could not be classified or lived inside— it made him an exile.

She nodded. She said, gently, "I'm very sorry, Sam. I'm very sorry about that."

She picked at the hem of her dress.

"I don't feel right," he said. His mouth was dry. A shimmer in his peripheral vision.

"Yeah, you don't look so hot. Your lips are white." She brought him a cup of water. He took a small sip—it was warm; he tasted blood. He spit it back into the cup.

"I'm not diseased," she said. Her voice was itself again, shot through with disdain. "I'm not contagious."

"I know that."

Did he? He was a little dizzy. He thought about Helen. She hadn't drowned, he knew that. She was living and breathing and writing a composition about the War of 1812 right now. It was he who was dead. His life was meantime. He drank the water. She said, "You want to know something else? Q left me for a man. He's a homosexual. A vampire."

"What do you mean?"

"I mean he's a fruit bat. I did all of it, whatever he asked, and he goes off and leaves me—what?" She opened up her hand, showed him a few bills. "Can you sit here for a minute?" She patted the mattress next to her.

He did what she asked.

"I wish you were a little uglier. Q was ugly. You can't trust beauty, you know what I mean?"

He didn't, not yet. He said, "Yeah."

She said, "But I think I can trust you. Promise you'll never lie to me."

He nodded. It seemed an easy thing.

Her yellow dress, one strap slipping off her shoulder. The stack of tarnished bracelets on her wrist. The slump of her shoulders, the dark bristle on her bone-white legs, her scowl and vegetable breath and how she sat with her legs a little too splayed, like a boy. He was close enough to smell her breath—to feel it.

The door was locked. Her breath in his face. You must imagine what it does to a boy.

She tilted her head, said, "Do I look like a bad person to you?"

"No." He answered out of instinct, then, remembering his promise, reconsidered.

"I don't know," he said. "Maybe a little bad. In a good way."

She snorted. "Bad in a good way? Poor puppy. I turn you on, huh? Is that what you mean?"

It was and it wasn't. What he could not say was that with every passing moment he suspected *he* was the bad person, that all the goodness he'd worked to cultivate—the manners, the grades, the clean clean room—they were just a protest against his true nature. When it came down to it he was bad. The idea entered his body in the quick, overriding manner of a muscle spasm. He was bad not because of sex in the woods with Helen; that was good. That was by-the-book goodness, he realized. That would have been easy, that would have spelled a life in Ringdale and a couple kids and a job at the hardware store. He'd pretended it made him bad but really it was what they all wanted for him, Constance and Joe and his teachers and everyone. Sex by the river would be an extension of his goodness, a confirmation of it, a sealing of it once and for all.

Did it make him bad that he wanted his uncle to suffer? Did it make him bad that what he felt when he saw his uncle's nervousness and damp flush was—it was pleasure. That was the word. There was pleasure in seeing his uncle banished, exiled from this room, in knowing that his uncle was afraid. His mother had not been a good woman. Perhaps Sam was bad too. Perhaps this was his true self and it had been waiting all along, here in his room, for him to claim. It was like he'd discovered some secret, long-forgotten box in the basement, moldering behind the furnace, and inside was a letter his mother had written him.

Judith said, "I would commit hara-kari for a single cigarette." She held two fingers to her mouth in a wistful V.

The letter said, *For god's sake do what you want. I am giving you permission, which you never needed.*

It said, *Look at what is right in front of your eyes.*

Here was a bad girl. Here was a ruined person whose words were barbs, whose demands were clear and mean, who murdered Helen with a blink of her eye. He looked down at her parted thighs. His heart was a chattering mouth.

Now the knock at the door. His uncle: "Kids! Time's up. Let's hit the road."

Neither of them moved or spoke. He kept his gaze on her lap.

"Time's up," Joe called again. "Kids? We'll get milkshakes."

But he wasn't ready to leave this room. It was like a mirror version of his own room. All his life it had been here, in its simple filth, a doppelgänger room, and he'd never known it existed. And that made him think: what other things and people and places were out there, echoes of him which he needed but would never be able to find? It wasn't fair making him leave so soon.

"Sam?" Joe called. "You ready? Sam?"

And he loved Joe so much! He did! Loved him with every part of his being! As a child he had a fantasy of living inside Joe's workboot, somehow miniaturizing himself so he could curl up where the toes belonged, and now he wanted only for his uncle to disappear, drop dead in the hallway if it had to be that way.

Joe knocked harder.

Sam didn't answer, didn't go to the door. He did nothing.
Judith whispered, "I'd like it very much if you kissed me."

Finally he lifted his head. She was looking at him, her mouth
open a little. He saw her glistening teeth. He saw the scab at the
corner of her lips, like a crumb she'd missed. What could he do
but what she asked, again and again?

PART 3

LEONORA

The man on the street said, "Can I ask you something? Can I have your ear for a moment? I'm having some trouble."

They faced each other in the cold. Her brother was gone. The school was four blocks away.

"As a father, see. I'm have some difficulty as a father. I've reached a wall. It's been a trial. It's been the worst six months of my life to date, if I'm allowed to be candid. I'm not allowed to be candid, I know. You're on your way to school. I need some help with my daughter. Can I be candid?"

Leonora said, "Be candid."

His plaid scarf was the same as her father's. The briefcase, the black shoes—they were same as her father's too. He was her father's age, clean-shaven, a nick on his cheek the size of a word in Bible print. He smiled like someone forgiven for breaking a rule—like a boy forgiven who can't quite forgive himself. She liked this. It felt appropriate, given the rule he was breaking by talking to her—his goodness inhered in his discomfort. His face was gentle, small greenish eyes, a wide chin. Maybe he was a teacher? She pictured him sitting behind a desk, stroking his chin, talking about history. His eyebrows were pale and full, his hair blondish-red. He looked like he got weekly trims, that kind of shipshape hairdo. She told herself she was a good judge of character. He said his name; she said hers. She did not hesitate or give her last name. He did not offer to shake her hand, which confirmed her sense of his goodness. He explained his problem, spoke in a clear, exact, slightly nervous voice, like someone new to the debate team. Faintly she smelled soap, a brand she recognized, and so she agreed to meet him after school to help him with his daughter.

She thought about the man in Spanish, in math, in English where they were reading a novel about the sole family to survive a nuclear war—about their youngest child, a girl, who taught the family in her breezy, ingenuous way how to be happy in spite of the apocalypse. She got so lost in thinking that when Ms. Nicholiason called on her she did not hear her name and could say nothing about that lovely girl in the book, that last happy child left on earth. She had been thinking about how men always wear the scarves their wives give them. She had been thinking about how sad it was that so many people get divorced, and about how her own parents would never get divorced. She had been thinking about the man and his daughter, this girl who had no idea how much he loved her, but who would be shown how much, would come to know it, with Leonora's help.

At last the day ended. Her brother waited for her at the foot of the steps, wearing the hood of his coat but not the coat itself, smashing the tines of two plastic forks together. "I'm going to walk alone," she said.

"You can't."

"I can do what I like."

"Mom'll get mad."

"I walked alone this morning. You left me—don't you remember?"

He didn't remember. The days blurred. A smear of ink on his chin, a vocabulary quiz crumpled in his back pocket. She told him to walk with Jeremy Jeffries, said she'd meet him at home shortly and they'd make ants on a log. They found Jeremy. He lived down their block, a pipsqueak, freckled, giddy, scorned— someone had drawn whiskers on his face with magic marker but no one commented because it happened all the time. Everything gets ordinary after a while. The boys ran off. Leonora waited a few moments on the steps of the school, watched other children disperse, watch the caged, shivering trees on the sidewalk, the flow of traffic. Her nose began to run. Her throat hurt, but not too bad. The sky was glistening white, perfect, a clean sheet of paper, and then a couple oily pigeons moved through it like misspelled words. The old crossing guard with the potato nose moved and swayed as though music played in his head. Children were being kept safe. The limo arrived for that rich foreign girl, but people no longer gawked. It was colder now than it had been in the morning. Leonora felt free and happy and blessed.

The coffee shop was just a few blocks away. The sign claimed: EXTRA SUPERIOR FOOD! Red vinyl booths clashed with a pink floor. It was nearly empty and smelled like Thanksgiving. An old guy sat at the counter writing something on a notepad. At a table in the window, three women shared one piece of pie, jabbed their forks at it with guilty eyes, like they were testing the deadness of a body. The man she'd met that morning sat at a booth in back, near the restroom. He had ordered her a hot chocolate. It sat there, steaming, where she was meant to be sitting. It told her what to do. In an instant she was allowing its steam to warm her face. They smiled at each other.

"How was your day?"

She sensed, from how he said this, what it would feel like to be his daughter—a little clobbered by stiff, hopeful affection. "Just excellent, thank you," she replied, and the way he smiled, kept smiling, the sadness he couldn't keep out of the smile, she understood that his own daughter had never given this kind of answer.

They looked at each other. The bell on the door rang—the old man was leaving. Behind the counter, a cook counted bills. Her companion tapped his mug, said he was already on his third cup of coffee and she should pardon his jitters. She said of course she would pardon him. She looked at the hot chocolate. A song about flying to Jupiter played on the radio. He rubbed his hands together, inhaled. She saw how nervous he was, which was proper.

"Like I said before, I'm in the final stages of a divorce. A messy divorce. Well of course all divorces are messy—maybe this one is a normal mess, I don't know."

"A normal mess," she repeated quietly, soberly.

"I can't lose my daughter as well as my wife. I can't. I won't, Leonora. I can handle the other losses, fine, take it, my bank account, all the photo albums, the furniture *I* picked out, *I* bought, she can have it all, every last thing. But I draw the line at my daughter. My wife—my ex-wife—for some reason she's under the impression that my daughter can't love us both."

"But she can!"

"Right?"

"Of course," she said, meaning it, wanting to say something wise, wondering if this was her job. Did he want her simply to listen, to confirm his daughter's capacity for love? What did he need from her? He went on:

"See, my girl is like any girl. She likes stuff."

"Stuff?"

"I see how her eyes light up. I see how they light up, but I can't pinpoint what, exactly, makes them light up. You know?"

Leonora nodded, but she wasn't sure what he was getting at.

"So what should I buy? Let's pretend money isn't an issue. Makeup? Clothes? Books? Music? Which music? Which objects for her new room? I want to give her a room like in a magazine. Pull out all the stops. When she's all grown up I want her to look back and think: *That was some room my father gave me.*"

He was probably a lawyer, she saw now. He spoke like he was reading aloud from a long, dry book he secretly wanted to throw across the room.

He was not good with kids, he told her. He knew that about himself. He didn't trust his instincts, and money wasn't an issue but you couldn't buy instincts, could you? She concurred: you could not buy instincts. It flattered her that he seemed to assume her instincts were good. Good instincts, she believed, mattered even more than beauty. Also it flattered her that he seemed to assume she was a representative of her age—she felt relieved, somehow, to be seen this way, an ordinary girl, a girl who could articulate the needs of other girls.

"Oh," he said suddenly. "You haven't tried your hot chocolate yet. Do you like hot chocolate? I shouldn't have assumed."

"I do." She grasped the cup.

"You don't have to drink it. I just thought—I thought it'd be good on a cold day."

She took a sip of the hot chocolate. This seemed to settle the matter.

He said a few things about his ex-wife, about how she had the empathy of a calculator, about how much money she spent in order to remove the hair from her body. Then he seemed to realize he was getting off track and began to describe his daughter, her pretty eyes, curly hair, her—he paused, as if unsure what else to say.

"Beatrice is her name," he said finally. "We call her Bea. She hates it. Wants to be Traci. With an *i*. Or Patli. *Patli?* I said, that's not a name, honey. She tells me I have no imagination; well, she's right on that count. Guilty as charged. But: Patli? She says we're the worst parents in the universe to give her such a monstrous name. An old fart's name, she's called it. On more than one occasion."

"I'm sorry."

"It was her grandmother's name." He said this apologetically.

"I think it's lovely."

"Do you? Yeah?" He smiled again in that sad way. "My mother loved that her granddaughter carried her name. But Beatrice—the younger Beatrice—she couldn't stand my mother. Called her Fussypants. To her face, I fear."

Fussypants! Leonora couldn't imagine saying such a thing to a grandmother, anyone's grandmother. She thought of her own kindly, rosy-cheeked nana, her crochet supplies in a basket, her particular smell (Dew of Morning face cream; laundry soap; roast chicken), the tidy way she arranged her hands in her lap, like a child in a pew.

"My mother bought Beatrice a teddy bear, a fancy one, shelled out a wad over at P. E. Fleiss, you can imagine. And Bea—you know what she did to that poor bear? No. Forget it. I can't say." He took a deep breath, craned his neck to the ceiling. Then he looked back at Leonora and said, "She's a tough cookie, my bumble Bea. She's got—what's the expression? Moxie? She's got moxie."

Leonora didn't know the expression.

"That poor teddy bear," he sighed. "It wore an aerobic suit."

"Mine was dressed up as an astronaut."

"Yes." He spoke this in a resigned, breathless hush, as if she'd confirmed some terrible news.

It wasn't Leonora's business, it was beside the point, but this daughter sounded just awful. She didn't want the girl to be awful! She wanted the girl to be sweet, oblivious maybe, but a basically sweet person who needed to be enlightened. Not a spoiled brat. Not mean to the elderly. The man looked at Leonora now with such a frank, open face that she had the abrupt and strange sensation that *she* should become his daughter. It lasted just a few moments, this feeling, but there it was: *Take the girl's place.* She felt a rush of generosity, and then a seizing in her gut, a mounting pressure, like her body was not a big enough container for its own munificence. She knew exactly what the man needed.

She took out a piece of paper from her notebook and, in careful script, wrote down the name of a magazine he should purchase a subscription to. Then she listed a band led by boys with bleached hair, then an expensive bottle of nail polish in a shade of red so deep it was nearly black, a shade called FANG that would require a half a day of babysitting for Leonora to afford, she wrote down the brand, the color, the store where he could find it for the best price. She did all this knowing what he needed was Beatrice, under an afghan, up too late, covering her eyes when the killer appears, and that it wasn't very likely he'd get this.

"You might want to consider getting the expensive kind of TV."

"Okay, good."

"The movie channels."

"I'll upgrade."

"And Jumpin' Sumpin's." These were a cheesy potato chip snack; the advertising campaign featured a hysterical, sombrero-wearing kangaroo.

"Right, yes."

"Junk food and good TV, she'll want to bring her friends over."

He closed his eyes, as if picturing the scene.

She made a few more suggestions, spoke seriously, gravely, hoped to communicate that she was above these gimmicks, these silly trends, even as she was deeply familiar with them. Her own mother would never buy Jumpin' Sumpin's, but Leonora enjoyed them at sleepovers.

When she'd exhausted the list he said, "You're very sweet, aren't you?"

"Thank you." Blood warmed her cheeks.

"Like—you're not quite a normal girl. Oh, but I mean it in the best sense. You're *kind*. I'm not so sure most girls are kind."

She said nothing. She knew how to take a compliment—silently.

Their beverages were gone. It was time to go. He told her that he couldn't overstate how helpful she'd been; also he wanted her to know that *he knew* how strange it was he'd asked her to come here. "Desperate times call for desperate measures. Have you heard that expression?"

"Of course," she said.

He thanked her two, three more times. "Truly, the pleasure is mine," she said, and liked so much seeing his bemused, sad, grateful face.

1

"Don't tell me you're one of those tub-thumpers."

This is how she greeted him. It was Jade Grant, behind the Come & Go. Paul had come here for a cigarette and found her sitting against the dumpster, her legs pulled up to her chest, a massive fountain drink between her knees. She chewed on its straw like on a piece of licorice, her pale, narrowed eyes suggesting a boredom so habituated it had become mere accessory. Her posture and baggy shirt hid her stomach.

It was rumored that Jade—daughter of Thomas Grant, the abortion nurse—was pregnant.

"They're so devastatingly *clean,* aren't they?" she said. "From West Liberty Baptist is my guess. Jabbering self-righteous fools. They claim they want to help. To help! The filthiest stuff comes out of their mouths, filthy, mean as hell, but they're always showered and powdered and perfumed and I'm sure that lady douches twice a day."

Then she said, "You're Paul, right?"

So she knew his name. They had only one class together, algebra, but never spoke—she sat with Kitty and Frick, passing notes and exercising the smallest muscles of her face with various expressions of disdain. Mr. Winslow was scared of the pretty girls, let them pass notes and look as disdainful as they wanted, but if a boy did the same, or an awkward girl, he was all over them. Jade was the best student in the class. That she knew Paul's name—though it wouldn't be his name for long—sent a wave of pleasure through his body, a shiver along his spine like a breeze on some unbearable summer day. Beetle got terribly hot. But he wouldn't ever have to spend another summer here. He reminded himself of that.

"Right," he said, "Paul." But it was really "Paul," not Paul. That's how he thought of himself now—in quotation marks. As soon as he got on the bus he'd take a new name. He wasn't sure who'd he become. Pierce? Patrick? He felt, despite himself, attached to the P. It was "his" letter, the first one he'd learned as a boy. P would be the very slightest connection to his mother. No. Forget his mother. But he'd keep P anyhow. He liked its force—he wanted more force, needed more, could not relinquish the little he had. Percy?

"I'm Jade," she said, and then smiled to imply she knew he already knew it. You couldn't not know it.

They were sixteen.

The smell of soggy cardboard drifted from the dumpster. He felt too warm, too loose. Spring did to the world what a hammer's claw did to a nail. He said, "We're in algebra together."

"Those West Liberty freaks followed me from school. It's not the first time. Jabbering self-righteous fools. Keep an eye out, will you? I have the feeling that woman carries a gun. If they come down that alley, say something. A code word. *Rooster.* Say rooster and I'll run."

He couldn't read her tone; she spoke mockingly, as if they shared a history of facetious chatter behind the Come & Go, but he saw a rigidity in her body, tension in her shoulders, and sensed she wasn't joking. Her reddish hair was wound around itself, pinned to the top of her head, an old-fashioned hairdo which made him think of England, of another century, of a woman in long skirts swishing through tall grass. Her clothes belonged to today: tight black jeans, a man's oxford shirt, white tennis shoes. On the left shoe someone had drawn the outline of five toes in black ink and colored the toenails with red marker. On the right shoe a single green letter, written so she could read it: *J.* She wasn't wearing any socks; he kept his eyes on her bony ankle.

She said, "You going somewhere?" for he was wearing a backpack and holding a sleeping bag and a pillow.

Was he? She was the first person who'd asked. He looked from her ankle to her face, saw the freckles strewn across her nose. Their eyes met, held. He looked away. He didn't know what to say. He was running, yes, or in any case wanted to be running, had already been gone three nights, was sleeping in the woods behind the abandoned factory, sleeping in a copse of slender birches that glowed in the dark like kindly ghosts. He'd run but hadn't gotten anywhere yet—this made him feel meek, childlike, like a kid who's escaped to his treehouse. Also he stank. He didn't want her smelling him. He took a step back.

"What's your deal? You blowing this joint? Splitting the scene?"

Had she noticed he hadn't been in school for three days? Of course not. He could vanish and no one, not his mother or stepfather or Jade or Gideon or the police or anyone, would come looking. It was time to get on a bus; that much was clear. "I heard you're pregnant," he said, then regretted saying it.

She spat the straw, gave him a stern look. "Mary Mello started that rumor because her boyfriend told some guys he wanted to—" She threw the empty paper cup into the weedy lot. "Mary Mello is a liar and a thief. First she told everyone I pierced my nipples. Her boyfriend has a fouler mind, if that's possible. They belong together. Nasty things which I *never* in a million years would agree to do."

"It's not my business." The feeling of regret wasn't going away.

"If the world was populated by rumor babies they'd be filling the streets. Their wails would keep everyone awake at night. We'd feed them to cattle. Maybe then those West Liberty numchucks would leave me alone."

She was doing something with her hands, a waving, clawing gesture that made him think of his mother, of what Goldie did to make her nail polish dry.

He said, "I didn't mean—"

"You want me to tell you all the nasty things I've supposedly done in the bathroom on the third floor next to the teachers' lounge?"

"No." He already knew.

She squinted at him, still waving her hands.

"It's none of my business," he said. "I'm sorry, Jade."

She nodded, and her hands came to a rest. She said, "If you're running away, I should join you."

His heart kicked.

"But I got this rumor baby to raise." She cradled it in her arms, rocked it; she cooed.

He saw them coming, a woman and a man, nearing the Come & Go, saw the woman point to Jade. The woman had waist-length hair and a long neck. The man was balding, chubby, and stroked a neat goatee. The woman towered over the man.

Paul watched them approach, still struggling with his awareness that he smelled wicked, thinking maybe he should go inside the Come & Go, wash up in the restroom, change undershirts, wondering if she'd be here when he was done—

But she had jumped up, grabbed his hand, and was pulling him, yanking his body through the lot, through a tangle of brambles, and into the woods. "You're a crummy lookout!" They ran together down the strangled path; he let himself be pulled through the lashing woods. Her hand was small, sparrow-boned, and miraculously cool. They ran faster. Trash littered the path, magazine pages, candy wrappers, cans, gum. He had no idea what was happening or what it meant. He'd been lingering for three days but was too scared to get on a bus. His failure to buy a bus ticket, to do anything but hide in the woods and smoke behind the Come & Go and wonder if anyone was looking for him—it made him despise himself. It was all just a pantomime of escape. And now, like that, he was running full bore through the woods of Beetle with a girl whose hair, as she ran, loosened, fell down her back, golden red, a shimmering cascade. They raced along, the path crusted with debris, fast, faster, until they came to the dirt turnout, a cool, shadowy clearing where people dumped bigger trash, broken appliances and old furniture, where, at night, kids sometimes came to smoke and scream at nothing and grope at each other. She let go of his hand and collapsed onto a rotten sofa. She threw herself across its springs and trash and leaves with grace and familiarity, as if onto her own bed.

He stood above her, not sure what to do with his body. They panted together. Their lungs heaving in union terrified and aroused him. He suspected that now he smelled even worse. Ten feet away, in a heap, lay a charred refrigerator, a smashed TV, mangled lawn chairs, a cast-iron tub, so that the clearing gave the impression of a ruined home.

Jade said, "'The fruit of the womb is a reward.' So sayeth someone."

Paul couldn't speak yet.

"You should have warned me! Who knows what these people are capable of."

"I'm sorry."

The Baptist woman entered the clearing from the other side. She did not seem out of breath. Jade saw the woman and covered her face with her hands. "Can you leave me alone for five minutes?"

"I'm your friend," the woman said, stepping toward them.

"My boyfriend's not going to let you talk that way to me."

Paul expected the woman to laugh, but she just looked at Paul, nodded, and said more decisively, "I'm your friend. I talk like your *friend*."

Jade said, "You know how you fucking talk."

"Honey, I haven't said a single cuss. Not one."

"There's more than one way to talk dirty."

The woman made a hand into a visor and squinted, though the sun couldn't reach them in the woods. "My speech is clean. Right speech is a gift to the world. Have you heard the story of the man plucking a chicken in the windy marketplace? The feathers are the speech. They fly and fly, and you can't get them back. It's an old story, like a fable. It happened long ago but it's still happening, always happening, one of those stories." Her voice glinted, a pretty voice.

"We don't need more of your stories."

The woman was older than they were—maybe thirty, with a plain, dour, earnest face. Her hair was so straight it appeared to have been ironed. She was thin and tall, elbowy, had the narrow pelvis of a marathoner. She wore running sneakers, tan pants, a white blouse, a braided leather belt that was too big for her. The belt's tail fell down her thigh.

"Does your boyfriend believe murder is a crime?"

"Don't get going with him."

"Do you?" the woman said to Paul. "Do you believe murder should be allowed in our society?" She seemed like a teacher— the plain clothes, the air of staunch, fatigued sacrifice. It was hard to not answer.

Paul said, "She wants nothing to do with you. That seems pretty clear."

The woman removed something from the pocket of her pants. A business card. She held it out to him and he took it. THE CHOICE BELONGS TO YOU. There was a drawing of a cherubic baby beneath these words, and a phone number.

Paul stared at the card. He said, "What do you want?" He realized what a fantasy it had been to be alone with Jade now that he no longer was. He longed for it again.

"I want to help, that's all. I want to right a wrong," the woman said.

Once Goldie had affixed a magnet to the refrigerator: U.S. OUT OF MY UTERUS! She had placed it there to upset his stepfather, who said it was gross as hell and was her intention to make him puke up his egg sandwich? Paul pictured his mother in bare feet on the kitchen linoleum, her red toenails, red robe, and felt a sudden burst of compassion for this Christian.

"Look," Paul said, "we understand your point. We'll keep it in mind."

"You certainly *don't* understand the point," the woman said. "If you understood the point you'd know it's not enough to 'keep it in mind.'" She pointed a finger at Jade. "She needs to act. She doesn't have the luxury of time. She has all the power, all of it. It's a sin, to have that power and to look it in the face and to not give a lick."

Jade said, "Oh for fuck's sake."

"Leave her alone," Paul said. "She's not pregnant, okay? It's a rumor is all. Go bother someone your own age."

The woman's outstretched hand fell back to her side. She said, "Pregnant?" Her face softened, her eyes got wider, so that for a second she almost looked pretty. For a second she had the sort of stunned, generic prettiness of a doll. "Are you pregnant, honey? Is that true?"

"Leave her alone," Paul said.

Jade said, "I'll kill you. I mean it," and suddenly she was standing up, a foot away from the woman, her hands on her hips. "Do you hear me?"

"I think you should go now," Paul said.

The woman seemed to think about his suggestion, but only said, "Paul's a good name."

"Please go," he said. "You've made your point."

"Paul was an important person, a missionary, a friend, a man of true and abiding faith. It's funny, because he was such a big deal, a real major hero, a Hero with a capital H, but you know what his name means? Paul? I bet you don't. It means 'small.'"

"We'll hurt you," Jade said again, but quietly. Her eyes were closed.

The woman turned to Paul. She said, "Paul won't hurt me. He's humble. His name means 'small.'"

"Don't be so sure," said Jade. "He's full of surprises."

The card in his hand was damp. They looked at him. His heart was going crazy. "I'm full of surprises," he said.

2

Ralph ran through the woods searching for Libby, for the kids—they were too fast, they'd outrun him, and somehow he'd taken a wrong turn, gotten lost, spent ten minutes running down a path he was sure was the right path only to find himself back at the Come & Go. He'd run in a circle, a big stupid loop, and now stood drenched in sweat and out of breath and back where he started from. He needed to drop fifteen pounds. The next time he wanted to cheat on his diet with a pack of strawberry SnowDevils he'd think of this moment. He braced a hand on the dumpster, wheezing, wondering if Libby had found the girl, hoping she had, but also wondering if maybe it'd be better if she didn't find her. The sun beat down. He thought they were making some progress with the girl. Maybe. But he sensed, if he was to be honest, that *he* was the one the girl was listening to.

He saw something in her eyes when he spoke to her, a flicker of warmth, a new listeningness. He was coming to suspect she was the kind of girl who'd listen to a man more than a lady; he didn't want to say this to Libby, who'd take it the wrong way, who'd charge him again with chauvinism when that wasn't it at all. Some girls just respond better to men! Was that chauvinistic to think? And some men respond better to women. There. Equality. Plus—well, it pained him to think it, but wasn't Libby coming on too strong? So maybe it would be better if the girl got away, this one time. Was it getting too personal for Libby? Well sure, yes, it was supposed to be personal, that was the point, the personal is political, it's always personal, it's a *person,* we're all people, thinking on an *un*-personal level is exactly what makes poor girls spread their legs for murderers. It's personal, has to be, and yet he had been seeing in Libby's eyes recently something he didn't like, something like desperation, a need that, to be honest, was maybe the wrong kind of personal.

He wiped sweat off his brow. *Chugga-chugga* went his heart. No more SnowDevils. No more ice cream or animal crackers, even if the box said LITE, that was a Madison Avenue lie.

He wanted a shower badly, feared he was starting to smell. He knew he should look for them but had no idea where to go. Maybe it was better to wait here—Libby'd surely come back for him. But he felt foolish and fat just standing there sweating next to the dumpster, and the clerk inside with the buzz cut had already yelled at him when he'd dropped off the pamphlets. The clerk had said if he found Ralph loitering he'd call the cops, and Ralph didn't need more of that, no he didn't. He wanted to buy some apple juice but the guy wouldn't sell him anything, so he went back into the woods.

Ten years ago the girl's daddy, Thomas, had talked Libby into having an abortion. The girl's daddy was a nurse in the clinic. Nurses have more power than doctors, most people don't realize but it's true, it's the nurses who talk to the girls, look in their eyes, ask questions, hold their hands, and whisper reassurances. The doctor just comes in, aftershave wafting, lifts his tools and— presto—murders the innocent. The job takes minutes. It's the *nurse* who sees the girl. It's the nurse who has the power to persuade, who witnesses the girl at that pivotal juncture, it's the nurse who's the gatekeeper, the guardian. The girl's daddy had sat Libby down in a windowless room and wrapped a blood-pressure cuff on her skinny arm and said, as that cuff tightened, "How are you feeling?" And Libby had said, "Okay, I guess, thank you." Ralph could imagine her young voice like a sliver of light under a door at night. Then Libby had said, "I'm scared, maybe I shouldn't be here, maybe this is wrong?" She'd said the stuff that any human being with a soul, with half a soul, a quarter of a soul, could see meant she needed someone to tell her to go home. But what did he do, the girl's daddy, the man Thomas Grant, soulless nurse, what did he say to Libby, to Ralph's sweet snapdragon girl, to this nineteen-year-old who hadn't yet opened the Bible? He said, "I'll take care of you." Libby didn't know how God said "Before I formed you in the womb I knew you" or how God knit all of us together in our mothers' bodies. No one had told Libby that the womb is intended to be a place where God works His creative action, not where man works his destructive action! It wasn't her fault that she didn't know—her mother was a commie, after all, her mother drove a pink van and sold wind chimes fashioned from old gutters. How on earth could Libby have known? Libby was blameless, and in her belly was a *blame-*

less child, but she didn't know this, she didn't know how Satan works, and so she told herself she was bad, that the baby must be bad too.

The nurse, Thomas, had his own girl. No one had guaranteed the destruction of *that* life. He got to have his pretty redheaded girl, and it wasn't fair or right. Why was he allowed a daughter? Ralph felt an imbalance, an injustice, as clearly as he felt the ache in his feet, or the need to pee, or his thirst. Now he walked back into the woods and found the path he hoped was the right one. The girl would come to see the terror of it, what her father did, how it was a crime against humanity and a profanation of God's creation, and she would demand her father stop, demand he make public amends. If the father refused, the girl would have no choice but to abandon him, disown him or disavow him or whatever was that legal term for divorcing a parent, and then maybe the man would grasp the slightest fraction of what Libby had suffered—Libby and thousands of other girls. *Emancipation.* That was it. The girl would emancipate herself. Sometimes they thought about shooting her. That would be another way to make the point. Some of them argued for such tactics. Desperate times, desperate measures. Certain people made convincing arguments. Libby, sometimes, seemed convinced.

Libby cried at night. He'd wake up and flip on the light and see her clutching her pillow, see the heaving of her long, thin back, smooth as soap. He thought about what she did to her leg with a shard of glass. He'd applied antibiotic cream. It healed very nicely, no scar. He thought about this as he walked.

Jesus was a vase and they were the flowers. That's what Pastor Gold said, and that's what it felt like, it was the right analogy. Jesus made life seem packed with good people, stem against stem against stem. He made of the crowded world a community; he made of the wilderness a bouquet. Could Ralph help the girl feel this too? Could he somehow communicate how much better and simpler it was once you were inside that vase?

That Ralph's sperm seemed not to work, or that Libby's womb was barren, Libby took as proof of God's rage.

3

There had been a fight at Paul's house, but he wasn't going to think about what happened before or during or after the fight. He left. The point of leaving is that you never have to think about the fight. He wouldn't think about the terrible cold that settled over the household afterward, the slammed doors and tight faces and the way he came to feel he was a stranger to his own mother, as though he hadn't emerged from her very cunt. *Cunt!* Why would he pick that brutal word? Because his mother was too selfish to have a vagina.

He wouldn't think of Gideon either, or biology class, or the model ship, or his stepfather whose dirty fingernails on his mother's arm would forever turn his stomach. Even now the thought of it made him want to save her, his mother who didn't need saving.

Jade and this Christian in the woods were the confirmation that he was leaving, proof that he had no place in Beetle, that it was a town of strangers. He'd leave and never return. He'd never have to set foot again in that cluttered cottage with the sad-eyed owl door knocker and the smell in the air like a kitchen sponge gone bad. The longer he lived on earth the sadder and more perverted and just plain *weird* people seemed. He believed that if he'd been raised in a white-picket suburb, if he'd lived in a house with aluminum siding and clean gutters, if he'd had two parents with steady jobs, if he'd been given books and a lawn-mowing business and a baseball mitt to oil—he believed he'd be happy. But that hadn't happened.

Once certain stuff got into you, it was hard to get it out. He was only sixteen, but he knew this.

The woman was saying, "I could have had a daughter just like you."

"Not likely."

"Red hair runs in my family on my father's side. Could have had a little girl I'd put in dresses and braids. But I was scared and young and your daddy—"

"Don't say 'daddy,'" Jade said. She just sat there listening, her head resting on the decimated upholstery, while the woman presided like a new teacher, awkward, breathless.

Jade said, "I never wore dresses or braids."

"Don't be so sure."

"I know what I wore!"

"Well, my daughter would have had dresses and braids. But your daddy—"

"I've never called him 'Daddy.'"

"Your daddy."

"I love him," Jade gave a steely, dignified smile. "I'm proud of him."

The woman took a step back, seemed to be losing confidence.

Paul suddenly understood that the woman was truly unwell. Was Jade right, that she carried a gun? At first it had seemed impossible.

"The world's broken, shattered to bits, but we can repair it if we do certain things. Like knowing God. Like protecting the innocent."

"Save the whales," Jade said.

"All the meanness in the world, its broken bits, can come back together, possibly, if we do the right things, say the right things, it's very possible."

"Hearing you talk about decency, that's funny."

"Take a vase and break it," the woman said, and now Paul heard tears in her voice. "Make a video of this. Then you play it backward. Can you picture that? That's what we must do for the world."

"Let's go," Paul said. "I'm going."

They ignored him. They were looking carefully at each other, looking at each other with an intensity that disturbed him, for all the sudden they seemed—how was it possible?—like lovers. Their faces held love and rage in equal measure. He wanted to look away, but he didn't.

"I know what you feel." The woman stepped closer. "We'll help."

"C'mon," said Paul. "Let's get out of here."

Now Jade stood. She rose weakly, as a person after an illness, steadying herself on the sofa.

"I know," the woman said softly. "I know just what you feel."

"Then you know how badly I want to kill it and leave it on your doorstep."

The woman shook her head, said, "How broken you are."

"Strangle it."

The woman kept shaking her head.

"Break it to bits."

Paul said, "Enough already."

It was time for him to go. The bus was the answer and always had been.

The woman's voice rose up, sprang at them—"Your father is a killer and you're a killer too. The world is dying at your hands. I'm sorry it's come to this." Her hand went toward her side. "There's something I want to show you." She took a step closer. Her chest rose.

Paul didn't see where Jade got the rock—suddenly it was in her hand, but it was too big to be in her hand. Mossy on one side, gray-green, the size of a bowling ball, and she raised it up like it weighed nothing at all, and then higher.

4

Ralph wanted to take Libby to see a doctor in the city who did miraculous things with ovaries. His cousin had told him about this doctor, a man in his early thirties, supposedly a genius, who'd recently been written up in *Conception Today*—a long, admiring article about the magic of the doctor's work and his incomparable success rate, plus several pictures showing him dandling delighted babies on his knee. Black babies, white babies, Chinese babies: the whole gamut. The doctor had a square, clean-shaven face, arrogant but reassuring. *I'm a lucky bastard,* the face said, *and I do good work—let me help you.*

Ralph wanted the doctor's help. His cousin had money and was willing to pay for a consultation. But the cousin was an atheist and single—what's more, she *wanted* to be single—and she wore fringed boots and lipstick and had joined a book club where women in fringed boots and lipstick got together each week to drink wine and discuss the sex scenes. The cousin's name was Christine; for several years now she had gone by "Chloe." Ralph made the mistake of telling Libby too much about Christine/Chloe, such as how she said she loved Ralph "despite the God thing." Libby despised the cousin, under no circumstances would she accept her money, and anyway it was God's will, not a doctor's, etc. And Ralph had said, "Yes, sure, of course—but, I mean—God put that doctor here, didn't he? God made the technology that lets that doctor look inside you?" Libby had practically torn his head off. "Your reasoning is disgusting, *Ralph*"—she said his name, when she was angry, like she was swearing—"I mean you can use the same reasoning to defend Doctor Foley or Thomas Grant, can't you? *Ralph*? Don't you believe in free will? Don't you believe we're vessels made by God but our actions are our own and no one else's?"

"Of course I do." He'd tried to touch her hand but she'd pulled it away, and then she was crying again.

She stopped crying and went to make them tuna sandwiches.

She was hot and cold, his girl. She was something else. He admired her resolve, admired her rigidity. Her belief was inviolable, stark, it didn't serve her, didn't make her happy, but she maintained it anyway—this was, he knew, the real deal.

He walked through the woods, looking for her, feeling confused, wanting a shower, the wind in the leaves bringing him back to the days of his own childhood when he'd played in woods like these. He'd preferred the rainy days, loving to dig holes in the sulfurous muck, to come home drenched and freezing, and to allow his mother to pretend to be angry while she dried his hair and made him hot chocolate with real whipped cream.

He hoped, if they had a baby, it would get Libby's height, Libby's metabolism, and his patience.

He was getting deeper into the woods now but saw no sign of anyone. He'd reached a place where there was no more trash on the path, where there was, in fact, hardly a path. This is when he heard the noise. First a yelp, which could have belonged to an animal, which he told himself was just an animal—a dog or a bird. Then—clear as day—a scream. Human screaming. It was Libby. He ran toward the sound, tried, but the sound was place-less and the path was gone. She screamed; he screamed back. "Libby!" Foliage lashed him. He called her name. He ran. The scream got fainter. He ran the other way.

He said, "Oh Libby oh Libby."

As a boy he'd dug holes in the ground and anything had been possible. Life was expanding infinitely. He called his wife's sweet, childlike name. Her screaming stopped. Then it started again, faintly. He spun, branches and leaves in his face. The woods did something strange with the sound, broke it into pieces, so it was coming from everywhere at once, so that he could only stand there, in one place, and take it in.

5

The bus was idling at the station, the driver chewing a tooth-pick and rubbing his temples. Paul ran toward it. He'd accidentally left his pillow at the clearing, but he still carried the sleeping bag, still wore the backpack, which thudded against his back as he ran. He wouldn't witness it, whatever it was. He wouldn't become complicit in this by seeing it through. He knew he was supposed to stay, to help, to be a man, but once he saw Jade raise the rock, once he saw the woman collapse, heard her screams, saw her cover her head, he'd been alone with his instincts and ran. All the while a gutted voice inside him said: *Be a man a man a man*. This word, this awful, liar's word—*man*—clanged in his head. He was terribly hot, savagely hungry, wanted just to get on the bus. That's all he'd ever want again as long as he lived. He vowed it. No one was allowed to expect anything from him!

When he reached the road he paused, squinted in the sunlight, pressed a hand to his chest, and felt with some horror his tumbling heart. Then his hand went to his hair, which was soaked and greasy. He was wearing too many clothes. He was half a mile from his house. Would his mother be home? He had the urge to check, peek in a window, see her one last time. But what was the point? Two hundred bucks in his pocket, plus a rabbit's foot. In his backpack were some playing cards, a few books, underwear, an old eyeglass case holding his nail clippers and safety pins and a coin from the sixth grade that said MATH CHAMP. He walked along the shoulder of the road toward the bus station, his body calming down, the sweat on his face evaporating, and then at once he thought: *What the fuck? What have you done?* These questions were not of him, did not emerge from his depths; it was like they were pressed into his head from the outside. *What have you done, you stupid boy?* He stopped. If a car came he'd have stuck out his thumb, but no car came. He stood there a moment, and then he willed himself to turn around. He willed himself to go back to that clearing. *Be a man! Sixteen isn't too young to be a man!* That's what his stepfather would say, that asshole. So he went back. By the time he got back, twenty minutes, half an hour later, there was no one there. He was as glad about this as about anything else in his life. The clearing was deserted. No blood, no evidence of a scuffle, of a body dragged away. The sofa was empty. The woods silent. His pillow wasn't where he'd dropped it. Who took his pillow?

"Hello?" he said.

Nothing.

"Anyone?"

No one.

That woman would be fine. Just a little cut up was all. Right? Yes. He didn't know. Maybe she was dead in the bushes. Probably not. Or maybe Jade? Probably not. It wasn't his job to know. The rock, the fight, they'd been a part of a conversation he had no business in, didn't understand. It wasn't for him. It wasn't his job to save anyone. It wasn't anyone's job! Everyone was banged up or would be, so what could he or anyone do? Nothing. In fact, he felt suddenly sure that they'd both been faking it—acting something out for each other, trying to prove something. Like men. Like who had the bigger dick, that kind of thing. He laughed. First it wasn't a real laugh—first it was just an assembly of tense, halting notes, a forced thing, *ha-ha-ha*. Then, without his trying, it became real. He felt the pressure of a true laugh behind his eyes—an expanding, sneezy sensation filling up the cavities of his head, a simple lightness, a gust of weird, disembodied, whole joy. He was laughing. Women were insane. He was hungry as hell. He was free. He was sure of it all.

PART 4

LEONORA

The waiter brought him the bill, and the man laughed at it, or rather laughed at the line drawing beneath the sum, a doodle of a frizzy-haired, clown-nosed creature holding a giant cup of coffee, inked by the waiter as a method of asking for a good tip, a method of reminding them that he, the waiter, was a human being whose capacities exceeded serving drinks. "Cute," agreed Leonora, and laughed too, felt obliged to laugh, though it struck her as sad.

Of course the man paid for their beverages, left a big tip, and this pleased her, confirmed her belief that he was a decent person stuck in a bad moment; that he understood and accepted the social order; that he was telling the truth when he said he knew it was weird to ask her to the coffee shop. She liked him. He liked her too, and he said this, then blushed like someone who's shown up with a too-opulent gift and realizes it only then. They stepped together into the cold day. He replaced the red mittens. A bus lumbered down the avenue, on its side an advertisement for a new kind of dental floss. She pictured Beatrice walking into her new bedroom, gasping in pleasure and surprise at the sleigh bed and mango walls and teen magazines fanned out on the inflatable coffee table, and then lifting the receiver of the transparent Princess phone, everything inside visible, its complicated network of wires and plugs and loops that enabled, miraculously, the simplest thing to happen. Plus the new CD by Roger Ranger. The room would be made new, and the girl, too, and her father, all of it, brand-new, and Leonora, who'd been the helper, would never see it, which was proper.

They said goodbye. He seemed to have new confidence. He said, "I wish you the best of luck, Leonora. All the luck in the world." His voice was crisper, stronger, than it had been before, which she took as proof of the value of their conversation.

They walked in different directions. A light snow had begun. She moved down the street.

She wasn't clueless: she knew the man wanted to win. She knew that part of the joy of connecting with his daughter, gaining her love, was in beating the mother. They were having a war, Beatrice was the spoils. Leonora had witnessed this scenario on TV shows and in movies and in the families of some of her friends. But couldn't it also be true that the man loved his girl and wanted her to love him too? Things didn't have to be one-or-the-other.

She would surprise her brother by making marshmallow crispy treats. Even if their mother didn't like them to eat too much sugar, it was snowing and you were allowed to eat too much sugar when it snowed. Her mother would be proud of

Leonora, even though she could never ever tell her mother that she'd allowed a stranger to buy her a hot chocolate. But if her mother could know—could see past the strangeness of it, the danger—Leonora was confident she would be proud. It was nearly four o'clock. Her mother would still be at work, still making phone calls on behalf of refugees. Leonora picked up her pace, passed the public library, the bank, then the building with the mirrored façade, which allowed her to observe, peripherally, her posture, and to correct it. The snow was not sticking.

Another bus, this one featuring a spoonful of yogurt and the words: *Too Good to Be True.*

A woman approached her.

She was not clean or wearing red mittens or in possession of all her teeth. Her clothes were baggy, dark, a tattered wool coat, flared pants, black boots with pointy toes. She wore her hair in a bowl cut, like a child's. Her expression, too, was that of a child, a child up past her bedtime—red-rimmed, a little wild. The woman said, "Excuse me, dear." It was the voice of a librarian, firm, clear, civilized. Leonora stopped walking. The woman lifted a hand—the hand was elegant, oddly elegant, with pearly painted nails. She said, "I wonder if you could help us for a second?"

There was a man too, she saw him now, five feet away, standing with his back against a building, smiling, full set of teeth, wearing a ski parka, holding in his arms a sleeping orange kitten.

The woman said, "Cute kitten, huh?"

It was.

"Sound asleep," the man said. "Out like a light."

"Two days old." The woman shook her head in wonderment. "Just hatched."

"Right?" the man said. "Cute as heck. Doesn't even have a name yet. Just hatched. Bundle a joy. Down from the stork."

Cats came out of vaginas. She'd never say it, but the word rang through her mind. Biology wasn't disgusting until people tried to protect you from it. They looked at her, as if waiting, and she wondered if maybe she was supposed to offer a name for the kitten, if that was the help they sought.

They waited.

She said the first thing that came into her mind: "Muffy?"

Her friend had a dog named Muffy; it seemed a classic pet name. It wasn't very imaginative—but then she'd been caught off guard. She could've come up with better given more time.

The woman laughed, said, "That's my girl. That's great. Muffy! Too much."

The man rolled his eyes at the woman, as if for Leonora's benefit, as if they had a history of siding together against her. His teeth were nice but his skin was rutted, rashy; the woman had nice skin but horrible teeth.

He said, "Look here, sweetie. We're supposed to drop this kitty at a friend's. Over on Glasgow Street. You know where that is? Near the chicken place?"

"Wing Dings," said Leonora.

"Wing Dings! Right. You know where that place is?"

The woman said, "This new kitty belongs to a girl over there. We're the delivery crew. A nice girl's getting this baby kitty for a present. Except we're kinda lost."

Leonora knew the chicken place, which was half a dozen blocks away but required going backwards and making three turns on account of some one-way streets. They looked at her.

"Flipping cold," the woman said suddenly, and while the words were rude, or anyway close to rude, still her voice contained a primness, a librarian's pleasant pinch. A ribbon of fear fluttered inside Leonora's body. Then she reminded herself about the world being light and darkness both. Decency in the face of darkness was the only way it got turned to something else. Also, it was wrong only to help attractive, clean people. Ugly people deserved help too. She began giving them directions but the woman shook her head, said, "Not from around here. Can't follow. I've got a map in the car—you point it out on a map? Can you draw a circle around where we are and where the cat's supposed to be?"

Could she?

The man said, "We'd really appreciate it, sweetie."

The wind picked up. Her throat was tight now, tighter than before, but she wasn't sure it was the illness.

Two circles. Two circles was resonable. It wasn't too much to ask. The man walked over to her and put the kitten in her arms. It opened its eyes. She said, surprising herself, "Thumper! Hello, Thumper." She could feel the animal's body, its blood, its heart, all these tiny pulsing sensations on her wrists, beating with her own pulse, thumping, you couldn't tell them apart.

"Thumper!" the woman cried.

"Thumper's a good name," the man said.

"This one's a live wire," the woman said.

The man said, "Just show her the map, Sandy," and she showed Leonora the map.

1

Judith sent her daughter off to school in a denim jumper embroidered with ladybugs. They ran up her belly in a vertical line, splitting her stomach and breastbone in two. Green buttons in the shape of flowers along the hem. The child didn't care about her clothes, didn't want cute jumpers or patent-leather Mary Janes or Barbies or glimmering barrettes, and while this was a comfort to Judith, who hadn't wanted them either, it also frightened her, because did not wanting these things mean the girl would turn out like her mother? What *would* the girl want? Everyone has to want something; it's easier to want the regular things, though you don't get a say. The daughter, her name was Diana, never asked for anything.

It was a damp Tuesday in May. They were late for the bus, so Judith drove Diana to school. She was in the second grade; her teacher was Mrs. Hoop, round, dull, all cream and beige except for the gleaming red fingernails of a prostitute. Judith kissed the girl's head. She drove home in a misting rain. Then she ate half a tub of cottage cheese while reading a story in the paper about some local girls who'd started a Sally Ride Society. They wanted to be astronauts, wrote letters to NASA, to the President: *Send more ladies to space!* They were planning another bake sale to raise money for a trip to Cape Canaveral. The optimism and pride of those girls unnerved Judith. There was so much terror in the world, bombs and arms deals and famines, all those dead people in Oklahoma City for god's sake (the mother of one of the dead lived in the next town over, was regarded as a heroine for spawning a victim, glorious for her tie to the tragedy), and here a gaggle of preteens planned moon missions, baked cupcakes and decorated them with little stars. All hope was misplaced. The world needed hope desperately, but it always came from the wrong people and went to the wrong things. If she ever came across one of their bake sales she would not buy a thing. The dead son in Oklahoma was twenty-two, had a fiancé. Those girls had no right to the cosmos.

She went to the living room to watch television, a game show. Five minutes later someone knocked on the door. A knock? Who came out here? No one knocked. But that's what it was, a double knock, a pause, then another. Someone was in their scabby woods knocking on the door of the cottage.

Judith and Sam and Diana lived in a little cottage in a town called Beetle. It was an accident, Beetle—it wasn't where they'd meant to come. They'd been planning to live in the city, had in fact been moving to the city, on the road, but Judith got scared. This was before Diana was born; this was when Diana was a germ in Judith's belly, the size of a paper clip. They were on their way to the city when she'd told Sam to pull over, stop the car, and he did, and where he pulled off was Beetle. They laughed at that—who would name a town Beetle? Absurd. The town was nowhere, bland, empty of threat. They bought Cokes at the gas station, stood on greasy asphalt and drank and took in the smell of gasoline, and she said, "I'm staying here." Sam was still wearing his wedding shoes. "Here?" He didn't understand. They'd been man and wife for eighteen hours. Here, yes; right here. But the city . . . ? No. She'd changed her mind. She couldn't go back to that place. "Oh." She could tell he was disappointed, but the power was hers, wasn't it? She'd earned the right to her say. She'd paid her dues. So the next day they were driven down a rutted road in the station wagon of a realtor named Sasha, a sexagenarian with pencil-thin eyebrows and hair that floated around her head like a shower cap. She stopped the car. "It needs work," Sasha said, squinting at the property. "It's been empty quite a while. There's a better place over on Coswell . . ." It was a fairy-tale cottage, tumbledown, overgrown, mossy and wild, with a red door and a cast-iron knocker in the shape of an owl, a claw-foot tub, a stone fireplace, a crumbling chimney, everything swathed in vines and weeds and coated with dirt, so that the total effect called to mind something caught in a spiderweb, a thing stunned and wrapped up but not yet eaten. The price was right. Sam said, "Let's see the place on Coswell?" but Judith said, "I want this one." He raised a brow. He had recently taken to raising it. She didn't like this particularly; it reminded her of her father. Sam looked at the cottage, touched the rusted hinges of its door, its filthy window, sighed. "Well," he said. He wanted to see her in that big bathtub, so he signed the papers.

Now, eight years later, a knock on their door. Who would knock? No one came here. Their daughter was at school; Sam was at the accounting firm. Judith sat in the cramped living room, smoking a cigarette, still annoyed by the Sally Ride girls, wondering why she should remain annoyed—who cared about a bunch of stargazing kids?—while on the television a woman had to decide which cost more, a jar of peanut butter or a jar of olives, and if she was correct she would take home a catamaran. The deviousness of human boredom, that it pretends to be alleviated by the most meager of exercises. *The olives*, thought Judith.

The rain had picked up. Thunder, weakly, a mild comfort, like someone clearing their throat in the next room. A knock. Diana was at school learning map skills, Diana had lost one of the decorative buttons on her jumper but didn't bother looking for it, while across town in a strip mall Sam punched numbers into a temperamental computer and sipped burnt coffee, and here was Judith, already twenty-six, a few community college courses under her belt, a part-time job at the Come & Go, faith and fidelity like apple seeds she'd swallowed by accident, in her but not of her, working their way out. They would come out whole. They were not things you could digest. Or were they? She didn't know; not knowing was the whole shape of her life; not knowing was liquid; it takes the form of its container. It was May. The woman on the television looked to the audience to help her decide. The olives? The peanut butter? The audience roiled and screamed and gnashed. Then there was a knock on the door. Another.

She rose.

But what if she hadn't gone to the door? What if she'd stayed sitting in her wicker chair, feet drawn up beneath her, smoking and watching television, watching the woman whose bra did not provide adequate support while she leapt joyously in front of her new boat (the peanut butter)—what if she had remained in this chair and ignored the knock, which now came more urgently— what if she had ignored the knock and stayed in her chair and watched the game show and then her soap opera and waited for her family to return—would she perhaps have borne out the rest of her life just like this?

She'd never know. It's one of those questions that sits on a shelf in your brain and swings its legs all your days.

He was about her age, she thought, twenty-six, twenty-seven, gangly, wearing a filthy corduroy blazer, jeans, hay-colored scruff on his face. He cleared his throat but did not speak.

"Can I help you?"

He said, stiffly, "Why hello, ma'am."

She was not *ma'am*. She wore cutoffs and a pink tank-top, no bra. She didn't need a bra, even when she leapt for joy. She had never leapt for joy. On her ankle was a gold chain with a tiny heart, a gift from Sam and Diana. She waited for him to say more, but he seemed unsure how to proceed. The air outside smelled of ozone, grass, distant barbecues. They looked at each other. His nose was wide and blunt, like a boxer's, but his cheekbones were fine. He shifted his weight.

"Listen," she said at last. "I'm not interested. If you're here to sell knives or God or whatnot."

"Whatnot," he said. "That would be my category."

Near his feet sat a suitcase of worn brown leather, its hinges tarnished, the name of an expensive company branded on its side.

"I'm not selling anything. I promise. And I'm not a Christian." He tugged on the sleeves of his jacket. She saw that he winced slightly, as if preparing for a blow. He took a breath. He blinked. Then he said, "This is my house."

Behind her, on the television, the audience hissed with displeasure.

"Was," he said. "It was my house."

He looked at the straw mat under his feet, at the top of the doorframe, the owl knocker. He worked on keeping his eyes from going inside; he was trying to tell her, with his restrained eyes, that he had manners.

"Your house?"

"I grew up here." His mouth, at rest, made something of a pout. For some reason it struck her as faintly ludicrous that anyone had lived in these rooms before her. She didn't believe him. "I should have called first," he was saying. "Except obviously I had no way to know your phone number." He rapped on the doorframe, then looked at his hand quizzically, as if he'd not been in possession of it. "See, I haven't set foot inside this place since I was—" And here he paused, looked down at his feet. He said, "Sixteen." The word came out tentatively, softly, like the name of a friend he was ratting out. Still he looked at his feet. His shoes were a mess. He was homeless, it was clear, or something like it. He looked up again, now sheepish. "I was on a bus," he explained. "It was passing through. Old Beetle. What could I do? I got off. I couldn't help myself. I didn't plan it, but the bus stopped and I was standing up. Why was I standing up? Who knows. I got off. Here I am." He made a high, wobbling sound that might have been a laugh or a cry or a sneeze or a cross between them, but which he swallowed before she could decide. The sound was awful. That's when she knew he was telling the truth.

Now he seemed to be looking at her feet. She clenched her toes. He said, "I used to hammer those floorboard nails. Ten cents a pop."

If she found herself one day passing through her old town, would she get off the bus? Would she knock on the door that had once been her door, the door to that lonely house with its ant-infested cupboards and lingering charred-meat smell and those chugging, ineffectual radiators and carpets her mother neglected to vacuum, even though there was a perfectly functional vacuum cleaner in the closet? What did Grace have against clean carpets? No. Judith would not knock. Only a pathetic person knocks. She did not believe in investigating nostalgia, which is merely the costume self-pity wears. But in this stranger's sad gaze there was something else. Beyond the nostalgia, that baser sentiment, she sensed—what? She wasn't sure. Something.

She said, "All right then. You want some water?"

He said that he couldn't imagine a better thing at this moment than a glass of water.

She liked the duct tape on the toe of his sneaker. She liked his scruff, his contained filth. She invited him in.

On the television a woman was squirting canned orange cheese onto a cracker—it sat there in a dazzling pile, like a castle. Judith turned it off.

"Thank you for trusting me," the man said.

Judith turned to look at him, his pout, his greasy brow, and she felt a wisp of dread, a wisp of—what else? where? like a whirling sensation, faint, something veering through her stomach the way a top spins across a tabletop, going where it wants to go, captive to nothing—

Hope.

She said, "What the hell makes you think I trust you?"

2

Q said, "Sex is the boat you row all your life. The one with mismatched oars. Sex is a boat chained to the harbor. You call it ardor. You call it lust. There's an anchor that's turned to rust. The anchor—here's the important part—is *invisible*. You think you're going someplace but you don't move. Sex is the boat you row, but pleasure—now that's something else. Pleasure is a tiny stream of fish running underneath the boat. A flash of silver fish too fast to see, flying not just up your cooch but other places too, places you didn't know exist. Oh my girl. It's time to jump from that poor boat, to cease and desist. Judy, you're a beauty. You're a smart enough kid. But you're the Helen-flipping-Keller of pleasure. If you come with me, I'll treat you to a kind of pleasure you've never known, beyond your bones, behind your mind. I'm warning you it will take a long time. You want to get out of your rowboat? You want to get in the water and see if you float? I'll pick you up at six. Get ready to be fixed. I have to warn you of one thing, though—it's gonna hurt a little."

3

He winced when he had an orgasm, embarrassed, swallowed his sounds, turned his head. Poor Sam. How badly he wanted to be bad. It was his hidden desire, his vain and tender secret, but she knew. He couldn't cry out in pleasure. He couldn't smoke cigarettes. He couldn't take his whiskey straight. The guy had manners. He had manners and faith, when all he wanted in his secret heart was to be tough and greedy and rude, to *take take take,* to live in risk, to moan, to live like it didn't matter when it ended, it could end tomorrow for all he cared, *screw it, drop my ashes in the Sargasso.* He wore a leather jacket. He wore his hair long, until someone called him "Princess," and then he cut it. The way she figured it, he was bad in one way only: he had married her. Was it enough for him? It had to be enough. Badness is the marrow in a bone; he simply didn't have the strength to crack it open. But he could knock her up, could marry her, he could look at the sweet, wounded faces of his aunt and uncle, he could look at their faces and shrug, he could do only that much, so he did, and then he got his accounting certificate.

Their wedding had been at town hall, in a strange room with a checkerboard linoleum floor that went up the walls, concluding at waist level. The upper walls were the green of a chalkboard. They'd been out of high school for a month. She wore shoes that pinched and pink gloss on her lips. The room was hot. She looked at a poster announcing the dangers of marijuana and she wanted, more than anything in the world, marijuana. Another poster celebrated the history of the postal service. The ceiling had been painted yellow. The room didn't make sense, but that wasn't the job of the room. Sense was theirs for the making. What is a wedding but a declaration of sense? It is the possibility that good sense will bring peace. It is the possibility that you'll learn to stay still, stop fiddling, stop running, stop wondering what would happen if you just got on a bus and kept paying and paying and paying. This is what a wedding means; the marriage, of course, is something else. "All set?" They nodded like scolded children. In a box in Sam's back pocket, jammed into a single ring slot, were two plain bands. It was three o'clock in the afternoon. High school had just ended; for a little longer three o'clock would feel like freedom, like being released, returned to yourself. They smoothed their hair. She made one final complaint about her ill-fitting shoes. Then, under fluorescent lights, standing before a half-deaf justice of the peace, before her father, before Sam's aunt and uncle, on a day of low clouds that threatened but did not produce rain, they signed the papers and spoke the vows and were henceforth man and wife. No one said, "You can kiss the bride," but they kissed anyhow, chastely. He did not look like the same boy who had fucked her in his tiny bedroom while his aunt puttered and hummed in the next room. He did not look like the boy who had, with a raging cry (Jesus! did he not know his aunt was next door? did he not care?—this startled even Judith, who prided herself on not being easily startled)—reached down and tore the condom off his prick, tossed it in the air, *slapped* it across the room like it was a bee that'd been bothering them, and said, hotly, into her ear, "I want it like this." At town hall, on his wedding day, he had the clean, composed face of a church boy, patient eyes, combed hair, and an ugly tie he'd borrowed from his uncle.

The wedding took place in Copper Junction, where she'd grown up, and the reception afterward was in the backyard of her house. Her father tended a charcoal grill, wore an apron for the first time in his life. Sam's uncle erected a volleyball net. His Aunt Constance, pale-faced, in a new lilac dress, moved tentatively, haltingly, like a person getting over a stomach virus, like she couldn't turn her head too fast or she'd puke. She hovered around the food table, shooed bugs, made sure the paper napkins didn't fly away. The kabobs tasted like gasoline. Someone made a pumpkin pie even though it was the wrong season; it remained largely uneaten, as if in deference to certain laws. Endless cans of beer. That feeling of an ice-cold can from the cooler, dripping with water, the pinkness of the palm, the first sighing sip—this was the way she would remember the day. A sudden chill, a fine blurring of relief and discomfort. Hops. A deep swallow, another, a longing she thought might have dissolved but of course didn't. She felt stupid for holding that kind of idea. What inner thing truly dissolves? Why would some civic procedure, of all things, fix her? She was stupid, but she could forgive herself. That was another thing about weddings: forgiveness was encoded into them. A foil banner—CONGRATS! in shimmering red—brought down by the breeze. Later, as the wind picked up, it moved end-over-end through the yard, a serpent eating its tail, until it got caught in the brambles at the side of the road.

Someone had put pots of flowers around the yard and strung Christmas lights across the eaves of the porch. Someone had vacuumed the house, washed the windows, placed a rose-scented candle on the back of the toilet, poured bleach down the drain of the kitchen sink. Who had done this? It wasn't her mother, because her mother wasn't a person who would do these things and also because her mother wasn't there. The last time they heard from Grace it was a Santa Fe postcard with a Seattle postmark. Santa Fe, Seattle. She'd written *All is well, missing you,* a few other things, but these weren't the point. That image of the cactus, that cool blue postmark, these were the real message. *Who knows where I am? Not you. Not me.*

"Toast! Toast!"

Her father, a little drunk: "May you be found dead at the ripe ol' age of ninety-nine, shot by a jealous spouse!" It was not clear to whom he was referring.

The next morning they left. There were no tin cans trailing, no soapy sentiments on the windows. "Get us out of here," she instructed. Once on the highway, she screamed, grabbed his thigh, and they laughed until they couldn't sustain it anymore.

"I'm happy," Sam announced. "I'm as happy as I've ever been."

It was a sweet thing. Why couldn't it stay that way? For a moment she was pleased, proud to have bestowed upon him this happiness, but then the foul thing in her brain said: *He said it wrong. He's as happy as he'll* ever be—*he just doesn't know it yet.*

Everything they owned was in the backseat of the car, its trunk, or lashed to the roof. They were supposed to go to the city, find an apartment and jobs. That was the plan, which wasn't really a plan at all. They would simply arrive, figure it out as they went, adventurers, buoyed by faith, by the residue of the fortune that brought them together. But they never got to the city. She said she needed to pee, but also she needed to stop and think. *Here,* she said, *pull over. Now!* He pulled off the road. It was Beetle, but it could have been anyplace. They found a gas station and she sat on its scummy toilet and held her stomach. She was not showing yet, but the skin around her belly button felt harder, hotter. The stink of the room, urine and mildew and lashing floral sanitizer, filled the cavities of her head. She thought, *You are as good as dead and never has your life had more meaning.* She thought, *Poor baby.* Meaning the germ in her uterus; meaning all of them, all the unborn, for whom bad smells and sorrow and sense are waiting. *Poor baby, poor embryo,* but she didn't wholly mean it. She was envious too of the unborn thing she carried, desperately envious of this embryo who would become a baby who would become a person who possibly would bypass—correct?—human horror. Cure cancer. Be president. It was possible, right? That was the grand, fuzzy, pathetic hope of any pregnancy, hers too, already, she wasn't immune, even if the thing was nothing yet, a paper clip unbending, who knew what it could accomplish? It felt delicious to pee. Pregnancy made of urination a vitally pure, shivering pleasure. There was no toilet paper, so she wagged her ass over the seat to dry. The mirror above the sink was not really a mirror but a piece of metal, like a baking sheet, defaced by keys and knives over the years, clouded by dirty exhalation after dirty exhalation, rendering her image vague and indistinct, dark spots where the eyes were, veil of hair.

The city was where Q and his horde of monsters lived. The city was where she'd vomited lo mein and been tied to the bed-post ("It'll be fun! We'll let you go as soon as you say the word"), where that guy called Hester held his face above hers and let a bead of saliva descend. He sucked it back into his mouth at the last second, laughed like a hysterical child. That saliva, white and whorled, suspended above her cringing face, had been like a proof of the failure of her life to come.

Please? Now? Uncle? She didn't know the word to make it stop.

Could she go back to the city? She'd thought so. Her instincts told her to return. But she had to remember not to trust her instincts. That was the lesson, right? Do not say yes. Do not fol-low. When that thing leaps up inside of you and says *Go Go Go for the love of all that is holy!*—you stay.

You stay.

She left the bathroom, squinted at the brightness of the day, opened her mouth to the light as if to take in some nutrient. Sam was waiting in the car. His good posture irritated her. He looked like a church boy, dutiful and head-bowing, though he claimed not to believe in anything. Fucking her loudly in the presence of his aunt, refusing the condom, these things could not change his nature. His face contained belief even when he denied it, an openness, an uncanny patience—she couldn't locate it in any particular feature, but in aggregate his face said: *Jesus Be Praised,* or some nonsense. "God can suck my asshole," he'd once said, but she wasn't buying it. How badly he wanted to be bad; how badly he wanted to scorn the very conventions that constituted his essence. Poor boy. Poor love. He was bound to his goodness.

They were married. They were on their way to the city. She was carrying someone who would become, impossibly, their child, a blood relative to both. She was walking back to the car, and Sam saw her coming and grinned, and inside her came a violent thrusting sensation, like a knee to the ribs, though the baby wasn't bigger than her pinkie yet and still kneeless. She stopped walking. It was the day after her wedding. A feeling like a knee thrusting, a breath trapped in her throat, and then Q's face, clear and up-close, the pores, the meticulous beard, the cleft in his chin where once, when he was passed out on the bed, she'd placed a grain of rice.

Sam rolled down the window. "You coming, baby?"

Sam, her good boy, her hope, her little lark in his double-tied shoes, what would the city do to him? And what would happen to a child there? It was hard to imagine being there and doing ordinary things, such as making tuna fish or smearing cream on their baby's butt.

"Let me drive," she said.

He moved to the passenger seat.

But she did not go back to the highway. Instead she followed signs to the town center. They came upon a church, a bank, an optician's, a library, a funeral parlor, a park where some men were installing a swing set. It was not unlike the towns where they'd come from. A giant flag hung limply above a building that must have been town hall. Finally she drove back to the gas station. She bought them Cokes. They stood in the sunlight. She told him she wanted to stay here, in Beetle, and she hoped he might too.

4

The man waited in the living room while she got him some water. Ice cubes clinked against the glass. He drank with his eyes closed, the skin at his throat bobbing delicately, nostrils warbling. He was like a desert dweller, a sunstroked prophet. She could see now the presence of some zealous, irrational hope he'd been carrying around. He chewed each cube, smiled. His lips were chapped. He was not unattractive.

He said, "Holy shit. Pardon me, but that water. From those pipes. Pardon me. That water is exactly the same."

"Surprise, surprise."

"I'd forgotten how good it tastes."

"Does it?"

He smelled the empty cup. He shivered. Then he handed it back to her.

"Amazing," he declared.

She didn't know how to respond.

He said, "I have a deviated septum. It means my nose doesn't work so well." He sniffed. "I think the room smells the same, but I can't be sure. I smell—what is that?"

"Cigarettes."

"Behind that. Something else."

"We had pork chops last night."

He frowned. "I don't think they have a name for what I mean," he said.

They looked at each other for a moment; then, after a deep breath, as if gathering strength, he said, "This place. It's yours? I mean—you own it? Or do you rent?" He waited for her answer with the clear, suspicious gaze of a child at a magic show. She said they bought it. He wanted to know from whom. The bank, she said. He nodded, exhaled. "You never met the former owner? A woman?"

"No."

"Goldie, her name would have been. Or Maureen Lynn. You know someone by one of those names?"

When she said no again he appeared confused—furrowed his brow—but then relief passed across his face. He said this name again, now louder, mockingly—"Goldie!"—as if it were far from the realm of the possible. Then he spun in a circle in order to examine the room, its water-stained ceiling, fireplace, splintery floors. No photographs. No bric-a-brac save a single ceramic figure on the mantel, a girl in petticoats holding a shepherd's crook, which had been her father's odd gift to Diana when the child was born. Two windows faced the woods. Another looked to a clearing where Sam tried to grow turnips and squash, and where, on hot days, Diana sat in her plastic pool. The man went to the window, touched the glass, squinted at the clearing, turned away. Beanbag chair. Stained yellow couch. Struggling ivy in a macramé holder. Bobo, the panda bear, propped in a child-sized rocker. Crayons in a spaghetti sauce jar. Monopoly, Operation. A home. A homey mismatched flavor. It was not her room any more than her face was her face; that is to say, it was deeply hers, only hers, and only an accident. One of Diana's drawings, a girl with purple wings and a crown of feathers, taped to the wall. Draped over the arm of the couch was a checkered afghan made by Sam's aunt. It held the smell of their feet in its fibers.

The man's eyes moved from wall to wall, thing to thing. He touched the stone of the fireplace, touched it in three different places, three different stones, clinically, solemnly, the way a doctor moves a stethoscope around a patient's chest. Then he pulled his hand away, said, "I need to catch my breath."

She motioned to the couch and he sat, leaned forward, rested his elbows on his knees, his face in his hands.

He said, "I feel stranger than I usually feel."

"You want some more water?"

"I can't drink that water."

"I've got juice."

"Sometimes my mother gave me juice in a teacup so delicate I could've bitten through it. No. Thank you. I just need to catch my breath."

She stood in front of him. She didn't know what to do with her hands. She felt guilty, as if she had perpetrated his discomfort.

She said, "Are you hungry?"

He seemed not to hear.

"A different couch. Ours was stiffer. I used to sit here and eat olives. From a bowl. With a spoon. Like how you'd eat cereal. And you know what else I liked? It's disgusting. Bananas and sour cream."

She said she'd never tried it.

"This cottage. This place." His eyes widened. "Upstairs? The room with the slanting ceilings? That's mine."

"It's my daughter's room."

"A girl . . . ? He whistled a few sad notes. "Okay. A girl. Yes," as if granting permission. Then: "What's her name?"

She told him.

"Man, I loved that room. That big closet. I used to sleep in that closet sometimes. I used to sleep in the fetal position and imagine it was wartime and I was hiding from the Gestapo." He frowned. "Bananas and sour cream. That seems pretty nasty, right?"

She shrugged. "My daughter eats bacon and peanut butter."

"Kids," he said. Then, wistfully, "Diana."

"Right." She wasn't sure if she should have said the girl's name.

"My stepfather was German, you know. I can't imagine a girl sleeping in that room. It always struck me as a boy's room."

Next he told her that his mother had collected crappy art from tag sales, whatever was left in the grass at closing time. He pointed to where her paintings had hung, a farmland scene, a blooming cactus. Tacky shit. He recalled a braided rug on the hearth (he tapped his toes on the floor as he described it), and a swiveling armchair of avocado green. The mantel was full of photographs, mostly of her, his mom, arty shots, black-and-white, pretentious. A partial nude he always hid if a friend came over, but that didn't happen much. A crappy model ship.

Her mind tried to furnish this room with other people's junk.

"Sounds nice," she said. She didn't know what he wanted to hear.

"No." He shook his head. "It was not nice at all."

Sometimes she watched television all day. Sometimes she watched television with her hands down the front of her pants, like a man. Sometimes she masturbated with the vibrating handle of her husband's drill. She stole cigarettes from the convenience store where she worked. She had the crazy instinct to tell him this. He would take in whatever she said, absorb it, how a spill is blotted by a towel. Then he'd leave and she'd never see him again. Instead she sat down in her chair, crossed her legs.

"I never realized how pretty the church is," he was saying. "The park, too. Back then it was just a tire hanging from a tree."

"There's a new public pool by the high school."

"A pool. Man. We never had a pool. We swam behind the old mill."

"They still do that."

"Goddamn Beetle. It puts the P.U. in upstate New York." He leaned back in the couch, extended his arms, so that his elbow rested on the cushion tops. He clasped his hands over the crown of his head.

He is making himself at home, she thought.

"The barbershop," he said. "The bank. Dot's Ice Cream. Dot's flipping Ice Cream. Richard's Eyeglasses."

"He died a few years ago. It's Lenny's Eyewear now."

He said, "The Come & Go. Oh God, the Come & Go."

"I work there."

"No you don't."

"Part-time."

He frowned, said, "I loved that place."

They were silent.

"You know what's funny? I've been riding the bus so long, even sitting here, perfectly still, it feels like motion. I was on that bus for days. I sat next to this guy who hummed the same song for four hundred miles." Here he paused, grimaced. "You'll have to forgive me. I seem to be on a talking jag. It's like all these words were sitting in a net in the back of my throat and someone just cut it open."

"I love buses," she heard herself say.

"Yeah? Buses are hell. But it's a known fact women can withstand pain far better than men."

Once, a couple years ago, she'd walked the mile to the bus station. She had no suitcase, only a few loose bills. It was a lovely afternoon. When she got to the station she felt confused—what had she wanted? She looked around. A row of maroon lockers reminded her of high school. Against another wall sat a few chairs with attached desktops, also like school, except bolted to these desktops were miniature televisions. The station was empty. She had nowhere to go. A man at the counter was picking at his fingernails. He looked up expectantly. What did she do? She peed. She strode into the restroom like it alone had been her destination, and then walked home again.

"My mother," he said. "Take my mother for example. Childbirth, back pain, my old stepdaddy with his bad breath. She gave birth to a stillborn right in her bedroom and didn't utter a word of complaint and was back to cleaning the kitchen the next day. Can you believe that?"

Judith didn't respond. She was disturbed by the way he said "daddy"—a certain inauthentic, Southern-sounding sing-sing. She was disturbed, too, by "stillborn." It hit her later, flashed like neon, all that symmetry and paradox, and she felt a bit sick. That was her bedroom now. A dead baby was born in that room? Maybe she shouldn't have let him in. Maybe it was better to sit alone in your wicker chair and wait for your daughter and husband and to watch the soaps. On *Frosted Glass* Lanie was about to have a baby that wasn't Guy's, and he was planning to murder her once it was weaned.

"Your husband—is he a nice man?"

"Yes," she said.

"Is he—"

She said, "Don't worry about my husband."

He raised his hands in surrender.

For a few moments they were quiet.

The rain picked up. A long roll of thunder.

He said, "Please forgive me if I say too much, or the wrong things. I've been alone for a very long time."

She said, "I can understand that."

She was too easily tempted. She was too excited by his unnaturalness, his pout, his unwashed clothes. By—something else. His quality of displacement. By her awareness—it came on fast—that she wanted him to stay awhile.

She asked him if he was ready to see the rest of the house.

He lowered his head again. He said, into his palms, "I'm afraid."

"Just a house."

"I think I expected it to be—like, neutral. How stupid. Nothing is neutral, right? Nothing in your childhood anyway. Least of all the house you grew up in. Why in hell would I have thought it'd have become neutral?" He looked up. His eyes were the blue-gray of shale. He wagged his head. "Time. Time. It's all jammed together. It doesn't exist. That's what no one gets. Time collapsed a long time ago. It's dead."

"You're a philosopher."

"Be kind. Don't make fun of me."

She didn't understand what he wanted from her.

She said, "I'm not kind."

"I know." His eyes were damp. "I could tell when you opened the door."

She felt, strangely, a rush of pride.

She said, "You want a cigarette?"

He took one, but just examined it between his fingers. Then he told her his name, Pax, which was absurd.

5

Oh fucking fidelity. It took a shameful amount of effort. Even after the baby was born, even when Judith spent her days spooning puree and washing diapers, even when all she wanted was the eyes of a stranger on her body, the stretch marks, the ass, when she knew that nothing would restore her as much as witnessing a grown man's longing, a man she didn't know or care for, a man who could not help himself—even then she was loyal. The power of witnessing another's longing. The power of standing nude and indifferent before a person who is at the mercy of you and knows it. The sweetness of this, the grief. It was not hers anymore. Was it ever? No. It had always been a fantasy. She thought it's what she would find in the city, but she had found something else.

The baby was called Diana. She cooed from a seat fitted with a bar of beads for her to spin. She had dark, glassy eyes, and rosy circles on her cheeks as if they'd been rouged. Her body possessed the dumbly frenzied quality of all babies. When Judith laid her down in her crib at night, in that one moment when the child was suspended over the mattress but before her back touched it, a certain reflex sent her limbs upward in spasm, as if shocked. It reminded Judith of what happens to religious zealots when god talks through them, those ill-dressed finger-waggers with their ridiculous pride. (It is so much easier to be apoplectic than to be still; it is so much harder to come to doubt than to come to certainty.) Diana had a birdlike cry, a belly so tumid and translucent, so like a fishbowl, you could see the veins swimming beneath the skin, and she also had a tiny, tiny vagina that had leaked a tiny bit of blood right after she was born. Normal, said the doctor, who explained how a mother's rampant hormones sometimes trigger in her newborn girl a mini-menstruation.

Judith healed. The girl grew. One day, the carnival came to Beetle.

In the open fields behind the high school dozens of tents, a Ferris wheel, a rickety roller-coaster, strings of yellow lights, trailers with neon advertisements for lemonade and corn dogs and elephant ears. The air was candied. For five bucks you could hit a Japanese car with a sledgehammer. You could shoot at cardboard Indians and win something pink. You could be strapped into a chair and rotated for a while. They pushed the baby in a stroller through the humid crowd. It was past Diana's bedtime. Drunk teenagers, sugar-addled kids, a group of old folks from the retirement home who skirted the perimeter, who gazed at the crowd, wore their longing in the disguise of disgust.

Big-band music, songs of a bygone era fizzed with static, fell upon them from speakers mounted atop tall poles. It was a full world, a city, its own civilization, but it was temporary. It would be gone three days from now. This was a thrill Judith didn't know where to keep in her body. Her hands shook a little. She ate a slice of cherry pie, which made it worse.

Sam said, "You want me to win you a thingamabob?"

"I do."

Gravely, with the smallest nod, in the manner of a cowboy feeding his horse before himself, he stepped up to the booth. He was given a ball, which he turned over in his hands a few times. He had to get it through a dark hole in the wall. He missed. Again. Again. She saw a deeper seriousness come to his face—he squared his shoulders, chewed on his bottom lip. His eyes moved between the ball in his hands and the hole in the wall. It was a small hole, surrounded by red and yellow and black arrows. The kids behind him grew impatient. *Hurry it up, buddy. Throw it already.* Who was he to them? No one. Just another dude in a leather jacket trying to prove his manhood with a ball. For some reason she could not watch. She turned, pushed the stroller away, wandered into a tent where you could buy the hides of artificial bears.

The tent was empty except for a carnival worker, a young guy in a white tank top, motorcycle boots. By way of greeting he showed her his palm. His dark hair was slick with pomade. He had the wide, chin-thrusting face of a character actor. Silver rings on all the fingers of one hand, none on the other.

"Having fun?" He said this like fun was an absurd thing to have, but he wouldn't begrudge her if this kind of rinky-dink affair pleased her small-town sensibilities.

She said it was all right.

Diana was sleeping in the stroller, slumped, head on her shoulder.

Judith felt it immediately, a sort of charge. She saw him shift his body so that his hips faced hers. Then he made a bored expression, blinked slowly, irregularly, as if in code. He told her the prices of certain wares, though she hadn't asked. His voice was low, nearly mean.

The tent walls shivered.

He said, "What's the name of this town?"

She told him.

"I can't keep 'em straight."

He meant: *I won't tell anyone. There's no one to tell.*

He meant: *You are no one.*

The ecstasy of no-one-ness, the jungle of nothing it grows around you.

Gazing at her from his bicep was the head of an eagle, its beak savagely hooked. It would have been easy to kiss him. It would have been shamefully easy to touch his big face with her hands and put her tongue into his mouth. The disassembling of order. The feeling in her body, just thinking of it—something shot forth, like a fish released back into the water, a fast-twitch explosion.

She left.

People will tell you there's power in walking away, but it never felt like it to her.

She bought a Sno-Cone.

In his trailer would be candles, red curtains, a stick of incense in a cactus pot, a guitar, all you need to lure the lonely women of any sad town during any crickety summer evening. How fine it would be to go to him. The fair is closed for the night. The moon is nearly full. Cotton candy tubes littering the ground, a hushed air, scattered campfires.

When she found Sam he was standing near the Tilt-A-Whirl, a massive panda bear under his arm, scanning the crowd and looking terrified. She kissed him, hard, on the mouth.

"I thought some asshole carnie had absconded with you." He handed her the panda bear. It was lime green, with a white muzzle and belly. "I went to the lost and found."

"We weren't there."

"I know. There was a box of lost shit, wallets, baseball hats, keys. Also a set of salt and pepper shakers. Why would someone bring those to a fair?"

"Good work," she said, about the bear.

"You didn't even see."

"I saw!"

She gave him the rest of her Sno-Cone.

Cars jammed the single-lane road back to town. They sat in traffic for an hour listening to a ball game, and then Diana woke up and made her feelings known.

6

Back then, stuck in the hotel, waiting to be rescued, she had been a girl with a cigarette burn next to her navel. It made her look like she had two belly buttons, two mothers. She'd been born first to a flesh-and-blood woman, to a house on a hill in a sleepy town, and then born a second time to that hotel room. A sink bolted to the wall. A broken light fixture someone shot with the silver gun she'd assumed was a toy until it blasted a dime-sized hole in the ceiling, and even then the management didn't show up. You were allowed to do anything there. No one would knock. No one would come upstairs to make sure anyone was all right. You could make any noise—the place absorbed them all. The glowing tip of a joint. A coil of rope. You were allowed any implement with which to sedate or entertain yourself. She had been holding between her thumb and forefinger a fortune-cookie slip like some kind of ticket to another world. What did it say, that fortune? She couldn't remember. It was gone.

She was making a snack for the man, for Pax. Three pieces of toast, stacked one atop the other, sitting on a saucer. Strawberry jam. She rinsed an apple under the faucet. She thought to cut up the apple and then caught herself. Pax was not a child. She was not his mother.

He was like something from a fable, a wanderer. He had the air of a bedraggled saint, the tape on his shoe, the old suitcase, the strange elegance of poverty when you look at it from the outside. His name, too, was a myth. He was like something from a book. She replaced the cap on the container of jam, washed the knife, drank a shot of bourbon. In the kitchen window she saw her reflection—the hard set of her mouth, her unbrushed hair flipping at its ends in the humidity. She brought him the food. He thanked her grossly, extravagantly, as if she had offered him the deed to the house, and then he ate in enormous, savage bites. Again she sat in the wicker chair, arms crossed over her chest, watching him. She had the edgy, attentive feeling of a person waiting in a doctor's office—she felt like a patient, as if in a moment she would have no choice but to expose herself.

When he finished eating there was new color in his cheeks. He took a breath and said, "I'm on my way to the city. I want to find a wife. Can I admit that? I probably shouldn't. It sounds juvenile. Or old-fashioned. Going to the city, looking for a wife."

The bourbon had softened the edges just slightly.

She said, "What kind of wife do you want?"

He lifted a brow. "What *kind*? What kind are there? I don't know. A nice kind. A devoted kind. Maybe dark eyes."

He turned to look her square in the face. One of his eyelids drooped slightly, but only on very close inspection. A long, serious face, faint half-moons of darkness beneath the eyes.

He said, "What kind of wife are you?"

It was a stupid question, she saw, once it was aimed back at her.

He waited.

How to answer? How to describe the infinite restraint, the tenderness, the longing to be alone and gratitude that she wasn't and the fantasy of some other man throwing her in his backseat like a sack of trash?

She could have said anything. She wanted to touch his face. She wanted him to take off his shoes and his pants. She said, "A lousy kind."

He shrugged. "I'll probably be a lousy husband. I was a pretty lousy son, if you want to know."

She didn't want to know, but it was nice to hear him talk. It was nice to see him slouched there, newly sated, driven to recall his memories. His hand absently stroked his belly. If was as if she'd taken in a stray animal. She felt a sense of accomplishment, selflessness, as if her own worth might be measured by his willingness to stay.

"Tell me," she said.

"There's not much to say."

It turned out this was a lie. He spoke in a nervous hush, like a boy before a campfire. He gazed at his hands. What happened, he said, was this: one night his mother had come into his room, crying, and woke him up. Her new husband, his stepfather, had said filthy things. She could imagine, right? He said he'd been sixteen. And isn't sixteen like a magic age? Wouldn't she agree? A crossroad. Anything can happen. You're open. You're on a precipice. For boys, anyway. Maybe for girls it happens younger? He wasn't

an expert on girls. This night when his mother came to his room—
she was crying. Sobbing. Some kind of tangled-up sounds.

He shook his head, pressed his ragged hands to his cheeks.

"My mother. That poor woman. I half expected her to open
the door today. I half expected her to be waiting here for me.
Hair done up. Lipstick. She made the most amazing—no, I
really would rather not think about her food. Chicken dumplings. Chocolate cake. You could die."

She interrupted him. "Do you want a drink? A real drink?
Bourbon?"

"But I want to tell you what happened."

Judith's own mother's face came floating over her, Grace's
face, deliberately stripped of its charms. One's own mother
arrived in any discussion of mothers. There could be nothing
generic, nothing hypothetical, in talk of them.

"She kissed me," he said. "We kissed. Up there in that room
where your kid sleeps."

It was sensational and vile but somehow immaterial. It was
what she expected to hear. She said, firmly, "It happens."

"Does it? I don't think so. No it doesn't."

"Bourbon," she said.

"I could taste what we'd eaten for dinner."

"You want some bourbon?"

"Dumplings."

"Enough."

"I left the next day."

She wanted to return him to the present. She said, "How old
are you?"

"I'd rather not."

"Come on."

"Sixteen. I'm a kid. I'm a lousy, horny kid. Horny as hell. Lousy."

"Everyone is lousy and horny. We're always sixteen, if you want to look at it that way."

This seemed to satisfy him. He stopped talking.

She went to get them drinks. The rain had stopped. Now the sun was coming out; bars of silvery light came through the window shade. Why did he think he could talk about his mother? The mention of this woman, a stranger, filled Judith with a blast of longing for her own mother, who was far away. The last time Grace called, a few months ago, she'd said, "You're still happily married? Still living the dream with Sam?"

It wasn't how her mother talked, *living the dream.*

"Where are you?" Judith asked.

"Pittsburgh?"

"Pittsburgh?"

"That's what I said."

"You said it like a question."

"I did?"

"You said, 'Pittsburgh?'"

"Oh," Grace said. A silence. "Pittsburgh. A perfect fifth-floor walk-up with a window overlooking a hospital. I watch helicopters land on the roof. Isn't that something?"

"I thought Detroit."

"People are always getting saved. I see it happen. That was ages ago, Detroit. I'm painting helicopters. I'll send you one for Diana."

"That'd be nice."

"You know, I wrote your father a letter. I quoted Jung: 'In all chaos there is a cosmos, in all disorder a secret order.'"

"Poor guy," Judith said. "He won't know what to make of that."

It was true, he didn't—Hank called Judith a few nights later. What do you think it means? he wanted to know. He'd read it a hundred times. Does it mean she might be coming back? "Maybe," said Judith.

Now Judith splashed water on her face. Pax waited in her living room. Pax's mother kissed him in Judith's daughter's room. She imagined being sixteen and asleep in her bed and woken by her mother's lips. The idea of it made her sick to her stomach—it felt, at once, like her own memory. She heard Pax cough. But it wasn't her own memory—the past was immutable, it was, it was fixed, it was done, it was one thing and one thing only. Wasn't it? Of course it was.

7

She was faithful to Sam. She could be a regular person. She could be good, ordinary, a normal wife and mother, unhaunted, untempted. But then why did it seem sometimes that the house was talking to her? Why, sometimes, when the baby cried and she'd go down the hall, flip on the light, did she find Diana sound asleep in her crib? The birdlike, creaking crying could not be placed. And once, having sex with her husband, she heard him say something terrible into her ear. The words were delivered in a pitiless voice. She pulled away, cried, "What did you say?" It made no sense that he would utter such a thing. She cried, "Why on earth would you say that?" and grabbed at his face.

"I didn't say anything, honey. I swear."

It was true. That voice had not been Sam's. The voice she'd

heard was damp, cavernous, as from the dead. But mostly the house was a fine place. They filled it with their things, then got more things. Mostly Judith was a normal person. She bought a sewing machine and made a pair of curtains for their bedroom. The fabric was on clearance, multicolored paisleys that seemed to move if you looked at them long enough, to shimmer and twitch, that evoked the tumult of semen.

The baby was normal, that was for sure. She grew. She learned some words. Her voice was high and sanguine, like a doll whose string is pulled. Judith found it distressing, those twittering cadences. One day she said, "Honey, why do you talk so much? Sometimes it's better to save your words for something that really has to be said." A stricken look fell over the child's face, and Judith felt guilty. Why would she make such a complaint? Why could she not tame her instincts? Still, it worked; Diana quieted down a little.

Sam finished his accounting degree. They got along. He did what she asked, such as brush her hair at night. Such as bring her coffee in the morning, and allow her meannesses, and paint the kitchen dark pink, even the insides of the cupboards, like tongue.

Tuesday. Wednesday. Thursday.

May. June. July.

Before, when she was a girl, time had been a pricker, an irritant, a tiny sliver of wood stuck in her palm coloring the experience of everything she touched. Her finger went there without thinking, again and again. She wanted time to go faster or slower or for it to pause momentarily. She did a quiet sort of battle with it, always. Now the sliver had been removed. That was her adulthood. A smoothness where once was friction. As if someone had one day walked up to her and, unspeaking, lifted her hand and simply tweezed it away. The nerves there quieted down. She had little awareness of the movement of time anymore. That is to say, she saw the calendar and wore a watch, but her days assumed a new fluidity. The tension of her childhood, the sense of something about to happen or having just happened, the wondering if it would happen again, the hoping you could defeat the clock with the very power of your ardent heart—this was gone. She lived in a dull, bright, busy present. Days passed. She slept and woke. Her daughter had a birthday, another, etc.

Once, in the child's fourth year, Sam said he wanted to take them all to Orlando, to make the great American slog, three days in a car without air-conditioning so they could enter the gates of that ever-after-y cosmos, where for your effort you were allowed to stand in hour-long lines and marvel at gleeful electric puppets and get earnest tinkling songs stuck in your head for the rest of your days. Judith refused. She knew the place would demand she maintain a certain dazed and beaming face, and the thought of seeing crowds of people with the same face terrified her. But she wanted Sam to go. She wanted him to take the child away for a while. Judith had not been alone for a very long time. No, that wasn't true—she had *never* been alone, not rightly. What would she do, by herself in the house for a week? Two weeks? The prospect nearly took her breath away. The bed to herself. The bathtub. Or maybe she would go somewhere, take her own vacation? *Alone.* The word dispersed throughout her body like steam.

"You go. I'll stay here," she said.

"By yourself?"

"Sure."

It was ten o'clock at night. They were in bed. She was reading a mystery novel in which they kept discovering bloated corpses floating in some ritzy marina.

He said, "Aw, she'd have more fun if you were with us."

Judith didn't believe this to be true—Diana was an adaptable child, captivated more by things than people. She was the kind of girl you found fiddling with pipe cleaners, pressing her face against a fish tank, a reader of princess books, picker of grass, long hair in a prairie braid, rosy cheeks. She tested the water with the big toes of both feet, as if one might be wrong. A double-checker. A lover of solitary games. She had a cool, blunted prettiness often assumed to be sagacity. Was it? They didn't know yet. She collected rabbit feet dyed unnatural colors. Slowly, with infinite patience, she assembled puzzles depicting the Scottish Highlands or wet-eyed baby animals. She was in kindergarten. Her teacher called her "amiable"—such a pale word. Wasn't it? So treacherously pleasant.

"Have you ever considered . . ." Sam spoke lightly. A newspaper—he was doing the crossword—rested on his tented legs. He said, "Perhaps you're putting your own needs before hers?"

"What am I failing to give her that she needs?"

"I just think she'd like a vacation."

"I mean besides Donald Duck. What else am I neglecting?"

"You're a good mother."

"Was that in question? I didn't realize."

"We could camp out along the way." He scribbled on the edge of the newspaper to get the pen's ink flowing. He said, "S'mores."

"I'd rather go to—" But she couldn't think of someplace else. He shrugged, went back to his puzzle.

"In any case," she said. "I have no idea what that even means: *good mother.* Who can say? Not us, of all people."

She looked down at the cover of her book, a close-up of a heavily lipsticked mouth opened in fear or in ecstasy, you couldn't tell which.

She said, "I feed her. I love her. Enough. Do I have to wear mouse ears to prove it?"

He didn't bring up Orlando again.

She slept with her head on his chest. His body was trim, long. It had not altogether lost its boyishness. The knobbiness remained, the startled breath and hairless chest. But now there were things that were not boy. For example the ability to grow a mustache. In certain lights, the faintest touch of gray at his temples. The way his mouth curled when he was unhappy, or how his brow rose and the nostrils widened when he was pleased. The definitiveness of his expressions, that's what she meant. This was new. During their first days together, he could not utter a feeling or wish without questioning it, contradicting himself, squeezing up his face as if to say: *But is that right? Is that what I feel? What do I feel? Tell me. Tell me!* That habit had stopped. He had been a fast-breathing, guilty, horny, desperate kid. Now he was stronger, she believed, in body and in mind. But the boy was not fully gone. He underlay the man. In bed she could see him, the boy: he lay like a body within the body, removed as a corpse, but he was not dead.

She reached across his torso and grabbed his upper arm. His skin was warm and smooth. She was eye to eye with his Adam's apple, watched it beat. Maybe she would have been happier if he had more fully transformed. She wondered. If he had lost the boy in him, perhaps the girl in her (that hungry, charmless, unwashed thing, a shoplifter, a lover of dumb thrills, a nail-biter, an escape artist) would have likewise vanished. It was like the presence of boy in him confirmed the girl in her, and this was cause for great disappointment, because she wanted that girl exorcised. She wanted that girl strung up, wanted someone to poke at her with a stick, wanted a public ritual, a crowd to finish her off once and for all.

He told her to have sweet dreams, and she said she hoped the same for him. They lay in the darkness. Down the hall, their child dreamed of boats taking on water, of holes in their hulls she plugged with chewing gum.

8

Judith stood in the kitchen while Pax waited. She poured two glasses of bourbon, then combed her hair with her fingers. What was she doing? Why was she hesitating to go back in there? The rain started again. The pink kitchen, in the absence of sunshine, in the dusky light of a rainy afternoon, had become darker, not tongue but throat. Finally she returned to the living room. He said, "Man, I could go for some chocolate cake." He'd finally lit the cigarette. He took dainty, courteous puffs.

"I'm not much of a cook," she said.

In less than an hour her daughter would come home from school. Judith's body felt calm, calmer by the moment, but a certain urgency was building in her mind. He would leave. She would never see him again. What did she want? She sat down next to him, legs pulled under her, knees pressed lightly into the side of his thigh.

He said, "Basically I've lived my whole life on buses. I ran away at sixteen. Took the first bus I saw. Got off here and there. I made fruit pyramids in Seattle. Baked bread in Tulsa. This girl and I had a place for a few months. But sooner or later I always found myself back on the bus."

"Fruit pyramids."

"Her name was Becky. She was a good girl." He paused, said, "I feel like a voyeur. Like—how is it? Like a spy into my future. Like if I hadn't left—if I hadn't run away—this would have been my life. This old house. A kid. A wife. Maybe even you? It's like I'm seeing some version of the life I've run away from. It's like I'm a voyeur into my own existence."

She pressed an index finger into his ribs. He did not show awareness that she had touched him. What was she after? She was suddenly irritated by her passivity, and by his jabber, and by the clock which showed just forty-five minutes until her daughter returned.

"Listen to me. God knows I'm no philosopher. I'm just a wanderer. A mucked-up, dirty, hobo American. But this place"—he opened his hand to the room—"it's me when I was me, or when I could have become me. The me I was supposed to be. I mean I want to come back. It's such a shitty house! No offense. But it is, right? No place to raise a kid."

"Drink your bourbon."

But he said, "Keep your daughter safe."

"Don't worry about my daughter."

"Keep her safe."

"Don't!"

"I think I may be the ghost under her bed. My mother kissed

my cheek. In that room. Then my eyelids, my ears, my mouth, my neck, my—"

She said, "Stop with the mother already."

Did he not imagine she had one too? That they all did? That his was not the only one lurking?

He stopped.

Diana would come trundling home. And then Sam, the accountant, her cock-a-doodle, her one true everlasting, he would come home with his briefcase under his arm, sighing mightily like a man from the mines, and she would pour him a drink, and he would stay here until the day he died. Pax's was not the only sorrow in the house. You could tell him this, and he would say he understood, and he would think he understood, but the truth was he did not understand, and not understanding such an important thing is what makes a person ride a bus all his life. Judith leaned in close to him. She said, "There are no ghosts under my daughter's bed."

He nodded. "I'm sorry I said so." He seemed to mean it. Now she felt a stab of pity. He was still a boy. He'd dissected his suffering as a kid takes apart a car engine, emerges greasy, soiled— the car won't run, but signs of his effort are everywhere. There was silence for a minute, peace, but then he was talking again, on and on, about a kind of ice cream he'd been addicted to as a kid, about the dog he never got, about some guy he'd met on a bus with a peacock feather in his hat. Her pity went away. Would he shut up? Could she make him shut up? Who was he to come into her home and speak aloud any flitting thing that haunted his brain? Why had she allowed this?

Then it occurred to her that she was allowed to do the same.

She said, "What, do you think, would make a woman drive her whole family into an oncoming train?"

Because he did not have a monopoly on sorrow. Because she had never before asked it.

He raised his eyebrows. "Is this some kind of riddle?"

He had found, as if from a suitcase of disguises, a cool, professorial face.

"No."

"Is there a right answer, or is it hypothetical?"

She said, "Both. Neither. I don't know."

But it did not provide the release she expected. It felt, simply, like a betrayal of her husband, as if she had revealed what kind of underwear Sam wore, or had mimicked the sound he made when he ejaculated.

Pax's eyes were closed. He appeared to be thinking. He said, "Shame." He opened his eyes. "What are people ashamed of?"

Her mind was empty.

"Or—wait." He rubbed his temples. "I have it. What's the only thing stronger than shame?" The question hung like a cobweb between them. It had no obvious source or color or use. "*Fear* of shame," he said. "A fear of shame so strong you'll do whatever it takes to earn it. People do the sickest, weirdest things. Anything to lay claim to whatever feeling you fear the most. I wish it weren't so, but all the evidence points to it." He looked at her a long moment. He blinked. "You thinking of going this route?"

Now is when she kissed him. She leaned in. His breath was warm and sweet, strawberry jam caught in the corners of his mouth.

What had happened in this house? Just the same mundane horror that happened everywhere. It was an ordinary house. But of course there was no house that wasn't its own chamber of horrors, that didn't, somewhere, have a hidden door, a hidden mouth. Diana would come home soon. Judith would pour her a cup of juice. They would sit at the kitchen table and play Operation. When it was Judith's turn she would lift her instrument, pause before the body. She would retrieve the spare rib. The child would murmur encouragement, as Judith had done for the child. Judith would feel unnaturally in control of her hands. She could empty the whole body. She could! The Adam's apple. The funny bone. She could win, if there wasn't the unassailable rule that her daughter must win. The funny bone on the table. Her daughter watching solemnly. Why did the child have to win? Why did such a rule exist? What was its purpose except to fool the child, except to make her future that much harder to bear? The charley horse. The broken heart. The wishbone. Each and every blasted part. Would her hand have ever felt steadier? Would her hand have ever felt more *her hand*? No.

She tasted cigarettes and strawberry jam. As they kissed he made a sound like someone waking (a rising hum), and then like someone falling asleep (a descending sigh), these two sounds back and forth, as if entering and leaving consciousness even as he kissed her, here and nowhere, nowhere and here. Finally they pulled apart.

"That's exactly what I'm taking about," he said. "It's what I've been saying all along."

"What have you been saying?"

Disappointment passed over his face. "How shame makes you an outlaw. How it makes you an outlaw and a voyeur. That's me. Both. Plus—can I be honest?—lonely."

She took off her shirt. He looked impassively at her breasts. She took his hand, placed it on her chest; when she let go, his hand fell away.

"My stepfather came into the room. He found us. He saw it. I tried to hurt him."

"It's done. Whatever happened, it's done now."

"It's not. It's never."

She said, "Look at what is right in front of you." Her nipples were pale brown, faintly flecked with darker spots, like eggshell.

He squinted, said, "I don't know how."

She felt very little. He barely touched her, floated above her body, his motions resembling push-ups. The act concluded with a familiar sound, a creaking like an infant's mechanical squall. They lay on the splintery wood floor. What she felt was sad release, the cruel pleasure of knowing the world moves along without you. She said his name but immediately regretted it, because he took this as an invitation to speak.

"You know what's nice about you?" he said. "You're at peace. You know what you want, don't fight it. You've got no need for morality or theories or, shit, *buses*."

"What are you talking about?"

She felt the urge to hit him. He wasn't allowed to talk about her—he knew nothing!

Diana was walking home from school with a stick in one hand and a book about oceanic mysteries in the other.

He said, "You're a blessing, Judith."

She said, "I'm not blessing you."

"You don't need to try. It just happens."

She said, "Look at my face."

"I'm looking."

"You're not."

He was.

She wanted only Sam now.

"I saw it when you opened the door," he said. He stroked her cheek. "You have no use for shame. None. You're beyond it. You know how primitive it is. Me, it's all I've got. Tomorrow you'll wake up like it's any other day. You've got a girl to raise. Dishes to wash. That's magnificent, isn't it? That's what I call good goddamn luck."

PART 5

LEONORA

A few years before, another winter, her father took her out in a snowstorm. The brother was too young; her father made a big show about how her brother was too young for what they were going to do. It worked: Leonora felt proud and important. Ha! She stuck her tongue out at the boy as he sulked and whined; their mother had to placate him by letting him destroy a roll of cellophane wrap. But a little way into the walk it occurred to her that perhaps *she* was too young. For the weather was getting worse, and it seemed they'd gone much too far. What began as a quiet, peaceful storm soon became rigid, twisting sheets of snow and ice, a violent mix that stung their faces, burned the membranes of their eyes and noses. The wind picked up, and soon it raged. Soon you couldn't see the streetlights. No cars, no buses, no people. It became difficult to stand up straight. In the distance an awful sound, like a train stopping short, a thrilling, spangly, dangerous screeching. "That sound! What's that sound?" she cried, but her father couldn't hear her. Where were they? Nothing was familiar. Just sheets of white, and wind, and pockets of moony blue. She couldn't see her feet or her hands stretched out before her. Yet this was the city! Her city! She knew it so well. Her father grabbed her hand. He pressed his mouth to her ear, yelled instructions: "Walk backwards. Soldier on. Gut it out."

Soldier on? Gut it out? That wasn't how her father talked, not with that barbed-wire voice. He gripped her arm, spun her around so that the wind, now, was at their backs, and for one brief moment she could see where they were, which was in front of the dry cleaners, two blocks from home. The dry cleaners. *Their* dry cleaners. Yet seeing this, making out the familiar words (*Schneiderman's Since 1952*), frightened her more, not less; disoriented her more, not less. That you could feel so lost, so small, and yet be so close to home—this knowledge penetrated her body as mere coldness never could. *Soldier on. Gut it out.* Her father, an economist, bookish, quiet, with a thin and lank body, with eyes her mother called "Bambi eyes," he didn't talk like that. Now his hat flew off. The wind tried to take hers too, but it was tied beneath her chin; she was just a little girl, she still wore hats like that. She lunged forward, to rescue his hat, his favorite brown corduroy newsboy hat—she couldn't bear his losing that hat—but he clamped his hand on her arm with great strength. (The next day the bruise would show.) He pulled her backwards. She didn't know if they were in the street or on the sidewalk, feared walking into a telephone pole or a car or falling down the stairs of the subway. Her father led her this way—she was impassive, free of volition, and finally she closed her eyes. She found it

was easiest to accept her helplessness, to submit wholly to it.
Plus it didn't hurt so much when her eyes were closed. In this
manner they made their way home. Snot froze on her face. The
ends of her hair, where they'd flown into her mouth, froze too.
Her arm throbbed. She couldn't feel her feet.

Her mother seemed irritated but not worried, and gave them
mugs of warm milk. Her brother sat in front of the fireplace, cellophane wrap binding his legs together, chanting "I'm a mer-
man" and flapping his legs. Her mother wore sweatpants and a
big white T-shirt. That was all. No sweater, no socks. She was
always warm enough.

At home he became her father again, fast-blinking, distracted,
clutching a hot-water bottle, the afghan drawn over his shoulders, bloodshot eyes on a paperback in his lap. The other person
was gone.

Gut it out. Soldier on.

These words came to her in the backseat of the strangers' car.
She'd forgotten them for so long, forgotten her father's alien
voice, forgotten the ice striking her face, but now she
remembered.

Gut it out.

She was on the floor of the car. A green sedan. She was hidden underneath a blanket that smelled like balsa wood and mud.
Their car. She was in their car. Sandy and whatever the man's
name was. The man called the woman "Sandy." She needed to
remember this name, feared that in the blast of details, in the
rush of smells, voices, sounds, colors, she'd lose it. She hadn't
heard his name, the man's, she didn't know his name, which
made his touch—one hand on her back, one on her head—
criminal. He should at least have introduced himself, she
thought. Or was that crazy? What did his manners matter? But

they mattered. Everything mattered. The smell mattered. The car mattered. The woman with the bowl cut, Sandy, Sandy, drove. Sandy complained about the cold, about the flipping broken heater. It was horrible, all these flippings, flipping this and flipping that, it was worse than the word itself. Trash on the floor, newspapers, fast food debris, batteries. She was down on that floor, mustardy Styrofoam for a pillow, a blanket on top of her. Three points of pressure: his hand on her back; his hand on her head; the floor hump pressing into her stomach.

Gut it out.

She had never been hit before. She had never ridden in a car this way before.

He said, "I wish there was another way, sweetie."

He said, "Don't get the wrong idea."

He said, "This is no good, Sandy. She's gonna get the wrong idea."

At first she knew exactly where they were. This was her neighborhood, the back of her hand. She followed their turns, visualized their route, said the street names under her breath. She would remember everything! When they neared Wing Dings she had said, "There it is," though of course they didn't care about Wing Dings. They'd passed her school. They'd passed the place where she'd once been tempted to shoplift an eraser in the shape of an ice cream cone, and she hadn't—hadn't! She'd wanted it badly, wanted it desperately, but she hadn't taken it. Very soon she lost her sense of direction. Her cheek didn't hurt anymore. Then he pulled the blanket off her and said she could sit on the seat next to him, provided she sat very still, provided she was a good girl, he knew she was a good girl, he hoped she didn't have the wrong idea. She sat up. He clasped her, his right arm around her shoulder, its hand squeezing her elbow, his other hand across his lap and pressing her hand to the seat, like they were at a scary movie.

Brown sheets hung over the windows in the backseat, obstructing her view—or really, she knew, obstructing others from viewing her. The car was dark green, a beat-up sedan with white pinstripes on its sides, the gray felt lining inside the roof coming down, pinned in places with thumbtacks. It smelled mildewy, heavy, like a car in summertime after a rain when someone's forgotten to roll up the windows. It smelled—*hot*. Which didn't make sense, given it was freezing. Yet the cold air had the fullness of heat—an air dense with sweat and grease and mildew and something sweet, like butterscotch. The windows back here were covered but she could see through the windshield, could see the road before them, the darkening sky. She could study the profile of the woman, Sandy. She could see her own breath, the man's breath, their breath joining. She was colder without the blanket over her, but she'd rather be cold and sitting up than crammed down there with the trash. She was gutting it out. She noticed her cheek was not hurting anymore. She noticed a gold star stuck to the steering wheel, a single gold star such as a child would receive for a job well done. She noticed that she was making sounds. Soft, flapping noises, like laundry on a clothesline in a summertime wind.

The man said, "I wish I hadn't had to do that, sweetie. I didn't hit you that hard, did I? Does it hurt? I'm a nice person, I promise it. Don't get the wrong idea."

She'd seen it before, in movies—the person who won't stop screaming, whose screaming is only stopped by a slap. That had been her.

"He is," said Sandy, in that clear, prim voice. "It's true, he's a nice person. It'd be a better world if it were full of hims. I mean that." Hers was the voice of a librarian. No—it was a voice like the card inside the library book. The card you use to sign it out. Lines waiting to be filled. Nothing but order. A clean, empty voice. It was not right, a voice like that.

"Please stop the car," Leonora said. "I won't tell anyone."

"Soon enough," said the woman.

Terrible order. Leonora saw the empty card inside the library book and then saw her name written across the top line, saw her own careful, right-leaning script. She'd always got gold stars for handwriting, never anything but.

"Don't be scared," said the man. "Can you agree not to be scared? I know it's a lot to ask, but can you try to relax? Would it help to hold the cat?"

She couldn't see the cat from back here but could hear him scrambling around the front seat, mewing now and then.

"I'm not going to hurt you," the guy said.

"It's true," the woman said. "He's not."

The woman dangled the cat over the backseat by the scruff of its neck. The man took it, set it down in Leonora's lap, then grabbed her arms again, so she couldn't touch the cat. The cat cuddled into her. Of all the names of all the girls in the city, it was her name, *Leonora*, on the card inside that library book. What was the title of the book?

The woman complained some more about the heater. The man ignored her. He said to Leonora, "Think about something pleasant. Am I hurting you?" He loosened his grip. "Can you do that? Think about something pleasant?"

She obeyed. It was in her nature. She automatically pictured her mother's face, pictured her mother getting ready for a party, begrudgingly applying makeup, grumbling about the tyranny of the male gaze; then, afterward, her face painted, her mouth a deep, matte red like an old movie star's, black liner around her eyes, looking into the mirror, inhaling, exhaling, silent, happy. She carried a teeny mirror in her purse for touch-ups.

No. Not this. It wasn't pleasant to think about her mother's party face. Instead she willed herself to think about Beatrice, that girl she'd never meet, the daughter of the man with the red mittens, Beatrice who lived somewhere in this city, who'd come home tonight to find a present waiting for her. She had a feeling Beatrice wasn't very pretty. Her father would have mentioned it if she had that going for her.

She wondered: Was this, what was happening now, like a punishment for trusting that man? For drinking the hot chocolate? Was God teaching Leonora a lesson about feeling too satisfied by helping? Would she still get to be a nurse or social worker? Would she still get to be a person? Would she get to pick onion off a sandwich or stand in front of a mirror wondering if her bathing suit was the right kind or learn how to say "gesundheit" in even more languages? She thought about picking onion off a sandwich. About lemonade. About flossing her teeth. About the kind of bathing suit she'd like to get. These things were better to think about than her mother or Beatrice or God. She pictured eating a plate of fried scallops while wearing a new bathing suit, and she felt better.

They were moving toward a bridge. She could see it now through the windshield. The bridge. She did not want to be anywhere near a bridge. But there it was, coming closer, suspended over water, black, lacy, like a leg in a stocking, a woman's leg thrown out in invitation.

"The sheet, Frank," Sandy said, for—look!—the brown sheet on the window next to her had begun to fall down. Leonora could see another car, a car alongside their car—she could see the driver of the other car, a man in sunglasses, bobbing his head to music. She turned her own head to the window, leaned closer, opened her mouth, but before she could do anything— what could she have done?—the man reattached the sheet and the other car was lost. Frank reattached it. Frank was his name. Frank. Frank and Sandy.

"Flipping sheet," Sandy muttered.

They crossed the bridge—she could do nothing to stop their passage. On the other side, just over, she caught a glimpse of another Wing Dings through the windshield. It was a chain restaurant, Leonora knew it was a chain, but its presence, its same sign, its same chicken on whose head sat, slightly askew, a crown—the same chicken with the same bubble emerging from its mouth, and in the bubble the words I REIGN SUPREME—this slowed her racing heart. It was home. Of course she'd never actually eaten at Wing Dings, it wasn't allowed (empty calories; corporate anthropomorphism), but in its familiarity, its recurrence, it soothed. It felt a little like a nickname, reassured her the way a nickname did, sweetly, vaguely. It gave her the feeling of home.

"What's going to happen to me?" she asked.

Her mother called her "Ladybug."

"I don't know," the woman said.

Her father, "Lee-Lee."

"Nothing at all," the man said.

Her father could be a soldier. She could be a soldier too. She could gut it out. If her father could be a soldier, could find inside him on that stormy night the thing they needed; if he could later return so easily to his other, his real self—well, so could she. No one was bad or good. Beatrice could become a nice girl.

Frank, Sandy, they could find love in their hearts. Then and there she made the decision not to panic. She was a thousand people. Right now she would be a solider. The sun was setting, and she would not panic, and everyone had everyone else inside of them.

1

He took the name "Pax" from someone he'd met on a bus out of Topeka, a scroungy guy in a big leather hat that flopped over his ears. Tucked into the hat's band was a peacock feather and an old note, folded in quarters, from a girl. Paul had admired the guy's rutted voice and easy generosity. He had torn the paperback he was reading in two, gave Paul the first half to read. It helped pass the time. It was a long bus ride, through plains, over mountains, town after measly town. The book was about a beekeeper who falls in love with his sister's best friend, a girl who happens to be a lesbian. They read together, Paul at the beginning, Pax near the end. It felt important, somehow, that they were part of the same story, Paul following Pax's trail through this odd book, his eyes where Pax's eyes had been, hearing the voices Pax had just heard. Things didn't end well for the lesbian.

Pax smelled of cooked meat, greasy, homey. He was tough and gristle-voiced, but read books about love and bees. *I should have been a Pax*, thought Paul, and right then and there endeavored to be more like Pax, and so he took the other man's name once he got off the bus.

Her name was Leonora Marie Coulter. She would never take another person's name. She was twelve years old, five foot two, last seen wearing dark green pants, a gray turtleneck, boots. Her coat was maroon corduroy with yellow lining. In photographs her smile was broad, crooked. Her real smile, her mother insisted, was much more subdued. She was a shy girl but attempted to hide her shyness. Her true smile was small, carried her chin downward. Her skin was pale and fine. She was proud of its lack of blemishes. Her long, dark blonde hair she fastened with two mother-of-pearl barrettes that had belonged to her grandmother. This is how she was wearing her hair the day she vanished. And her bangs had just been trimmed. And, said her mother hopefully, she carried a little pot of lip balm in her pocket, as well as a nail clipper. She was fastidious about her nails, which were short and clean. Her mother repeated this information as though the investigation would hinge on it.

A silver ring around her index finger. A string bracelet she made last summer at camp. A bra. She didn't like to wear a bra, but she'd recently resigned herself to it.

Wednesday panties. Panties that said *Wednesday* in cursive around the waistband. She disappeared on a Wednesday, was the kind of girl to wear Wednesday's underwear on Wednesday, Thursday's on Thursday. It made you sick in the heart. She was orderly. She was tidy. Her manners were impeccable, her voice soft. They feared this might not have worked to her advantage.

She liked badminton. She liked mocha swirl. She liked those orange circus peanuts in cellophane bags, but only a few, too many and she felt like vomiting. She liked clean nails. She liked yellow roses. She liked that song about *hey there little red riding hood.* Her mother produced this litany of preferences for the television camera while the newscaster nodded his head, affirming each: *Yes, clean nails. Yes, sleepaway camp, badminton, yellow.*

This was winter. For several months she was a missing person. They prayed that she'd just run off, gone to seek her fortune, followed a boy, that kind of thing. But it was highly unlikely that Leonora would run off. She'd been a happy girl, quiet, not a risk-taker. She lived with her family in a spacious first-floor apartment in a turn-of-the-century brownstone. She had her own bedroom, a double bed, a pile of plush bears, a few girlfriends. Summers at sleepaway camp. She and her younger brother liked Monopoly and practical jokes. Once they sewed up the fly of their father's boxer shorts; once they put vinegar in their mother's morning coffee.

Have you seen her? Have you seen this girl? Her mother, on the local news, opened her palms to the camera. *If you can hear us, honey—*

Winter became spring. Then summer, with its window boxes and cleavage, and still she was nowhere.

2

Pax got off the bus and stepped into the street. The air was humid, dense, rich with the melony gas of decomposing garbage. He stood on the curb, suitcase at his feet. He watched people come and go, traffic, wheeling birds. The sky was dull white, like a paper towel. Shirtless men in hard hats climbed a scaffolding with slack, simian grace. You might have thought them drunk, or else fully at peace with the prospect of their death—they dangled, laughed; their disjointed babble carried across the street. A fire truck with nothing to hurry to. A stream of cabs. A woman with a toddler strapped to her back pushed a stroller containing two more children, all freckled, yawning, in sunbonnets. Someone was playing a harmonica: an old bum, eyes closed, his song antic and grating, past its day. He wanted you to put spare change in a bedpan by his side. A bedpan!

Pax loved this place. He hadn't been back for a couple years and had forgotten the noise, different noise from other cities, here it was a bluesy huffing din which, in its constancy, its oppressiveness, was not sound so much as temperature, stunning the body as high heat does.

Also it was hot. Nearly ninety. Already he needed a shower.

He wandered and did not stop wandering for several days. This was his favorite part of arriving in a city, that first interval when it feels so open, full of weird and perfect and singular charms, when you weave among people, sleep where you can, eat greasy food from vendors, piss in bushes. After a while it gets more particular. You start to see the sour faces. You notice eyes. You know which cops monitor the library, which cop's got the hard-on for the vagrants, you know the bullies, the swearing streetwalkers, start to hear the curses, start to see panic on the faces of the city's dispossessed. You start to realize you're one of them, a guy on the fringe in shitty shoes. But at first, during those first few days in any city, you can be ragged and unbathed, watching the sadness but not of it.

Then, at once, you're part of it. You wake up one morning on a cot in a shelter and there's a social worker looking down at you, and he asks your name, and you make something up, and he starts to write it on a clipboard, but you're gone.

He liked the subway of this city. Liked its echoes, its heat, its moldering gusts, its congregation of musicians and deadbeats and tourists, how its eggy oily stench got into your mouth, into everyone's mouth. The democratizing force of the underground, its unavoidable suggestion of the death that's coming for all of us, somehow this was reassuring. Perspiring tile. Gummy cement. Massive, trembling rats with tails like car antennae. He stayed underground for days at a time. He rode. He walked. He watched. He liked waiting on platforms, trapped in crowds, liked the collective breathing and sweating; the faces people made when crowds pressed them together—or rather, he liked the faces people tried to hide, the averted eyes, pinched mouths, he liked a face that betrayed its owner.

He saw one face everywhere. A girl's.

Flyers on subway poles, on the walls of the trains, a big poster of her face next to an advertisement for a movie called *Gateway to Paradise II*. This girl's face right next to the face of a famous actress in massive sunglasses. Why was the simple, predictable prettiness of this girl so much better than the beauty of the actress? She made the actress in sunglasses look ridiculous. The girl was a human, maybe more than most people. Her face could not fully compose itself. It could not achieve what it wanted. It never would. The girl's face was everywhere. At every stop. At every turn. It was a face that was trying hard not to betray itself. And yet she was a child—what did she have to betray?

He was looking for a wife. That was his mission, he wouldn't let himself forget. As he walked the streets, rode the subway, he kept his eyes open, someone gentle, pretty but not dominated by prettiness, someone who'd maybe be carrying too many grocery bags? He could offer to help. He could hold her milk. No one paid him much attention. He showered at the Y. He played basketball in the park. The women he saw were too serious-looking, or bored-looking, or ugly, or had their arm entwined with a man's, or another woman's. Anything went. Wives, it seemed, were out of fashion. He browsed the bookstores. He visited museums. A billboard, too, hanging in the city's biggest square, her face, her name, HELP US, an exclamation point, another.

3

Male newscasters are allowed to have imperfect skin. This one had white hair (no woman newscaster was allowed to have white hair) and a faint trace of rosacea on his cheeks and nose. He sat face-to-face with the girl's mother. Behind them, on the studio wall, an image of Leonora stared from the happiness of last October. She was flushed from jump-roping, wore a patchwork coat with rolled-up sleeves. Her arms were thin. She stood under a bare tree, orange leaves at her feet. The newscaster took a breath, leaned forward slightly, said, "Our viewers are naturally wondering how you're holding up. There's been an outpouring of support." His voice was smooth and even. It held concern like a small ball balanced in the palm. He could hold the ball forever. His tie was striped. His glossy hair resembled, in its neatness, with its stiff bang, a newsboy cap.

The mother said, "What do your viewers expect me to say?" But before he could reply: "We're holding up as well as can be expected."

"Our viewers are wondering—"

"They want to see me cry?" It was delivered as if with genuine curiosity.

"The outpouring of support has been truly remarkable."

"Because I cry," she said. "Someone wrote a letter. A stranger. Asked why I wasn't crying more, publicly. I cry. I just want to be clear."

"People are really pulling for you and your family."

"I can't cry on television."

"We've never seen such an outpouring of sympathy."

"Someone out there knows something. Someone." She turned to the camera. "You? Maybe you saw something? Maybe you want to share what you know?" She stared into the camera as if into a mirror. She knew who she saw. She knew everything.

"How is your husband holding up? Our viewers would like to know."

She said, "You? Are you watching? Can you hear me?"

"The number's on the bottom of the screen, folks." He pronounced each digit carefully. "If anyone knows anything, there's a reward."

She said, "I want, also, to send a message to—to whoever took her. I want to say—" But she stopped. She wore red-framed glasses, a navy blazer with a circle pin on the lapel. She looked more like a newscaster than the man did. Her face was stately, serious, with good bones, a fine brow, a face showing abundant awareness of the ills of the world.

He said, "I understand there'll be another prayer vigil?"

Her eyes widened. You could see the powder they'd applied to her skin. She opened her mouth. "The message—"

Again she said nothing.

"A candlelight vigil? By city hall?"

"I—can't."

He leaned in closer. Would he touch her arm? He seemed to want to. But his hands stayed on his lap, held his index card.

He said, "What is your message, dear?"

"Dear?"

"Say what you need to say. This is your opportunity."

She squinted. Silence.

The newscaster turned to the camera. He lifted his jaw. He pouted. "Give her back," he said. "A mother's plea. A family's wish. A city's hope. Give. Her. Back."

4

He took a flyer off a telephone pole. He kept it in his back pocket, looked frequently at her narrow face. He couldn't stop looking. He recognized her. She was like the sister he hadn't had, a familiar something in the eyes, a quiescence, a longing, a studied blankness. She looked like she was struggling to find the right thing to say, the one perfect thing, in a crowd of yammering idiots. No one was listening to her. Plus they had similar eyebrows, she and Pax.

Once, at a bakery, he brandished the flyer, asked the proprietor, "Have you seen this girl?" like he was a relative, an uncle, even the father.

"I'm sorry. I haven't."

Pax nodded.

"Tough," said the baker, shaking his head. "Real tough. I've seen her on the news. I had a cousin once, disappeared too. Turned up in a casino, broke and high. Hope that girl's off somewhere hitting the jackpot. That's what I hope."

Pax pictured this girl sitting on a vinyl casino stool with a bucket of coins on her lap, coolly sipping a Shirley Temple.

"What's her name again?" the baker wanted to know.

"Leonora." He made it sound Italian.

"God bless her," the baker said, and then gave Pax a box of cookies on the house.

For a while he slept in the park. Now he was staying with Ricky Maroon, a guy he'd met during a pickup game of basketball. It was a good arrangement. Ricky was lonely, a talker, needed someone else's presence, needed for his own incessant chatter to reach someone's ears. He gave Pax the spare couch in his little apartment in exchange for Pax's nodding company. He served Pax plates of meatloaf and mashed potatoes, beer. For dessert there was a saucer spread with maraschino cherries and a couple stale cookies, like in a Chinese restaurant.

Ricky had decided he was a poet. It was his calling, and since he'd accepted it he said he felt two hundred percent more alive. He was stocky, with black uncombed hair, a uniform of hiking boots, cutoff jeans, polyester short-sleeved shirts like math teachers wear. He carried a notebook in his front pocket, a bitten pencil behind his ear. The meatloaf was dry, the beer cheap, but somehow this sharpened the pleasure. It had been so long since Pax had a home, since someone else made sure he had a beer in his hand and a clean blanket and some socks.

"Let me read you a poem. Hey buddy. Can I read you a poem?"

It was six o'clock in the morning. Late July.

Pax, in his underwear, reclined on Ricky's yellow velour sofa. Yellow light burned through a window shade made fragile by the sun; a single touch would disintegrate it, so it stayed down all day. A spider plant hung from a hook in the ceiling, its leaves the color of burlap. Ricky knelt on the floor next to the couch. Pax could smell his dandruff shampoo in the room's awful heat.

Pax yawned. "What time is it? Maybe later?"

But Ricky had already begun to read: "It's too late for the boogeyman. He's come, gone. Leather face, faux-jeweled eyes, won't bother you. So keep your superstitions. Petty inklings. Faith. Even the monsters are done with you. He came to your window. He saw you sleep. Your drool didn't stir him. He said: Your dreams are free. And you woke and said: Oh God. Come back."

Pax said, "Come *back*?"

"Come back. Come back." Ricky stood, snapped his fingers. His knees were indented from the carpet, pink and pocked. Pax wondered how long he'd been kneeling there, watching him sleep.

"I used to worry like hell about the boogeyman," Ricky said. "I used to fear everything supernatural. *Damn* I wish I could be like that again. Now what do I worry about? That there's no such thing as the boogeyman. That's worse. If there's no boogeyman there's no god to save you from him. You want some juice or something?"

Pax said yes. Ricky went to the kitchen, returned with a jug of grapefruit juice, no cup, a pack of cigarettes and an ashtray. He lit a cigarette, gulped some juice from the jug, but didn't offer any to Pax.

"I was dreaming about a girl," Pax heard himself say.

"It goes on—" Ricky read: "It's too late for the boogeyman.

Too late for the rheumy goblin. Rotten-toothed zombie. Were-wolf with his too-tight dungarees. Erection."

"Erection?" Pax said. "That came out of nowhere." But really the stranger word, he thought, was *dungarees*.

Pax rolled over.

"You want to get back to sleep? Get back to some girl? Huh?" Ricky pressed a fist to Pax's head, moved it around a little.

It was true. He wanted to get back to a girl. But he didn't want to ruin this thing with Ricky, this—what would you call it?—home life.

"No. I want to hear more. Keep reading."

"That's all I have. It's not done yet."

Pax closed his eyes. He saw Leonora's face, that poor missing girl, her bangs. It was always most clear to him just as he was waking up.

Ricky said, "Yesterday I saw the loveliest chick walking down McGregor. Asian. A little girl, and she was smoking a cigarette. No hips. No tits."

In Pax's dream Leonora had matted hair. She'd lost one of the barrettes. Her lips were chapped.

"I said to her, 'Can I buy you a cup of tea?' I was perfectly pleasant. I was nothing but a gentleman, Pax. And you know what she said? She said, 'I don't drink tea.'"

Pax knew it was a terrible poem, that it wasn't a poem at all, just a cluster of urgent insomniac words battened together with spit.

"Girls these days. They expect everything plus twenty," said Ricky. "I used to think it'd be better out in Utah. Have a whole bunch. Now the thought of just one gives me heartburn." He tipped his head back, smoked his cigarette like a man onstage. No one knew how vain he was: he put hairspray in his eyebrows to keep them in place. He plucked the hairs that grew around his nipples, examined the pores on his nose with a special magnifying mirror. "You ever been in love?" Ricky asked. "The whole shebang?"

Pax didn't answer.

"Not me. Not me. Not ever. It's a shame. I have a lot to offer." He stubbed out his cigarette and lit another. He said, "You need a little boogeyman inside you to fall in love."

5

The girl's mother was right there, on a park bench, knitting. He said hello. Her clothes were elegant but wrinkled. The hems of her pants were damp. It was early morning but already hot. The radio warned of a scorcher.

"Hello," Pax said again.

"Good morning." She did not look up. She was knitting a sweater. Its sleeve, a ghostly pendulum, swayed above her lap. Pax straightened up. He hadn't brushed his teeth.

"I know you." He couldn't help it. He felt a rush of panic, as if meeting a celebrity. "On TV. I saw you." A star. He was flummoxed, wet-palmed. A star. But she was not a star.

"You're her mother."

"You've got the wrong person."

"Leonora."

He didn't mean to say it. His blood swam behind his eyes. It was like giving away a secret. One couldn't say the name. Not like this, not in the sunshine, not while the woman was knitting. She was trying to be a normal person making a normal thing out of yarn. Saying the girl's name was uncouth, pitiless—worse than asking her for an autograph. And yet—*not* saying the name, wasn't this a crime too? He wasn't sure. The dead, the gone, they want their names to be spoken. The living can't bear it. Or maybe it's the other way around? He didn't know. Only after he spoke the girl's name did the mother look up from the yarn. She narrowed her eyes. Then, lulling and cruel, she said, "If you have something of relevance to say, go ahead. Otherwise leave me alone."

Her needles clicked in time. Her glasses were perched on top of her head. Pink pearls glistened in her earlobes. He was pretty sure he stank. He felt a sudden, tremendous, galvanizing hunger. He said too loudly, "Let me buy you a hamburger." For a moment he held hope that he'd found the one thing that could satisfy the great mouth of her loss. "Can I do that for you?"

The needles stopped moving.

"I detest meat." She closed her eyes. "Meat is a crime. The last time I ate a hamburger was in 1982."

Never in his life had he been in possession of anything relevant to say.

She opened her eyes again. "You want to know something? You want to know what I think?"

He said he did.

"I think people are lunatics. Kids go missing. You know this. You watch the news. You see the poor parents. You see the picture of the poor kid. You think: *What lunatic is responsible?* You focus the lunacy on the one who took her. The rest of the world is okay. You do this; I did it. Right? Don't answer. But then, when it happens to you, your kid . . ."

She looked at him with dull expectancy. He wasn't sure if he was supposed to speak.

"You get letters," she said. "Accusations. Weirdos calling on the phone. Packages of voodoo dolls. Stick this pin here. Eat this herb. Say these words. Abracadabra shazam goddamn. Praise the moon. Praise the goddess praise Jesus praise the FBI. Never mind the strangers who want to search for her. You know what I say? I say it's lunacy everywhere. I say damn the church. Damn the helpers. Their armbands. Their weird patience. They want to be assured their own girls don't get stolen. It's an insurance policy, their help. Damn them all, every one of them, and damn you too."

Then she resumed knitting.

"Damn me," he said weakly. He felt light-headed and shamed.

She said, "A man who wants to buy me a hamburger, for example."

"I don't want to give you anything," he said. "I'm sorry. I'm leaving now."

But he did not move.

He said, "Forgive me."

She flushed. He thought she might yell. Then, shrugging: "I am hungry, actually."

"Really?"

"In 1982 I got some kind of worm. I puked for days."

"A salad."

"You offered a burger," she said, "I'm taking a burger," and she went back to her sweater.

He ran to a restaurant half a block away, bought two cheese-burgers, fries. He spent nearly the last of his cash. When he returned to the bench she was gone. He sat where she'd sat. He was hungry, wanted to eat the food, but that would be wrong. It wasn't his. Eating her food, it would have been like touching her.

Traffic blurred on the avenue. The sun throbbed. The skin of his face felt stretched too tight—his nose had burnt, peeled, was burning again. He wondered what happened to the girl and if there had been a witness. It was better if there was a witness. One can't be one's own witness. That's often the belief, that one can split oneself and watch and later, coolly, fairly, tell the tale. But it wasn't true. One needed someone else. It was especially important if one was dead.

He hadn't just come upon her mother. That was a lie. He'd gone to her apartment building, which was not too far from Ricky's. No, that wasn't true either. He'd taken three trains and walked five blocks. He'd gone there, stood before the brownstone, saw the purple peace-sign sticker in the window. He'd watched her emerge. He'd followed her to the park, where she lifted her face to the sun and stepped like a bold child into the fountain. Then she'd selected a bench. The grace of her hands on those knitting needles baffled him. Why did he feel his fate mingled intimately with hers? Why was he consumed by thoughts of her child? His dreams were mostly awful and not annihilated by daylight. Usually they showed the girl bleeding, her forehead slashed, but he didn't fully trust them, because twice they showed her waiting for a train, and once holding a fishing rod, once on a clean white bed in only her panties.

He returned to the apartment building three days later, watched the mother descend the steps. Now she was wearing a pink dress with billowing sleeves, sandals with straps that wound up the ankles. She bought a hot dog at a sidewalk vendor. She took a bite, chewed, and spit it onto the street.

6

Ricky ruined the couch. It was an accident, he said. He must have dropped a hot cigarette butt between the cushions. The couch smoldered all afternoon; it smelled poisonous. They dumped water and baking soda on the cushions.

"I guess I'll sleep on the floor," Pax said.

"Naw, I've got a big old island of a bed."

Pax hesitated.

"I insist," said Ricky. His grin revealed his gums.

Pax dreaded the wafting smell of dandruff shampoo. He feared Ricky's hand alighting, in the brief incidental manner of an insect, on his hip. At the same time, it had been years since he'd slept in a bed with a person, since he'd lain with another human being on a proper mattress, on a set of sheets, in a room designated for sleep. He was touched by this man's generosity.

He remembered his namesake, the Pax on the bus, placid, stoic Pax, who would have accepted the invitation.

They lay on their backs, untouching. The heat wave was crippling the city. It was a couple hours past sunset. The delicately oppressive scent of ozone lingered. Through open windows they heard traffic in the distance, the bullfrog bleat of tractor-trailer horns, and, closer, electric guitar music. There had been a baseball game on the radio; the city's team beat their rival by a landslide. Intermittently a gloating cheer rose to meet them from the street below. It was a queen-size bed, with soft, threadbare blankets, though it was too hot to lie under them. Ricky wore his cutoffs. Pax wore jeans and a damp t-shirt, which he'd run under the faucet. They'd each had several beers. Pax felt slackened, clammy, and loosened by these drinks and by the landslide victory and by the dim noise of the city. He said, "I'm kind of thinking a lot, quite a bit actually, about that missing girl."

Ricky grunted. "Who's that?" He was chewing on a toothpick.

"That girl, Leonora. Leonora Marie Coulter. That one."

"Pretty thing, right? They say she's probably dead. Nine out of ten, they're dead."

"That's what they say?"

"That or smuggled to Thailand. But then again, kids run off. You know, my sister Trish ran off for a while. They come back. Or they don't."

An ambulance sped down the street. Its siren, the inconsequential dire nature of it, triggered a seizing in Pax's gut.

"Mexico maybe. Caught up in one of those rings, high on smack. My sister went to California with her dumbass boyfriend. She called a couple weeks later."

"Smack. I hope not. I don't think she's in Mexico."

"Or some kind of pills, maybe, uppers. Get more work out of the girls. My sister called from a phone booth. She was pregnant. She called when her boyfriend ditched her. My dad wired her money for a train back home, but she used it for an abortion instead."

"Huh."

Ricky snickered. "My idiot parents."

"She's just a kid."

"Naw, she was nineteen."

"I mean Leonora. She's twelve. That's all."

"It doesn't really matter how old. You're never too young to get chewed up."

"I feel like I'm meant to do something. Why do I feel that way?"

"Because you're a big old softy. You feel for all people. I used to be like that, but I quit. I quit it for poetry."

"What if she was the one? The girl I was meant to marry."

Ricky flicked his toothpick across the room. "You believe in that kind of thing?"

Pax didn't know. He wanted to see what would happen if he said it.

They were silent then. The siren grew fainter and fainter. Pax wondered what person was lying in the back of that ambulance. Perhaps they'd found Leonora—trapped in an elevator shaft, legs broken. Or sooty, beaten, crawling out of the subway on her hands and knees. Of course it wasn't Leonora, just another soul hurtling through the city.

"I've been thinking about talent," Ricky announced. "I'm a poet, right. But do I have talent?"

"Sure you do."

"It was a hypothetical question."

"Sorry."

"You're right, though. But it doesn't matter. Talent's just a platform. The question isn't can you find the platform but: Are you willing to jump? I'm standing on the platform. I've got that far. But that far is trivial. That far means nothing . . . What are you doing?"

Pax gripped his hands together. He tensed his legs. "I feel like I'm meant to save her."

"The girl? Oh man. That's rough. You're a wounded little pilgrim, aren't you? But don't blame yourself. There are far worse things to be."

"What's worse?"

"A poet." He faked a laugh.

Maybe she was in an elevator somewhere. Maybe she had starved to death in a broken elevator, the bones in her hands fractured from pounding. Maybe she was stuffed in a garbage bag, in one of the millions of dumpsters of this city, or sleeping soundly in the back of a station wagon under the country stars. Maybe she was happy. On safari, binoculars strung around her slender neck, a zebra grazing nearby. Or sitting by some harbor. Maybe she was eating clams from a plastic basket. Maybe Pax had taken her himself. Maybe she was in a river. Pale fish nosing her knees. Maybe he'd put her there.

Ricky said, "Will I jump from the platform? That's the question. Do I dare jump?"

"You will," said Pax, not caring at all.

When Pax had disappeared, his mother had not hung signs. His mother had not gone to the news stations. She'd done nothing. He was gone. He had vanished. He became, immediately, a ghost, for what is a ghost but a being no one expects to see walk the earth again? It is a shock, a sign of ill nature, when one sees a ghost. No one expected to see Pax, and so no one did. Maybe he'd done it. This would explain his shame, the little knife of guilt he'd carried with him all along, on all those buses, all those roads, state by state. Our acts are waiting for us.

"I need a cigarette," Ricky said. "Did I hurt your feelings? You're a wounded pilgrim. A bleeding heart. So what? I like that about you."

Pax said nothing. The lighter clicked and rasped. Ricky puffed.

Had she seen fit to report his disappearance, what would his mother have told the newscaster? He was last seen wearing jeans, a plain white T-shirt. Tube socks with orange bands at the calves. An expression of the faintest concern, always. A fisherman's bracelet of braided rope, on his left wrist. His hands were soft, slender, a bit girlish. He liked books about aliens. He liked books about unsolved mysteries, vanished ships, ESP. He liked cheesecake. He liked spice gumdrops. He was a good baseball player. He had a white scar at the base of his ribs, shaped like a dagger, from falling into a rosebush as a small child. He enjoyed sour cream and bananas. He was too skinny. He was polite. He was last seen. He is prone to. He should be approached with. He may be. But his mother made no report.

Ricky said, "Maybe she just ran away."

"I think she was taken."

"Who knows? No one. It doesn't matter anyway. In the long run, there's not much difference."

"There's a big difference."

"In the long run it doesn't matter, I'm saying."

"In any run it matters."

Ricky blew smoke through clenched teeth. "It amounts to the same thing. For the people left behind. Not for the girl, I suppose. Yes, for the girl there's a difference. But for the rest of us it amounts to just about the same thing, I'm afraid."

"You're wrong," said Pax.

Ricky touched Pax's ribs. He walked his fingers up Pax's side, pushed his fingertips into the wet hollow of Pax's armpit. It was what Pax feared, but it made him sink into his joints. He said Ricky's name.

"Yeah?"

"Ricky," he said it again, louder.

"I'm right here, man."

Pax said, "I might need a little help figuring some things out. I don't know what's going on."

"Nothing's going on, my friend. Nothing at all." And with a yawn, "It's hot. It better rain. Nothing else."

It all felt real, all of it. That was the problem. Everything felt real, including what he knew for sure wasn't: graduating high school, the party his mother might have thrown him, a barbecue, balloons, a handful of guests complaining about mosquitoes, his loudmouth stepfather and that dude from the bar with his accordion and gym shorts and Jade Grant—why not?—in a cotton sundress, a boom box playing songs of love and good news. But there hadn't been a party. Some things had happened and some things had not. He knew the difference.

His skin was slick, and Ricky was touching him.

7

Ricky wanted, for all intents and purposes, to fuck him. On first glance, Pax wasn't his type. But as you got to know him, his overcompensating manners, his weird, almost senseless patience—it changed your mind. He was handsome, as it turned out. He had a strong nose. He was thin, sinewy.

They lay in silence, Ricky's gut bloated from the beer. Electric guitar licks rang out, faded, rang again, an adolescent's talentless tirade against his parents who would not be able to sleep in the room next door, whose father would finally rise from bed, unplug the guitar, threaten loss of allowance or love or some other privilege. Ricky wanted to fuck Pax, but he hadn't taken Pax in for this reason. The desire had risen slowly. He'd been here five weeks. It happened over time. So many languorous evenings drinking beers and listening to ball games, so many glimpses of Pax biting his thumbnail with pinched-faced concentration, or blathering about the dead girl, or drooling on the arm of the couch in his sleep—they had the effect of softening Ricky to him, and also, conversely, making him want to throttle the guy. Pax was strange. He was rootless. He had weird fixations, and he knew nothing about himself. This endeared him to Ricky, and it annoyed him too, Pax's lack of insight, his superhuman naïveté. The guy had to be nearing thirty. He was a grown person, bright, he'd read the right books. Age certainly doesn't predict self-knowledge, but it usually predicts some awareness of lack of self-knowledge. Pax wasn't aware of the fog, of that dense, ever-gathering cloud, enclosing his very head. Ricky both admired and feared this. Ricky wanted to kiss his neck, his honker of a nose, possibly his mouth.

He regretted speaking of his sister. Why had he done that? He had not spoken of his sister in years. He had not written about her either, even when a poem seemed to demand it. He was afraid of the images that would emerge. The poem about her would be bad or, worse, it would be good.

"You awake?"

Pax didn't respond.

Ricky said, "It does matter, all right? What happens to the girl—what happened—it matters enough. Also, forget I said anything about my sister. Can you do that?"

"I'd already forgotten."

"And forget about that girl while you're at it. You want to torment yourself. You look for avenues of torment. She doesn't exist. She can by no means be saved."

Pax said nothing, but Ricky perceived new gravity in his breathing, a meaning in its rhythm that wasn't there before. Ricky put his hand on Pax's stomach.

He said, "I'm going to write a poem about you, but I'll give you a different name. Yours is very cool, man, and loaded with meaning and strong and all, but it doesn't quite fit. You're a Jack, maybe, something classic. In my poem, I'll call you 'Jack,' and I'll say: *He held his sadness the way big men hold their booze,* something to that effect. And I'll get your mouth in there too. Your chewed thumbnail. Your suitcase, I may conclude with that; it's a strong image, that beat-up suitcase, old clothes, everything mismatched, worn to the nub. Or your fantastic shoes. Your shoes are ridiculous, by the way, with all that tape. They may really be too much for the poem. I have an old pair you can have. I may say: *He was a man without a razor.* I know you use my razor, Pax, and that's fine, I don't have a problem with that. *He was a man without a razor or a bar of soap or a scrap of history.* It's fine that you use my soap as well. What's mine is yours. But what I'm trying to get at is that I won't mention this girl. You're stuck on her because it suits some unwell purpose. It's a kind of elaborate distraction. She's a red herring. I'm saying she doesn't belong in the poem."

Pax rolled over to face Ricky and, in one impulsive motion— the motion of one who's suddenly flattered, who feels the thrill and burden of flattery, who must act in this moment if it's to happen at all—Pax kissed Ricky on the mouth.

For a second Ricky felt surprised, but then he thought: *Why are you pretending to be surprised?*

Their teeth clicked. The sound to Ricky's ears was the click of two glasses, the chime of a toast. Their kiss felt like that, a toast, awkward and full of appetite. *Oh man,* thought Ricky, *oh man oh man.* But he was surprised. He knew it would happen, hoped it would happen, but the Pax who was kissing him, the Pax who had made this sudden move, was not the same man who'd been whimpering next to him five minutes ago. Something had shifted between then, and Ricky was glad, but he was also aware that it could shift back just as fast. The kid next door who before strummed meaninglessly now played a hit by Roger Ranger. Pax was making these high, churning sounds, similar to laughter, close, but not laughter, Ricky realized, not laughter at all.

"I've done this before," Pax said.

Ricky pulled away, chuckled warily. "I thought so."

"With a boy." Pax pressed his face into Ricky's neck. "I've done this."

"I had a hunch."

Pax burrowed further into Ricky's neck. Ricky thought he was trying to get closer, to declare some kind of intimacy, but then Pax said, again, sorrowfully, "I've *done* this," and Ricky realized that he was trying to hide.

"All right already," Ricky said. "We've done it. We're sick. We're delicious."

"With Gideon Booth."

"Yes," said Ricky. "I've done it before too. It's okay."

He patted Pax's back in what he hoped was a friendly, assuring manner, rubbed his ropy spine, his narrow waist.

"My mother came in." Pax spoke hotly into Ricky's neck. "She found us. Me and Gideon. He had a rat-tail. His hair had a rat-tail I mean. He was a kid. He was a nice kid. No, he wasn't nice. He was cruel."

"My mother saw me once, too," Ricky said. "She was a spy. She looked. She asked for it. She wanted to see, no matter what she says."

"And Gideon said, 'Hello Missus—' but he didn't know my last name. He said 'Hello Missus, uh, Missus.' I thought he knew my name. My mother did something stupid."

"Yeah, what's that?"

Pax rammed his lips into Ricky's chest. "She called my step-father in."

"Shit, kid. Stop biting me."

"My stepfather came. My stepfather broke Gideon's neck."

"His neck! No shit."

They were still for a moment.

Ricky said, "No he didn't. I don't believe you."

"His collarbone."

"Fine, his collarbone. I'll buy that."

Ricky felt bracingly alert, a little nervous. He listened to Pax's startled breath.

Ricky said, "My mother pretended it never happened. Fine. Fine with me. My dick in Claude Sullivan's mouth, there's an image for the mama. There's one for the scrapbook. But it never happened, she says."

"It never happened," Pax said.

"Never."

Ricky extricated himself from Pax's hold. The air hosted a new smell: Pax's sweat. Ricky recognized it as fear sweat, that peculiar spikiness belonging to fistfights and alleys and fucking in bars and under bridges with people whom one isn't supposed to fuck. It was a sour, ringing smell. Ricky inhaled, pleased that he could inspire that kind of perspiration.

"I once had a rat-tailed haircut, too," Ricky said. "Ugly as sin."

The boy next door was not really playing Roger Ranger. He had turned on his stereo and, in the mirror, mimed the lead guitarist, fingers hovering above the strings. He was growing his hair out. Soon his father would confiscate the stereo. The losing baseball team's bus was rumbling down a dark highway, moving further from the city. In dark windows the players pretended not to look at themselves.

8

ideon was a head taller than Paul. This is when Pax was
still Paul, sixteen, still a kid who hoarded spiced gumdrops
and read books about ESP. Gideon didn't read books. He had
no sweet tooth. Olive-skinned, with wavy brown hair and a lan-
tern jaw, he brought to mind an Olympian. He had a casual,
innate grace, walked with a fast loping stride, backpack slung
over one shoulder. His hair was neatly trimmed save for a wispy
braid, the rat-tail, which fell nearly to his shoulder blades. Gideon
had said, "Hey Paul, you want to study for that biology test
together or what?" as if they often spent their afternoons
together, study partners, when in fact they seldom spoke. Paul
wasn't even planning on studying but he agreed. "Your house,"
Gideon announced. He didn't smile.

After school they walked together in silence, past the church,

Gizmo's Video Palace, the eyeglass shop, then stopped at the
Come & Go for red vines and sodas. Finally they turned onto
Route 22, walked on the muddy shoulder, and then stepped over
the guardrail and onto the clotted path, the shortcut that led to
the cottage where Paul lived with his mother and stepfather. The
path was a mess. Most of its litter was Paul's doing—soda cans,
candy bar wrappers, bits of Styrofoam, crumpled magazine
pages, scratch-off tickets. His English teacher called him "tenderheart"; he wanted to show that he wasn't, *not at all, not at all!*
so he discarded a thing a day, devoted himself to this petty crime,
a potato chip bag, a lollipop stick, until the trash overwhelmed
the thicket. Was he tenderheart? Gideon didn't seem to notice
the litter. They walked in silence. Paul, made nervous by Gideon's
cool expression and swift pace, by the murderous way he had
guzzled the soda, finally said, "So what about Jade Grant?"

Gideon sighed. "Who the hell's that?" Then: "What about
her?"

"I heard she's pregnant."

"I don't care a lick about Jade or her fetus." He kept his eyes
straight ahead, increased his stride. Paul struggled to keep up.

"I don't care about her either." But Paul did care. He thought
of her often, all the time. He wondered who impregnated her,
and when and where, and imagined possessing the kind of power
she did. How could Gideon not care? Everyone cared. They
watched her with new attention, gave her a wide berth in the
hall, studied her belly and boobs and the hold of her face. In
algebra, Paul watched her sigh as she completed her equations,
watched her wind a hank of glossy red hair around her index
finger. She finished her worksheets before everyone else, then
examined her fingernails, the veins of her wrists. Sometimes she

doodled on her hand, or shoe, or just stared at the wall clock, stared hard, as if her gaze, if applied right, might set it on fire.

The cottage was empty, his stepfather at the plastics plant, his mother at the bowling alley. They went inside. Gideon surveyed the cramped rooms. He touched each object on the mantelpiece, touched the hem of the robin's-egg tablecloth, ran a finger along the spines of the books.

"Who reads these books?"

"My mom. The romances. The others are my stepfather's."

"Crappy books, huh?"

He picked up the model schooner that occupied the place of honor on the mantel.

"My stepfather made that."

"It's not very good."

"Yeah—well. I guess not."

"No one knows how to make anything anymore." Then: "Chinese machines, they know how to make things. *Robots*."

"The sail is torn. It's been sewn up. I ripped it."

He'd been punished for that. He'd been flipped over his stepfather's knee. He'd been too old for spanking, fourteen, but it worked: he hadn't touched the model since.

Gideon examined it with vague disdain. "Shitty," he said.

It was thrilling to have a veritable stranger in the house, and for this stranger to say things that Paul himself could never say.

"Just put it back, man, yeah? He's funny about that thing."

Gideon replaced it carelessly. Its bow edged off the shelf.

They went upstairs to Paul's room; Gideon collapsed on the bed, his head on Paul's pillow, like it was his own room. Paul stood by the doorway. He was embarrassed by the painting that hung over his bed—a soulful clown holding a parasol. His mother had bought it at a tag sale. Gideon didn't seem to notice it. He said, "You got any music?"

There were some cassette tapes in a shoebox, but Paul didn't want Gideon going through them. He pressed Play on the tape recorder—the song was a ballad, sappy, about being stuck on a person, about a feeling down deep in your soul. It wasn't what he wanted to hear. Gideon chuckled, pulled himself up on his elbows, said, "You like the mitochondria? You good at biology?"

"I'll pass it, I guess."

"I got a D on the last quiz. Mister Mason can fuck me sideways."

Paul gathered his materials together, notepad, textbook, a couple pens. He sat on the floor, his back to the wall.

"The body," Gideon sighed. "I guess the body's fine. It's when you go too far inside it. I like the outside stuff. I like the pores. I can go so far as the blood. But dendrites? Ribophones? Who cares about that shit. People worry way too much about what's invisible. People want to name every last piece of dust."

"Ribosomes," Paul said.

Gideon grinned. "I knew I picked the right study partner."

Paul nervously started to describe cell function. Then Gideon got off the bed, sprawled out on the floor in front of him. He lay on his side, propped on an elbow—he flicked a dust bunny under the bed, said, "You got yourself a girlfriend?"

"No," Paul said.

They were the same age, but the way Gideon asked the question, the effort he took to keep a straight face, the implicit mockery—Paul felt like he was being ribbed by a rude uncle. But then Gideon said, "Me neither," and this came out earnestly, even sadly, and he put a finger on the button of Paul's pants. He said, "Me neither, man."

Gideon's finger moved from the button of Paul's pants to the fabric of his crotch. He said, "This your dick or a nut?" It was the same toneless, vaguely irritated voice he'd used to say *dendrites* or *ribophones*.

"My dick," Paul whispered.

"Cool." Gideon glanced at his own groin, shrugged. "I got two meatballs and a cocktail wiener."

Paul could say nothing.

"Let me," Gideon said.

Paul's blood rushed to meet Gideon's hand. He felt his stomach drop, felt his mouth go dry, felt—did not hear as much as feel—a series of words tumble from his mouth. The faint pressure of the words, their lightness in his throat—they emerged, one by one, to the same rhythm that Gideon's hand worked the fabric. But they weren't words. They were sounds, syllables, articles: *oh—the—buh—ah—sah—an—the—*

Gideon went about it with a certain sighing duty, like a kid forced to clap erasers. "Wait," Paul managed to say.

Gideon stopped. "You gonna come?"

Paul couldn't answer.

Gideon said, "Endoplasmic Reticulum. Is that what we're waiting for?"

Paul heard something downstairs. Or was he being paranoid? The boom box sang *I wonder where you are, I wonder what you do.*

"I mean, is that your idea of a good time? Golgi bodies? Say so if it is. Say the word and I'll stop."

"Don't stop."

When Gideon undid Paul's pants, yanked his zipper, Paul experienced a moment of panic. Gideon would mock his dick. But Gideon said nothing. His face maintained its indolence. He put his mouth on Paul. He went and went. Paul's own mouth, now, was empty, free of words, syllables, articles. His brain was empty. He felt as if he'd been opened, as if someone had opened him up and removed everything, blood and bones, the whole soup of him. He felt a terrible, consuming lightness. Then the door opened.

Someone took the name of the lord in vain. Someone else laughed. It was hard to know which person made which sound. The whole of his life would spin around this moment. What a stupid moment it was! Being so light, so empty, it was hard to get to his feet. He staggered. His vision blurred. His hand was buzzing, numb, couldn't manage the zipper. Someone said, *That's the end of the road,* or maybe it's what he thought, or what someone else thought, the moment was so wholly crude and exposing it would not have surprised him to hear another's private thoughts. His dick hung out. His heart battered his rib cage. His mother—why was she so stupid?—called out his stepfather's name.

Even when Gideon left, clutching his collarbone, his body rigid with pain, even then he looked bored. On his way to the door he stopped at the mantel. With the hand that wasn't holding his collarbone he swatted the model ship to the floor. He didn't close the door behind him, just strutted away, a gambler, strides long and calm. Paul's mother was holding her neck, both hands gripping it, as if strangling herself. His stepfather, who smelled like plastics, like a new shower curtain, whose hair was oiled and face seemed gentle but who was not gentle, looked at Paul as if about to scream, opened his mouth, but this time he did not scream. He closed his mouth. He returned the broken ship to the mantel. It was only a matter of time before Paul ran. His stepfather wanted him out. His mother, too, though she didn't know this or couldn't say it. When she came to his bedroom some nights later, pressed her hand to his forehead, to his mouth, when he could see her breasts through her nightgown and could smell the sweat under her perfume, what else could she have wanted but for him to get out of there? She kissed his face, his cheeks, forehead, eyelids. The kisses were fast and hard and not tender. It was how one kisses a baby. It was how a new mother, unsure if she likes her infant, kisses him, an attempt to generate tenderness, to prove the child, to prove herself, worthy. Every kiss said *Get out*. Every kiss said *Go on go on go on go*. Her breasts brushed across his chest. This is what a boy does. Not that. This. And this. "Get out of here," he said, but she wouldn't. He couldn't push her away. She was his mother.

"Oh Paul. Paulie," she murmured. "I wanted so much for you. I hoped so much. We all did. You were the only one. We hoped so much," like he was dead.

He said, "I'm not dead."

9

But his mother wasn't stupid. Or if she was stupid she had willed it upon herself, it made things simpler. It made it easier to marry the new man, to stand at the altar in a dress with a bodice like a pile of suds, to pretend that she had not overheard that bitch waitress Felicia say under her breath, "Wearing white, huh?" Being stupid allowed her to stand at the altar and look at her betrothed's falsely gentle face, to kiss lightly his pale, too-small mouth and accept his word that he'd care for her forever. She wanted to be cared for. It wasn't unreasonable. Helplessness had been bred into her, she knew this, just as plants are bred for different characteristics—height, color, juiciness of their fruit, whatever. She had been bred to be helpless, which had its advantages, which, at its best, was like living as though you were always being carried by a happy groom over a threshold; and at its worst—but that wasn't worth thinking about. Paul was getting older. She needed a husband. Paul said to her, on her wedding day, "Are you sure about this?" He said it with such care, such patient, practical tenderness, like he was her mother. He was twelve. She had a benign growth in her uterus that now and then sent ribbons of pain down her legs. The doctor wasn't too worried. She had a phobia, too: she feared thunderstorms with the indomitable, righteous purity of those who will not ride in planes or enter elevators. She had given birth to Paul during a thunderstorm. Since that day, whenever she heard even faint thunder, whenever the air assumed a staticky, floral charge and the wind lifted the leaves and set their shadows upon the wall, she would bite her bottom lip and grip the nearest sturdy thing, preferably the hang bar in her closet. Her new husband scolded her: "Be a grown woman, love," or "Stop whimpering, love," or "Get that fat ass out of the closet, love." He added *love* to his harshest statements, and it worked. She nodded. She gathered herself. She stepped from the comfort of the closet, where the absolute darkness and laundry detergent smell kept her from remembering what it felt like when Paul was born, when his mushroom head tore her apart.

She had held him in the damp crook of her arm. His face was like a sheet of balled-up paper. "All babies look like that," said an aunt by the bedside, knitting booties of contemptuous green. The power flickered all afternoon. Thunder snapped like a leather belt. The baby was ugly. She had wanted so badly a girl. The next baby, who was stillborn and a girl, appeared on an afternoon of fierce sunshine and blue sky, but his mother did not come to fear these kinds of days. She told Paul this set of facts in an unblinking manner, a manner of *See what I have done for you?* A manner of *You have taken more than your share, but I'll forgive you.* She stroked his hair as she said it. She came to want him. She made it clear. She hadn't always wanted him, but now she did. It was like a parable, he thought. It was not a life but a tale.

10

He felt Ricky's prick on his thigh. It was surprisingly light, unsure, in the way of an empty puppet. He heard a moan emerge from his mouth—his mouth which had been open from the start, which had found the shape of the moan and been waiting to expel it. There was a certain uncomplicated familiarity, as between old friends. Ricky wore the expression of a person trying to find a word in a foreign language. A soft rain began. A single word rang though Pax's body, and of all things it was a girl's name. Nights like these permit one to believe in fate. At once he had a path. It was his. This night was part of it, and Ricky's prick was part of it, and Leonora, and her mother. Gideon had a rat-tail. That gas station attendant Burt what's-his-name had a tattoo of a lion on his pectoral. He never touched Burt. The original Pax, his namesake, had a book about beekeepers and lesbians and a perfect voice and a better name, but he had never touched him either. Never Burt or Pax or Ed or Ray, who offered to pay for it, or Donald, who took him clamming. He had always said no. The rain picked up. The city was desperate for it. He had never been quite as at peace, nor as lonely, and he said so. He said a few more things. He said something, stupidly, about having sex with a woman in his old house, about the way it had freed him for this, prepared him, as a pan is cured for cooking. Then he said he'd once loved a girl named Jade, that as kids he and the girl had been accosted in the woods by a crazy Christian, that years later he'd tracked her down—Jade, not the Christian—that he'd made some phone calls and learned she was married and a neurosurgeon and living in a great European capital. A goddamned neurosurgeon! He'd never felt more proud or more alone. Now she was gone. Everyone was gone. And yet knowing she was a neurosurgeon, knowing that his glorious red-headed nymph worked inside people's heads! Stared at their minds! It gave him a wild sense of hope; it made him big and dizzy with loss. He said he'd once had a job making fruit pyramids. He said he loved his mother, loved her still, always, but that she'd probably never forgive him for leaving. He said a few sentimental things. He quoted a German philosopher. He was trying everything out. He bucked beneath the poet. Then he was still. He screamed. He was trying everything. He spoke with a husky, affected bravado, like a bad actor, and then with a whine.

"Shut up," said Ricky, "can you manage that?"

"Be kind," Pax begged.

"That's not what you need."

It was true. That wasn't it.

11

The newspaper said *Missing Girl Found Dead in Lot* and, below this, *Grand Slam for the Good Guys*. Pax read both articles through. A taste in his mouth like orange rind. He read them again. The catcher had hit the grand slam. Leonora had been wrapped in industrial carpet. Perpetrator unknown. No leads yet. He spit into the sink but the taste remained. He wanted to run to her mother's home. He wanted to see her mother, whom he loved. But what comfort could he provide the mother? None. Absolutely none. "Good morning," Ricky said. "Sleep well?"

He needed to get on a bus. He wouldn't find a wife here. He would not find a wife anywhere. He stood in the kitchen, arms loose, his face dim and resigned, as a man stands before a heartless judge. Sticky linoleum beneath his feet. Ricky, small and dense and bloated, looked upon him in a faintly admonishing manner.

"Bad news about the girl," Ricky said. He was leaning back in a kitchen chair, shirtless, smoking a cigarette. "I really thought she'd run away. Most of them run."

She was dead. He'd known it all along. His certainty, his fixation, all his visions and dreams, these were like proof of his guilt. Then last night, in Ricky's bed—it was like he had given up on her and she had known. It was like he had willed it. There was still sleep in his eyes but now he was wide awake. He said, "I did it."

"Yeah?" Ricky blew smoke out of one side of his mouth. "That's sure some news."

Pax said it again.

Ricky laughed dully. "Oh buddy, you're one guilty son-of-a."

Pax gathered his things.

"Delusions of grandeur, my man." He was still laughing. "I saved you some toast."

"I have to go."

"Sure, sure. Coffee first?"

"But thank you for everything."

The laughter stopped. "Don't be a fool, Pax. And don't you dare thank me. Don't you dare, man."

Pax shook his head. "My name isn't even Pax."

"I don't care what on earth your name is. You think your name tells me who you are? You thought you could hide behind a phony name?"

He considered it. "I don't know."

"Poor thing," Ricky said, with gentleness. "I know you better than you know yourself."

Pax packed his suitcase. Where was his belt? It was nowhere. He looked everywhere, ran around the apartment, sweating, heart pounding, found it finally under the stinking yellow couch.

12

Pax discovered the heat wave had broken. The air was newly fresh. He walked past children on stoops. He walked past pretty women in high heels, a man belting words from the Bible in a spit-infused voice that reminded him of Ricky, that inspired—too soon—a burst of nostalgia. He walked faster. It was much, much too soon for nostalgia. Pansies and geraniums, wilted, flattened by rain, filled the city's million window boxes. He walked past many dogs, diners, hydrants, over subway grates and sleeping bums, past flower vendors and hot dog vendors and peanut vendors and magazine vendors, men selling wares with the same untroubled, wholesome greed they've had for thousands of years. Bottle tops and ticket stubs and a diffusion of broken glass, so much glimmering trash in the road, in the gutters, a rubber ball, a pink pacifier with a ribbon tied to it. All these relics of the world were lost to him, to them both, him and the girl. He paused before the precinct for a moment.

13

Joanna Coulter entered her son's bedroom. He was sitting on one of the twin beds, cross-legged, holding a tan plastic soldier in each hand. He made them crash into one another, on his face an expression of routine hostility. She sat on the spare bed. The room, she noticed, smelled odd. He was only eight, but a faint musk was palpable, a whiff of something fleshy, semisweet. It wasn't the smell of a child. On the wall above his bed hung a pennant of the city's baseball team. The curtains, which she had made by hand, were navy blue and patterned with yellow stars. When she said, "I have some bad news," he looked up. His face was puffy, small-eyed, tired.

"She's dead, huh?"

"I'm afraid so." The words in her mouth were hard, falsely small. She coughed, to put something between herself and them.

He played the words over again, quietly, in his own mouth.

Then he said, "What happened to her?"

She could not think of a word, not a single word. Her head flashed with color. Her hands found the tops of her thighs, squeezed.

"I mean did somebody hit her?"

Joanna worked on unclenching her hands. She worked on a word, just one, if she could get one word out it would return her to the world of words, to all of them. She inhaled. She said, "Yes." The boy nodded, smiled faintly, seemed somehow satisfied and disappointed both, smug, like he'd been told the secret of a magic trick. She didn't like the smile on his lips. Now there was a rush of words, they came easily, words to remove his smile, words which would be plaster on the wall between them and what happened. She told him she loved him so much. She told him she promised to take good care of him forever, and that they would go see a person called Doctor Grayson who would ask him to play in a sandbox, and she told him that they would always have Leonora in their hearts, and that he was allowed to say whatever he wanted, to cry, or not to cry, or to be mad, or not mad. The words were a wall, and on the other side of the wall was the crime, but also on the other side was Leonora. She wanted to be quiet now.

The boy made a circle with his thumb and forefinger, held it to his eye, like a spyglass. He made a little squeaking sound.

She said, "Let's get you some lunch."

"I've been farting in here," he admitted.

"That's okay."

"Poor Leonora."

She explained that there would be a funeral. Perhaps he could choose a favorite toy to put in her coffin, or he could write her a letter? He didn't seem interested in this. He tossed the plastic soldiers off the end of the bed. He lay down, crossed his arms neatly over his chest.

"Do I look like Dracula?"

"Yes."

"I bet she'll look like Dracula." He spoke with new hoarseness.

They didn't say anything else for a few moments. She heard the shower running in the bathroom down the hall. Her husband had been in there for nearly an hour. By now the water had to be cold. He would emerge shortly, pink and puckered.

"Will they catch him?"

Not a single moment of her life could prepare her for the question.

"I don't know."

"I don't understand," her son finally said.

She said, "I don't either."

"I don't get it."

"We will never get it."

"What I don't get is how she eats. If she's dead, she doesn't get dinner, right?"

"That's correct."

"How does she eat, then? Where does she get food?"

An image of lunch money flashed before Joanna's face, her hand pressing a bill into her daughter's hand. Usually she had denied Leonora dessert.

Joanna said, "Well, she doesn't need to eat."

"Oh right, dead people don't eat," as if he'd simply forgotten.

He seemed a little old not to understand this concept. Why had she even once refused the girl dessert?

"Did she go all at once or in pieces?" he asked then.

"What, honey?"

"When she died," he said. "Does a person die all at once or bit by bit?"

It wasn't a question she could answer, and she told him so. Suddenly he reached for her, took her shoulders, stiffly, uncertain, like a kid at a middle school dance. She took his shoulders too. They held each other this way for a while.

14

He climbed its stately granite steps. He stepped into a cool, white-walled room. *I swear, she didn't suffer,* something like that. *It was so fast. She didn't feel any pain.* He would make himself her witness, which is all anyone could hope to have. He stepped into that place of ringing phones, frosted glass, and ticking clocks. He understood how childish he was, how desperate to feel important, how much he longed to be something at once better and worse than himself. Yet this knowledge did not dilute his relief. The waiting room was full of plastic chairs, and in these chairs were people, wearing bold or bored or sleeping faces. A woman at the front desk, talking on the phone, placed her hand over the receiver and looked at him with uncanny warmth. He resented this immediately. He wanted no warmth. He wanted to be taken by the throat. He wanted a cell. He wanted someone to grab him so they could see how heavy his limbs were, how utterly without urge.

"I need to talk to a detective." He cleared his throat. "I have some information about a crime."

She smiled, took his name, asked him to sit. He took the last chair, between a young blonde woman and a dark-skinned man. Pax kept his eyes on the floor, its scuffed, pale green squares. Next to him, the woman's toes tapped the floor lightly. She wore white sandals, her toenails pastel pink. The man on his other side wore black wing tips; his feet were firmly planted. No one made any noise. Across from him a couple held hands. An old man in seersucker checked his watch every thirty seconds. It was impossible to imagine what they were all waiting for. Had they witnessed crimes? Were they waiting to bail out their friends? It was unlikely that they all had confessions to give, yet for a moment his stomach tightened and he felt immense anticipation, as if someone here would tread his terrain, would lay claim to the crime before he could. He tried to make eye contact with the receptionist, but she was still on the phone, writing something on a notepad.

"They tell me to wait, but I should be out looking," the woman next to him said softly. It took him a moment to realize she was speaking to him. "I think I should be out looking. That's what my gut tells me. A mother is supposed to trust her gut, right?"

Pax didn't want to talk to anyone. He nodded.

"My kid. He ran off. He's lost. I lost him."

"I'm sorry," Pax said.

She blotted her eyes with a tissue.

"He's so young. Just five. We're visiting, you know. From Indiana. Indiana is a lot simpler. Indiana doesn't smell like this." She had a moonish prettiness, bleached hair. Her mascara had bled.

Her bangs were tall, crisp with hairspray, like a small hood lifted by a breeze. "We were walking along. There was a crowd of people. Tourists. We're just tourists. We don't live here. Oh—do you live here?"

"No," Pax said.

"Then you won't be offended if I call it a hellhole, which it is."

"They'll find your son," Pax said.

She shook her head. "I've been here forever. It happened yesterday. I've been here the whole night."

The whole night, while the baseball game was played, while he and Ricky lay in Ricky's bed, while he and Ricky—call it by its name—fucked, while Leonora's body in the roll of carpet was dumped in that parking lot, this woman had been sitting in this plastic chair.

"Forever," she said.

"Yes."

"He's just five."

"I understand."

"He's always running off. I said, 'Johnny Maxwell Trim, in the city you don't run off.' I told him it was dangerous. He wanted to know dangerous how. I told him there were bad people here. He said, 'Like monsters?' I said, 'Yeah, monsters, so hold my hand. You better hold my hand.' But I knew he'd run off. Monsters don't scare him. He won't stay still, never. Especially when there's something foul to see."

She dabbed at her eyes.

"He's a nice boy," she said, "but he likes odd stuff—monsters, liver. What kid likes liver? I never met one before him. I never knew a child to eat liver. Have you?"

Pax shook his head.

"His favorite color is green. Everything green, towels and

sheets and shirts. He's wearing a green shirt now, in fact. That's what I told the police there. And green sneakers. Monsters, he's all about monsters and blood, all that. He likes vampires, goblins, ten thousand leagues under the sea. I told the police he may be in the sewer system."

"He sounds like a nice boy."

Now he had no choice but to remember the day he'd gotten lost in the city when he was a child. Why were people always intruding with their stories and complaints and making you remember? He thought about that day and its freedom-peace-fear-grief-thrill-hope-guilt-fear—what could you call it? It was the first feeling that defied a name. How wonderful and right this seemed at the time. But soon it became a curse, a sorrow; soon the impossibility of finding the right name was not a pleasure, soon *all* his experiences felt too big, unsortable, a massive glare. That crazy woman who had taken him into her shack, that oddball with the dogs, she was gone and the shack was gone. He went there—it was the first thing he did when he returned to the city. In place of the shack was a sign about the miracle of some unpretty flora.

The woman did not want to stop talking. "Nothing scares him," she was saying. "He's too brave. That's a problem, right? Between us, I think he's a little crazy." She covered her mouth with her hand. "I should be out there looking for him. I should be out there as we speak."

"I think you should do what the police say." Pax didn't sound like himself—his voice was sharp, knowing, impatient, like his mother's.

She nodded. "Yes, you're right, yes. You're absolutely right."

They didn't speak again. All along she'd wanted him to tell her to stay still, and once he did she was silent.

Half an hour passed. Beyond the waiting area the station grew louder. Competing music from several radios, walkie-talkie static. At one point a handcuffed woman was led by, a prostitute in a yellow dress, boots to her thighs. Pax closed his eyes. He waited. He was hungry but didn't care if he never ate again. Then the door swung open and a cop came in. He held a small boy around the waist as one holds a bag of groceries.

"Ma'am," said the cop, out of breath, and approached the blonde woman. "We found him on the east side. Is this him? Your kid?"

The woman stood and looked at the child. He was dirty, mouth slack, with hair that fell over his ears and a shirt stained with jelly.

The cop's badge said *Lowenbrau*. He pointed to the boy's head with his free hand. "Is this him? Your boy?"

The woman was shaking. The boy looked at her. He was no more than three. His face showed no recognition. One red sneaker was untied.

At last she shook her head. "No," she said. "No, he is not my son."

The cop apologized, carried the kid further inside.

She sat again. For a while she was quiet. Then she turned to Pax.

"I may not get him back."

"They'll find him." But he didn't really believe it. Who knew what happened to that kid, to any kid. Pax needed quiet. He needed to maintain his resolve.

She said, "You want to know something crazy?"

He did not. He made no motion or sound.

"I almost took that one," she whispered, leaning in close. "He wasn't my son, but I may not get mine back. That kid was just looking at me. Can you believe that? Part of me wanted to take him and be done with it. I almost took him. Is that crazy?"

She looked at him with widened eyes, waited for his shock.

He would not give her shock.

"Crazy, yes," the man on Pax's other side said suddenly. He turned to face them. He was Indian, maybe, with wide eyes, a face of exhausted indignation. "Boy run away. You go batty. Boy run from batty lady. I cannot blame boy." The man had the clear stare and wide shoulders of a baseball umpire. "You stop talking now?"

She blinked. Then, like a child, nodded demurely.

Pax looked down at his lap. His heart raced. The thing was that Pax could believe it very well. It was all anyone wanted, a substitute to stand in for a loss, it was the worst and most obvious part of human nature.

"I should have held on tighter," she whispered.

The man said, "All day talk to strangers. Steal a child! No shame. No shame."

"I'm shamed," she said. "Oh, I'm shamed."

"Batty," the man muttered.

"Batty," she agreed.

Pax waited to be retrieved. Another hour passed. The station grew louder. Finally another boy was brought in for the woman to inspect, a kid with a round and regular face, a face like a hamburger bun, the face of any kid, of all of them. This was her son. She stood up, clucked her tongue; she knocked him lightly on the side of his head and cried "You!" as though he'd drawn on the wall with crayon, and the boy grinned, made a face that said *You love me anyway,* and she did.

They left. Pax waited.

He wasn't a murderer but wasn't innocent either. No one was

free of crime—his crime was vague, elsewhere, nowhere, a crime
not of passion but of passivity, of indifference, of failing to see
people. And *someone* had to murder her. *Someone* had to confess,
to offer her family that relief, to bear the burden of the horror, to
be linked forever and always to the girl. That was the miraculous
prospect—being linked to her, married to her in history. Him, old
Paul Prickface Pussyhater Pax. Why couldn't it be him? It had to
be someone! So why couldn't it be him? Why not? He wanted to
do something good. That was the thing about goodness—you
couldn't wait for it to come to you. You needed to move to it. For
once he wanted to move to it. Not to flee, not to evade, not to
skirt the perimeter, and also he wanted so badly to feel close
to a person, a girl, this girl. She was pretty and young and
about to do everything. Here, in the station, a confession on
his lips, he felt brave and peaceful. He didn't deserve peace
either, but he took it.

He waited some more. From another room, a woman was
yelling: "Those hooligans stole my silverware! My fox-fur coat!—"
Then the sound of a door slamming, and her voice was gone.
People came and went. Sometimes his stomach made noises.
When he closed his eyes his stomach felt emptier. When he
closed his eyes the boys and girls of the world rose up in his
vision. Boys and girls like in some sort of a grand Soviet parade,
rows and rows, happy and innocent and so close to losing it all.
Every criminal was once an innocent. He closed his eyes, allowed
himself to picture his mother, and Jade, and Judith, and Leonora,
and Leonora's mother, all these decent women, would-be women,
and felt a surge of ardor, an amorousness, a longing not sexual,
or only partly sexual, for it resided in his stomach and heart and
head—it had a sexual part but something else, too, bigger than
sex, righter than sex. He felt a desire to smash love into his body,

to smash love into the world, to allow love to be the violent act he'd always suspected it was. Why did people pretend it wasn't violent? It was the most violent thing.

The Indian man was called into a deeper part of the station. Soon Pax would be asked to go deeper too. People came and went. He waited. Someone would retrieve him, someone with a notepad would record whatever he said. He planned his story, which would pass from someone's notepad to someone's mouth, to mother, to newscaster, to judge, mouth to mouth to mouth, and somewhere in this transit, possibly, it would become true. It would become an official thing. It could. It could. Pax straightened. Someone would come for him soon. The air was peace. He took it in, let it out. He would keep this feeling. He swore that he'd keep it, find a way to make it last, and it was true, he did. Even afterward—after the lie-detector test, after the psychiatric evaluation, after his mother came and sat with him and held his hand and rubbed his shoulders and begged him to tell the truth, to clear his good name, after the newspaper articles, after the cell, after the narrow bed he sat on with the candid silence of a monk, after his belt and shoelaces were returned to him, after he climbed up the jail's steps into blinding noonday light—even then this peace would remain. The receptionist called for him.

LEONORA

F rank called it a rumpus room, meaning it was a cellar but
didn't feel like one. It was a room she might have liked a
great deal under different circumstances, a room with soft yellow carpet, blond wood-paneled walls, a lamp made from a gumball machine. On a bamboo bar sat a glass bowl of drink
umbrellas. A big black-and-white photograph of a tree, unframed,
was pinned to the wall behind the bar. A clock in the shape of a
pineapple.

The kitten slept in her lap. It was a gift, the kitten. She had
been the girl getting the kitten. Neither of them had known it,
not the cat, not Leonora, but all along their lives had been veering together, moving toward each other, since the very beginning of time, since before either of them was born or breathed.

As the hours passed, she began to take a certain pride. She

imagined other girls, other people, would go berserk, lose their minds, which would only make things sadder and more dangerous. Beatrice, say, would shriek and claw and hurl insults. Others would vomit. Others—most people, probably—would leave themselves. She felt it as a distinct possibility, leaving herself, felt the invitation to close herself to the story. But that seemed wrong, a betrayal. She wanted to be—well, it was maybe strange—but she felt it was important to be a friend to herself. She didn't want to leave her body alone in this mess. This decision felt like a sort of victory, brought a feeling of woozy, helpless arrogance, like she'd won something big but had to keep her mouth shut about it.

Still, she cried a little. When the second hand came around again to the pineapple's tuft, she stopped crying.

The cat, all the while, was licking her hand. Its tiny, rough tongue. Its fluffy ears the same orange color of that candy they call circus peanuts.

She wished it wasn't happening—she would give anything for it not to be happening. "Anything"—was that true? She felt it was important to be honest with herself, and so made a list of things she'd be willing to give up: feet, hands, hearing, vision, hair, her brains, her beauty. She'd give up her grandmother, who was old anyway. There was no guilt in wanting to sacrifice her grandmother; Leonora knew that her grandmother would trade places in an instant. But people who take people don't take grandmothers. They take girls like Leonora. She cursed her face. No. She would love her face. She would love her face, her manners, would not regret even the things that brought her here. The easy path is not usually the right one. Her mother liked to say this, and Leonora always wanted to agree, though she never truly had occasion to understand. This was the occasion.

She thought about the kitten. How their little lives had been shuttling toward each other's. The purity of the kitten, that its beauty stayed intact no matter what happened, no matter who touched it—this made her feel better. A small rectangular window near the ceiling had been boarded up with plywood. Otherwise the place was cheery, sweet, a room ready for a party. Drink umbrellas! Once her mother had gone for Halloween in a shirt decorated with drink umbrellas; she'd called herself "Happy Hour." Leonora stroked the cat. She thought about the Underground Railroad. She made a list of all the unlikely victories of the world, Frederick Douglass, the 1980 U.S. Ice Hockey Team, penicillin, the Gutenberg Press, Sally Ride, whoever it was who'd first climbed Everest, the United Nations, carbonation, the suffrage movement. What else? There were plenty. The hugeness of the list, the fact that it never could be exhausted, helped. It made her calm. It made it easier to stay inside herself. The kitten helped too. She sat in the center of a tan leather couch with a blanket over her lap. The cat was on the blanket. This wasn't the same blanket that hid her in the car; this one was clean, white wool. It held no smell but the faintest chemical whiff of dry cleaning. They had given her a clean blanket. They had given her a cup of soda, but she didn't drink it. They had given her a bowl of quarters for the gumball machine, but she didn't touch the quarters. She heard voices upstairs but couldn't make out many words. Occasional footsteps. The man, Frank, came down now and then. He apologized that the soda was flat, stood before her in his ski jacket, baggy jeans, white sneakers that looked brand-new. He said, "Sweetie, you just take it easy now," as if she'd been wailing, when in fact she was sitting politely, unmoving, on the couch. The rash on his face was bad—she could tell he'd just rubbed some ointment on it; it shone. The woman never came down.

"Later on I'll swing by the grocery. Pick up some snacks. What kind of beverages do you like?"

She didn't reply.

He kept his gaze on her, bit down on his bottom lip.

"Any particular kind of snack?"

What was she supposed to say?

"Sweetie?"

She said, "Please don't call me that."

"I told you *my* name."

She said, "Your name is Frank." She tried to say it with confidence, the way she'd report it to a police officer, but it came out too softly. She said it again, tried to be harsher, to say it with disgust: "Frank."

He said, "So what's yours? If I know your name, I won't have to call you 'sweetie.'"

She shook her head.

"C'mon."

She stared at him levelly, heart pounding.

"You want me to guess? Is that it? Like in the fairy tale? If I can guess your name it means we're married?"

It was as if someone had rung a bell in her stomach.

"We are not," she said.

He sighed and went back upstairs.

Her poor family. Her father who'd wake up and have no one to read to, who'd have no number for this, no chart to consult.

Stay here. Stay with yourself.

Gut it out.

She examined the cat's tail. She examined the bamboo bar. She looked for a long time at the picture of the tree thumbtacked behind the bar, the only picture in the room. It was a dim photograph of a big tree on a hill somewhere, a tree in winter, without leaves, without birds, any tree against any sky. It was nothing special. A tree on a hill. But as she gazed at the tree, as she allowed her eyes to lose focus, allowed the tree to blur, she found herself remembering the tree she'd seen this morning on the way to school, that tree a few blocks from her house, its branches dark against the white sky. The tree she would have climbed this summer if she'd been that kind of girl. The tree near her house, suspended in her mind; the tree here, suspended on the wall.

Then something happened. She saw that the tree in the photograph in this rumpus room had the same curve to its biggest branch, had the same lump in its base, the same barely perceptible leftward lean, as the real one she'd gazed at earlier. Could they be the same tree? She looked. She forced her eyes to focus. They were the same tree. They were! It was impossible but true, and she thought: *Everything comes around again.* She didn't have to will this thought; it simply appeared. It made no demands. It didn't automatically present its opposite, as most thoughts do.

She used the bathroom that he'd shown her, a tiny room, no window, just a toilet, a sink the size of a dessert bowl, like a bathroom on a train. She peed, then washed her hands. It seemed to her a particularly grievous offense that there was no soap. She opened the tiny cabinet under the sink but found only a spare roll of toilet paper and one of those spongy rubber things used to separate toes when you paint your nails, like a foam brass knuckles. These objects, the presence of these objects coupled with the absence of the soap, filled her with rage. She opened the door.

There he was, Frank, and the rash on his cheek.

"There's no soap." She practically shouted it. "Get me soap."

He blinked. She said it again. She would never stop staying it. He went upstairs. Soon he came down again with a box of plain crackers and a bottle of soda and an unopened bar of soap. Right away the soap's jingle sprang to her mind: *Feel clean—squeaky—fresh—rise higher than the rest.* The soap was called *Soar.* He left again. She washed her hands, saying the alphabet in her mind like they taught her, A to Z, to kill all the germs. Then she returned to the couch; the kitten found her lap.

Pyramids. The Golden Gate Bridge. Movies. Frank Sinatra. Marvin Gaye.

She closed her eyes and pictured her mother at Halloween wearing a long black sweater, dozens of vivid drink umbrellas stuck into its knit, her whole torso covered with them.

Footsteps upstairs.

She opened her eyes. The kitten was sleeping.

They were the same tree. She looked again and it was true.

She could never explain what this meant to her, what it did to her body, a feeling not unlike relief. Could that be the right word? It seemed too terrible to think such a thing. She took a breath. Another. The word, the feeling, stayed in her body, suspended in her body like something she'd swallowed, moving through her system, like a pill dissolving, it was going everywhere.

Everything comes back to itself. They're all the same, every tree, every sky, every person. Meaning she wasn't alone. Meaning Frank had meant it when he'd said he was sorry the soda was flat. Meaning Leonora could drink the soda and would not be betraying anyone. She could drink the soda. Everything comes around again. She wished she could tell her parents, her brother, her nana, but she knew she couldn't tell them. And wasn't that kind of funny? That this tree is that tree and this girl that girl. That all along you think they're two different trees, or a million different trees, but really they're one huge tree that's been split again and again. What's funny is that you have to figure it out on your own, and by the time you figure it out it's too late to say it. She stroked the cat. She thought: *My sweet cat.* Its skull felt like a ping-pong ball. Miracles erupted in her mind. Amelia Earhart. Radios. The baby who'd been saved from the well. There was only one miracle. She was part of it, Leonora Marie Coulter. She touched the cat's tail, its paws. Pasteurization. Prosthetic limbs. She held the cat to her stomach. She told it what she knew.

PART 6

Byron tucked the list in his back pocket and put on his red mittens. He and the girl faced one other. He said goodbye, wished her luck, all the luck in the world. Her smile was lovely, moved across her face like a leaf on a river. They walked separate ways. It was snowing now; the air felt slightly warmer. Cable TV. Jumpin' Sumpin's. Nail polish. The combination of the snow, the big, swaying, papery flakes, and the less frigid air, and the list secure in his pants pocket—all this gave him a sense of new possibility. The rage he'd been carrying for his ex-wife (the rage that was a twin to witless, irrevocable ardor) was finally replaced by the simplest kind of hope. Hope was bigger, it turned out, than rage and ardor combined. In his soul he identified a kind of hope that felt—what could you call it except feminine? For that's what it was: a *girl's* hope. It was so without edge, so without asterisks

or variables or contingencies. It was the purest thing, no strings
attached, hard and shiny as a bottle of nail polish. He walked
uptown, past beggars, past drug pushers, past men selling pret-
zels as big as his head, past a woman in a wheelchair who sang
"Michael Row Your Boat Ashore" in a husky voice that made
him think of Etta James if she'd been white and an amputee
with a shoebox of change. All along, walking, his hair damp with
snow, his pulse increasing, these simple, bare, hopeful words
played in his head: *I love Bea; she loves me.* He would get through
to her. It was inevitable. Leonora made it so. Leonora looked at
him like she believed it was possible—like it was an eventuality.
So it was.

What a nice kid, Leonora. She took it all in stride. How weird
he'd been! How inappropriate! His cheeks burned thinking of it.
It was in such bad taste, the whole proposal, and she could have
run, or told someone, but she met him at the coffee shop, sat
before him with her contemplative gaze, blinking her long lashes,
solemn, patient, like a child nun, or like the matchstick girl,
that's what she reminded him of, a wisp of a thing, everything
inessential gone, like one whose poverty is simply a method of
revealing her goodness.

He spotted a grocery store and got excited about the Jumpin'
Sumpin's. The glass doors opened for him in a sighing, efficient
whoosh; he felt sure, stepping inside, hearing the jangling
Muzak, receiving a smile from the pretty clerk at the register,
that everything would be okay for all of them. He bought three
bags of Jumpin' Sumpin's, a copy of the teen magazine Leonora
recommended (on its cover a boy with bleached hair held a finger his lips—*Don't tell anyone!*; his eyes, half closed, dazed,
invoked less someone seductively stoned, as was surely the
intent, than a little boy trying to stay awake through the late

movie), gummy candies in the shape of worms, a certain sugar cereal Leonora said was all the rage, Coke, and a large bottle of carrot juice. The juice was for him. Bea always made gagging noises when she saw it. Bea said, "I don't give a rat's ass about beta-carotene."

It was not the job of childhood to give a rat's ass about beta-carotene. That's what she was telling him. And you know what? She was right. Byron decided, now, to admire her honesty.

He arrived to an empty apartment. Bea was at debate club. He laid his mittens and scarf on top of the radiator, hung his coat on a hook by the door. The apartment smelled like a shirt after a hot iron, the air dry and starchy. He poured the Jumpin' Sumpin's in a big bowl and put her Coke in the fridge. The candy and magazine he stored under the sink where she wouldn't see them. Then he sat at the table to wait. He rested his fingertips on the kiddie placemat (it had been Bea's as a kid, depicted the planets, the swirling cosmos, and for some reason he used it still). It would have to go—he saw that now, that he wouldn't win her over with mementos from the past. She didn't yet have nostalgia for an earlier life. In several years, when she needed such things, when such a placemat would wound and heal her in one fell swoop, would create the very injury it promises to heal (and vice versa)—well, then he'd pull it out and watch her face. Now he put it in a drawer. He swept crumbs from the tabletop, dropped them in the sink. Sat down again. He felt a little nervous. Outside, the surf-sounds of traffic ebbed and flowed. The place was too tidy—too spare, clean, dull. He saw suddenly, as if through Leonora's eyes, that it wasn't the kind of home Bea'd want to invite friends to. It wasn't at all *cozy*. But he'd change that. He would. He'd get a shaggy rug for the living room. He'd get an artsy poster, a Manhattan skyline or Ansel Adams-y deal;

he'd remove the heinous oil painting, an oversized squirrel in a pine tree, which his great-aunt gave him twenty years ago and he'd been lugging around since. *Enough!* He'd put the whole thing, frame and all, down the trash chute. Just the idea of it, the possibility of such a brazen act, allowed something to open up in him. It happened quickly, a narrow space that wasn't there before, a chute, like a new corridor between his mind and heart. He had to break the frame before it would fit down the chute, but he did it.

His allegiances were so silly. His allegiance to Great-Aunt Rita's awful painting; his allegiance to his rage/ardor for Shirley; his allegiance to the belief that Bea was beyond knowing. *Why why why?* He felt dogged by needless rigidity. Why hadn't he ever considered the notion that superficial changes could be real changes? That's what hit him now. Objects, surfaces, the veneer of life . . . they *are* life. He'd buy some bright throw pillows, plants, and a lamp with a red shade so the place would have, just subtly, the mood of an opium den.

Half an hour later Bea arrived, sighing, dropping her massive backpack in the doorway, and moaned that she needed two Tylenol right now or she was probably without question going to commit an act of homicide using only a mechanical pencil and her retainer on the next person she saw, which was sorry to say her father. Then she smiled at him as if at her dearest friend. He procured the pills; she took them with still-warm Coke, wiped her mouth, and said, warily, "You never buy Coke." Then she saw the bowl of snacks on the table, squinted, frowned, and dug in.

She was getting tall. He'd always assumed as she got taller the baby fat would melt away, but that didn't seem to be happening. It grew with her. Which meant, he supposed, it wasn't really baby fat. She wore her fat how a child wears a snowsuit—too busy to notice it, too excited by the landscape, the whole wide snowy world laid out before her, to feel encumbered. He wondered if this would last. He hoped so. She was a pretty girl, big with life; her spirit seemed to inhere in her fullness. He was reminded of Mrs. Pablonski, a chubby, creamy, vociferous woman who showed up at his elementary school to lead them all in a square dance. He remembered standing by the bleachers, listening to the staticky fiddle on the record player as Mrs. P. showed them how to do-si-do and bow and curtsy; her huge bosom swayed, swung, rose and fell, kept everyone dancing, everyone in impossible thrall to it, that great rocking bosom. He was uncomfortable thinking about Bea this way, but it was true, Bea shared something with that dancing woman, a density that seemed to bear her spirit.

Bea said, licking her fingers, "I thought you were opposed to sugar."

"Not categorically."

"Sugar does to the body what cartoons do to the mind. You said that."

"Not categorically." Then: "I like cartoons."

"What cartoons? Besides Zoot Suit Henderson."

He couldn't answer. Only Zoot.

"I thought you said at your house I need to comply with your dietary restrictions."

"Everything in moderation, right?"

She leaned forward and selected a Jumpin' Sumpin'. She stared at him while she chewed it. "I won't eat another prune," she said finally. "I can guarantee that."

"How was debate club?"

She rolled her eyes. "I had to argue for the legalization of prostitution."

"Oh?" Things seemed to be getting more and more out of hand. The craziness thrust upon kids these days—but he wouldn't take the bait. He couldn't trust his instincts.

"Just kidding. Euthanasia."

She nibbled at her cuticles. She wore jeans, a baggy black turtleneck sweater, and pearl earrings that had once been Shirley's. The earrings, their primness, their tininess, their implication of an ancestral order, had always reassured him. But she also wore two keys on her neck—two metal keys that clinked when she moved. On a shoelace. A shoelace! This disturbed him, which was of course exactly Bea's intent. She'd taken to wearing this necklace around the same time he and Shirley announced they were separating. Its purpose was to show the world she'd been abandoned. The necklace said: *I'm a latchkey kid now. I'm a child of the era.* It was tacky, he and Shirley agreed, and also risky, would attract the gaze of who-knows-who; it made Bea vulnerable when she thought it conveyed strength. But Bea insisted on keeping it around her neck. The dinginess of the shoelace was the worst part. Couldn't she have at least chosen a pretty cord? A ribbon? Or some bright gimpy thing like kids make at camp? Of course not. She had a sadistic streak, his bumble Bea—he was coming to admire it a little. It made sense to admire it. Otherwise it would kill him.

"Don't you think people should have the right to do what they want with their bodies? If I got a brain tumor, if I had six months to live, who's to say I wouldn't want to end it?"

"Oh honey. I don't know."

"I'd probably want to bungee-jump and eat heaps of chocolate. Where are people supposed to want to go? Mozambique? Disney? I'd take Disney. But if I wanted to die instead, it should be allowed. I own myself."

His mind spun. Then he understood. He said, "Yes, Bea, you do." That was the heart of everything.

"I'm glad you like debate club," he added. "I can't wait to come to one of your meets."

"Contests."

"Contests, right."

She waved a hand in the air as if at a terrible odor. "Please do *not come,* Daddy. I'd die of embarrassment. Who wants to be talking about prostitution in front of their father?"

"But I thought—"

"I'd get too nervous if you were there. Please don't come—oh and don't look all hurt. I told Mom the same thing. But do you think we could get me a new shirt? We're supposed to wear white shirts with collars. They provide red ties. Mom said she's already 'exhausted my wardrobe budget' and I should ask you."

"Of course. We can go to Gill's."

"Not Gill's. The Emporium."

"Listen, Bea. I was thinking if we got this place set up. Made it nicer. Made it—*cooler.* Maybe you could have a party here."

She started to laugh, then squeezed her chin and mouth as if to keep her face in order, as if to control herself, though the obvious purpose of this gesture was to underscore his retardedness. His heart sunk, but he soldiered on. He'd stick to the concrete.

"Look, I thought we'd get the movie channels. Find you a new bed. Some stuff for your room. A boom box, music, posters. I want you to feel *at home* here. I know you've been through a lot, honey, and so I thought—maybe we could work together, make it nicer, and then you could have a party . . . invite your friends. Like a housewarming. I'd stay out of the way."

"You'd stay with Uncle Kenny?"

He hadn't meant he'd stay out of the apartment. He was

pretty sure chaperones were still standard. "We can talk about that part later."

She looked at him skeptically.

He said, "What do you think?"

She said nothing.

"Oh, Bea. My sweet pea. I know the divorce has been awful. I'm sorry. I'm so sorry. I want to turn over a new leaf. Go easier on you. Work together! Of course you can drink Coke. In moderation. No more carrot juice. No prunes. Life's too short, right? We'll start with the apartment. Let's do that. We can go shopping." Suddenly he felt desperate. He said, "I got three bags of these things—" And he pointed to the bowl of Jumpin' Sumpin's, gestured with a hand like a game-show hostess, flourished his palm, and then, seeing what his hand was doing, let it fall like deadweight to the table.

She said, "Is that how you think you win over a fat girl?"

"Oh! No! Bea, I—"

"I'm kidding," she said. "Relax."

He saw the color come into her cheeks, a faint smile, saw her eyes widen, and he sensed he'd unleashed some new optimism. She scanned the room. She looked at the Jumpin' Sumpin's before her, licked the tip of her finger. She looked at the glass of Coke, at the clean tabletop, at her father's mittens and scarf on the radiator, at the silent TV, and then she lifted her chest, raised her head, and her face, at once, changed—seized, tightened, brow furrowed—so that for a moment it appeared she was going to laugh. Instead, to his horror, she wept.

He had not seen her cry since she was maybe—six? seven? The girl didn't cry. Not when she broke her ankle. Not when he and Shirley announced their separation. Not when she was suspended for a week for cheating on a math exam. Not when her grandmother, the first Beatrice, suffered a heart attack on Thanksgiving Day, right as those gorgeous pies were being set out down on their ancestral platters, or when her friend Donna moved to France, or when Ali MacGraw died in a trashy movie Shirley couldn't get enough of. Always Bea remained stoic, committed to the order of herself. Always her face belonged to a factory worker, to another era, a time before leisure, before self-help, before the invention of adolescence. Oh, she moaned like a teenager, that was true enough—she was petulant and grumpy and erratic like a teenager. But she never, ever, ever cried like one.

Now she wept. Her face broke into a thousand pieces, repaired itself, and broke again. This cycle continued as if it would never stop. Her tears dripped onto her sweater, landed on the wool, quivered there, like jewels, on her breasts. She made no effort to cover her face, or to wipe her tears, or to turn away. He felt stunned. He could only look at his sobbing child, panic stirring. He wanted Leonora to tell him what to do.

Finally, between heaving breaths, Bea spoke.

"I want to watch Zoot Suit Henderson."

He told her she could watch whatever she wanted. He stood, relieved, moved toward the TV, but she grabbed his arm. He sat down again. Her cries, at last, were remitting. She wiped her eyes with the heels of her hands. Her breath puttered.

She said, "I need a new shirt."

"I know it's been rough," he whispered, leaning close to her. "We tried. Your mother's a good woman, but it just wasn't meant to be. I know you're scared."

And what did Bea do? She shocked him once more. She laughed. A quiet, sniffling, head-shaking laugh. It went on longer than he thought possible. Then she ran her hands through her hair, fluffed it, shook it out, performing this motion with a glamour he'd never seen, with chic, disinterested poise, like a model in a photo shoot. Her hands returned to her lap. The glamour was gone. Very quietly she said, "My mother has a below-average IQ."

What could he say?

"Not true."

But it was—it was!

"She's petty," Bea went on. "She's cheap. She's got a crush on that janitor, Demeter or whatever his name is, the freaky guy with the long hair and the kazoo."

"Dimitri."

"Except supposedly it's from Asia so it's not a kazoo but an 'instrument of spiritual enlightenment.' I know why you pulled the plug. I don't blame you. I mean, you're not perfect. Lord no. But you're a good person. I believe you are. Does that surprise you? I think it might."

He never cried. Not when she was born. Not when he wasn't made partner. Not when he found Dimitri's long black hair on his own pillow, not when the smell of musk oil permeated his sheets, not when he kept smelling that musk even after the sheets had been washed, after they'd been replaced. Not when his mother died forever and always and on Thanksgiving Day. Not when he was married at sunset to the love of his life, not when happiness penetrated him so fully he was sure he'd never be free of the sensation, not when he kissed her and kissed her and would never never never stop. Not when he stopped.

He didn't cry now either. But, for the first time in years, his eyes got glassy.

"It's not the divorce," Bea said. "That's not why I cried."

"Then why?" That his voice was the same—that the wetness in his eyes did not affect it came as a tremendous relief.

"Adults think we're all so messed up when our parents split, but we can handle more than you imagine. Victoria Grassley has insane nutso Nazi parents who smash dishes and, like, frame *crimes* on each other. You know the King Solomon thing you told me? The baby he threatens to cut in two? Victoria's parents would *do that*. And she's fine! No one knows. Everyone's always like, 'Oh what can we do for you? How are you holding up?' Girls are strong. I don't know about boys. Boys fix everything by giving each other wedgies or whatever, but girls are stronger than anyone guesses. I'm glad you're divorcing. I am. It gives me more freedom and I don't have to listen to you fight. That's pretty much awesome."

"Awesome?"

He wanted to believe everything she said. He did believe. He didn't. He saw a flash of doubt on her face.

"You sure?" he said. "Awesome?"

"Mom spent my clothing budget. She bought herself a bathrobe with a holster for a remote control. She 'exhausted' the budget so now I can't get my debate shirt. You'll get me a shirt, right? I can't compete without it. Mister Fritz is a freak about dress code."

"Why were you crying, Bea?"

She rubbed her bloodshot eyes.

She said, "Cheryl Cloister hates me. She makes the rules. If I had a party here, you know what would happen? No one would come. I want a party here. I want a stereo. No one would come."

"That can't be true, honey."

"Cheryl is the devil."

"Oh."

"She controls everyone. Maybe Molly and Jane would come, *maybe,* but it's doubtful. And who wants to hang out with Molly and Jane anyway?"

"But what about the old gang? Lane and Petra? What about that girl with the glasses? What's her name? She was always a nice kid. We can make a list. You might be surprised by who's on your side."

"I want Cheryl," she said simply.

"Let's work on it," he said. "One step at a time."

She said, "Also I want tampons. Mom thinks they make you lose your virginity but they don't. It's like she was raised in *Little House on the Prairie.* She wants me to use *hay* or something."

She was trying to shock him now—she'd exposed herself and wanted him to pay for it. He gave her forty bucks every month for her hygiene products. There was no need to tell him about tampons.

"Buy whatever you like," he said.

"Tampons?"

She wanted him to say it. There was a meanness in her face he could not escape.

"Tampons," he said. He found the wetness in his eyes was now in his throat.

"God, are you *crying?*"

"No."

So he said it again, *tampons,* to prove he wasn't crying, even though he was. He was crying, but the strangeness of the word, *tampon,* the taboo of it, its weirdness, that was bigger than the tears, weirder than the tears, and so would defeat the tears. She seemed to sense this and said it again herself. Then she left to wash her hair.

While she was gone, he put the magazine with the bleached-blond boy on the arm of the sofa. Should he hold off a little, wait, play it cooler? But his instinct told him he needed to come on strong. His instinct turned out to be pretty good.

Bea shrieked with delight when she saw the magazine. She launched into a long monologue about how Christian, the bleached-blond boy on the cover, was obviously superior to the raven-haired BJ, who'd lived part of his childhood in a van and whose current romantic involvement with a woman called "Calico" defied anyone's understanding. Christian and BJ started Roger Ranger when they were in high school, but they sucked until Jon-Jon became their drummer. Byron knew better than to ask questions or make any sounds. He listened. Christian was the handsomest. Jon-Jon was the nicest. BJ was sort of handsome, Bea was saying, but he didn't care about the fans. And Roger Ranger's fans were the most devoted, the most deserving! It wasn't right. Christian, for example, would never be rude to fans. And Jon-Jon always signed autographs and posed for photographs even when he was in a hurry. BJ and Calico could fall off the face of the earth for all Bea cared. But that song he wrote, the one about the missing girl, the girl who's gone to pieces? It killed her, it moved her to death, it was like nothing else she'd ever heard, ever, and she had to give him credit for that. Byron, it was true, tuned out a little as she talked. He didn't take in the full meaning of her words but rather their frantic, lovestruck, rageful charm.

He made dinner while she paged through the magazine. The plan was going so well—so much better than he'd possibly hoped. But what would happen after he'd exhausted the list? Then what? He told himself he'd figure it out. He was building momentum. They ate pasta and green beans. Bea used a great deal of garlic powder and salt on everything, and she chewed with her mouth open. He decided to wait until things were more solid between them before pointing that out. After dinner, all on his own, he did something that seemed to genuinely please Bea: he served her a container of chocolate pudding with a single gummy worm sticking out of it. "Oh," she cried ecstatically, "that's disgusting!"

He felt a hope in his body he hadn't felt since the day he'd met Shirley. Except this hope was simpler than that, so much more obvious.

An hour later, he heard Leonora's name. Bea was sprawled on the couch in her flaming-dice pajamas; Byron was sweeping the floor. The word, her name, flew past him. *Leonora*. He turned. On the television the newscaster wore his gravest face. The word MISSING floated next to his head. Then someone switched a switch and her face, Leonora's, was fixed on the screen. Her smile was demure, patient—the same as in the coffee shop. *Leonora*, the newscaster repeated. Byron couldn't exhale.

"Huh." Bea squinted at the TV. "Don't know her."

He couldn't exhale so he tried to inhale, but that didn't work either. He dropped the broom. He fell onto the couch next to his daughter.

"Probably a prostitute," Bea said.

The newscaster told them what Byron already knew. He described her snow boots, the color of her shirt and coat and eyes and hair.

"Maybe a prostitute," Bea said. "You can never tell. Girls are currency."

He made a hideous noise he couldn't account for, a cross between a cough and a moan and an *oh God*, and at the same time his heart bashed his windpipe, so that it was impossible to speak, to offer an explanation for this sound. "Poor Daddy," Bea sighed, and leaned her shoulder into him. "Don't worry—nobody will take me." Her body gave off startling heat. He couldn't respond—there was nothing to say and no apparatus with which to say it. The softness of his daughter's flannel pajamas. The citrus notes of her shampoo. Her long hair, damp at its ends. Without thinking he took her hand. She let him. Her hand was warm, fidgety, impossibly soft; it was like a small animal. He held it. They kept their eyes on the television. Any minute she would pull it away. They listened. Any minute. The newscaster relayed the details, which were few. Then he turned to another camera. He announced that a famous gymnast had come from Russia to teach the lucky kindergartners of P.S. 34 how to turn somersaults. On the screen, little boys and girls tucked their heads between their knees and rolled. The clip ended. The newscaster shuffled his papers, cleared his throat, and moved on.

ACKNOWLEDGMENTS

For their support during the writing of this book, I wish to thank the MacDowell Colony, the Massachusetts Cultural Counsel, and the Rona Jaffe Foundation. I am deeply grateful for the wisdom and generosity of Eric Bennett, Jill Bialosky, Ben Braunstein, Bill Clegg, and Justin Tussing.